PRAISE FOR

"Another am...   ...l *Addiction*

"Great snark...   ...lent world-building and innovative twists on urban fantasy conventions are par for the course in Henry's series."

—*RT Book Reviews*

"Prepare yourself for plenty of snark, plenty of action and plenty of fun from this endearing and exciting series."

—*My Bookish Ways*

BLACK HOWL

"Maddy is a strong female heroine . . . The ending of *Black Howl* will probably leave you shocked . . . and dying for the next."   —*Fresh Fiction*

"This series reminds me of the Harry Dresden series by Jim Butcher or Rachel in the Hollows series by Kim Harrison . . . It has enough action, suspense and sarcasm to keep my attention. I look forward to seeing where Christina Henry takes us next."   —*Dark Faerie Tales*

"Action-packed. You are sucked in from page one and set on a roller-coaster ride of action till the end."

—*Paranormal Haven*

BLACK NIGHT

"A riveting adventure of a novel . . . *Black Night* has within its pages the most utterly believable and wonderful depiction I've ever seen of a character forced to face her darkest fears."   —*Errant Dreams Reviews*

continued . . .

BLACK WINGS

Ace Books by Christina Henry

BLACK HEART

CHRISTINA HENRY

ACE BOOKS, NEW YORK

THE BERKLEY PUBLISHING GROUP
Published by the Penguin Group
Penguin Group (USA) LLC
375 Hudson Street, New York, New York 10014

USA | Canada | UK | Ireland | Australia | New Zealand | India | South Africa | China

penguin.com

A Penguin Random House Company

BLACK HEART

An Ace Book / published by arrangement with the author

Ace Books are published by The Berkley Publishing Group.
ACE and the "A" design are trademarks of Penguin Group (USA) LLC.

For information, address: The Berkley Publishing Group,
a division of Penguin Group (USA) LLC,
375 Hudson Street, New York, New York 10014.

ISBN: 978-0-425-25659-6

PUBLISHING HISTORY
Ace mass-market edition / November 2013

PRINTED IN THE UNITED STATES OF AMERICA

10 9 8 7 6 5 4 3 2 1

Cover art by Kris Keller.

For Sarah,
even though there isn't
a kick-butt redhead

ACKNOWLEDGMENTS

As always, thanks to Danielle Stockley, the best editor a girl could have.

Thanks to my amazing agent, Lucienne Diver, for embarking on this journey with me.

Special thanks to the hardworking Einstein Bros. crew, especially Michelle, Guy, Kayla and Jessie.

Much gratitude to those friends who keep me sane—Anne, Pam, Sarah and Heidi.

A special shout-out to my number-one fan, Logan.

Love to all of my family, especially Chris and Henry.

1

"YOU HAVE TO GET OUT OF THE HOUSE—NOW," J.B. said.

"Why?" I asked.

I faced the front window, the portable phone tucked under my ear. A strange black shadow slid across the surface of the glass, like an oil slick.

"Sokolov has sent the Retrievers after you," J.B. said. "You have to go. You have to go now."

The side window in the living room was drenched in the same shadow. So were the ones in the dining room. I ran through the house, looking for an escape, but there was none. The things looked like nothing more than black liquid, but I could feel their hate. They wanted me, and they would not leave without me.

"It's too late," I said, backing into the dining room. I felt Nathaniel's arms close around me.

"They're already here."

We watched in silence as the black fluid oozed over each of the windows.

J.B.'s voice was in my ear. I realized I was still holding the phone to my ear and he was still talking.

"Don't try to fight them," J.B. said. I'd never heard that tone in his voice before. He was pleading. "It will be much, much worse for you if you do."

"I'm not afraid of them," I said.

But my bravado was false. I *was* afraid. The apartment had been sealed shut by darkness. The Retrievers would not leave an opening for me to escape.

Someone was pounding on the door at the bottom of the stairs. J.B. was still talking, telling me not to be dumb, telling me if I fought the Retrievers, then I would be returned to Beezle in a thousand bloody pieces.

"Beezle's gone," I said.

The pounding repeated. I looked at Nathaniel. He shook his head from side to side.

"Good-bye, J.B.," I said.

I clicked off before he could say anything else.

"J.B. says not to fight," I said. "What do you think?"

"He knows more of the Retrievers than I," Nathaniel said. "Perhaps you should heed his advice."

"They're not taking me," I said. "On the off chance that they leave me alive, they would surely take—or kill—my baby as soon as it's born. And I am not spending the rest of my life in some Agency prison."

There was the sound of splintering wood below. The Retrievers were breaking in.

"Surely Lord Lucifer will not permit this to happen," Nathaniel said. "Call for his assistance."

"Lucifer's a little busy right now with Alerian," I said.

"He owes you more than this," Nathaniel said angrily. "You would not be in this predicament were it not for him. He forced you to cross into the realm of the dead and retrieve Evangeline's soul."

"If you haven't noticed, Lucifer's not real big on helping out those in need," I said.

"Run," Nathaniel said. "I will stay here and hold them off, distract them."

"Run where?" I asked. "They've got the house surrounded."

Nathaniel murmured something, and a portal opened up in the middle of the living room. I stared into its swirling depths.

"Where does it go?"

"Someplace safe," Nathaniel said. "Run. I will close the portal behind you and ensure the Retrievers do not follow."

Heavy footsteps sounded on the stairs.

"But . . . how will I be able to get home again?"

Nathaniel grabbed my shoulders, gave me a fierce, hard kiss, then shoved me toward the portal. "I will speak to Lord Lucifer. We will find you. Go."

The door to the apartment splintered as the thing outside slammed into it.

"Go!" Nathaniel shouted.

He turned toward the door as it slammed to the ground and something awful came through. I caught a glimpse of darkness, terrible darkness, as I dove into the portal, a shadow reaching for Nathaniel even as I fell. I called his name once, but I was already gone.

The portal pressed in on me, making my head squeeze in agony. I had no time to wonder where Nathaniel had sent me. Before I knew it, I was falling out of the portal, crashing into soft moss below. I stood up, brushed off my clothes, gathered my dignity, and looked around.

Wherever Nathaniel had sent me appeared pretty primeval. I was in a lush forest, surrounded by ferns and moss and broad-leafed trees. Candy-colored flowers bloomed everywhere I looked. A little waterfall trickled over rocks and into a slender stream to my left. It was a completely alien world, as far from my urban jungle as I was likely to get.

My legs felt suddenly shaky, the aftereffects of the appearance of the Retrievers hitting my system. I sat down on the moss and took stock.

I was alone in a strange world with no food or water. I had my sword and the clothes on my back. And my last friend in the world might be slaughtered by the Agency's bogeyman for helping me escape.

No. I couldn't think that way. Nathaniel was powerful, even more so now that he had come into his legacy from Puck. I had to believe that he would be able to defend himself. I had to believe, too, that the Retrievers would ultimately leave him alone.

Everything I knew about the Retrievers said that they were like attack dogs that went after a specific target. *Kind of like the Hound of the Hunt,* I thought. So chances were very good that Nathaniel would be ignored since they weren't after him. But if he picked a fight with them, put himself in their way . . .

Every instinct I had told me to open another portal, go back home, and fight until the Retrievers were destroyed. I am not a runner. It is not in my nature to leave a fight. But J.B. didn't seem to think I would have a chance against the Retrievers, and J.B. understood pretty well what I could do.

Did that mean that the Retrievers were more powerful

than Lucifer? Than Puck or Alerian? And speaking of Alerian, what were his intentions now that he had risen from his long sleep?

I rubbed my forehead. There were too many problems. I could solve none of them from here. Wherever here was.

The first thing I needed to do was find some food and a safe place to sleep for a while. I'd had no rest except for a catnap in the backyard after I'd fetched Evangeline from the dead world for Lucifer.

I couldn't remember the last time I ate. Nathaniel and I were on our way to make pancakes when the Retrievers had arrived. Pancakes. I could go for a giant stack of them right now. Too bad there wasn't a handy pancake tree. I was going to have to forage for food.

If Beezle were with me, he would laugh his little gargoyle butt off at the idea of me foraging. When I was young I'd tried camping in the backyard once. I found an old tent in the basement and got an idea in my head that I would have an adventure.

Of course, I'd thought that backyard tenting experience would be a stepping-stone to an adulthood where I would travel the world with nothing but a backpack, sleeping on the ground in the Andes and the Pyrenees and wherever else my feet would take me.

I didn't even last the night. The rats scurrying through the yard from the alley kept me up for hours. In the darkness, my mind magnified the rodents to dog size. Around midnight I gave up and trudged inside the house.

Beezle was snoring on the banister when I entered. He opened his eyes just long enough to say, "I told you so," before closing them again. And that was the end of my camping adventure.

I felt a little pang, thinking of Beezle, and resolutely put it aside. Beezle had always been the constant in my life. But he had chosen to leave. Dwelling on it now wouldn't help me survive.

So I stood up for a second time. I pulled my sword out and glanced around the sky. The sun was hidden by a canopy of leaves. There was no guarantee that the sun here moved the same way as the sun did at home, in any case. I wasn't sure where I was, but it didn't *feel* like I was in my own solar system. Or even my own galaxy, for that matter.

I started walking in the direction I faced, following the meandering path of the stream. As I walked I made a small hash mark on every third tree or so, thinking it would make it easier to tell if I got lost and started walking in circles.

Insects buzzed in the trees and grass, keeping up a continuous cicada-like noise. Some of the insects flew from tree to tree, or flower to flower. They were disconcertingly large. I saw a beetle-type bug with an iridescent green shell that was the size of my hand. Butterflies as big as Chicago pigeons flapped around my head. I didn't see any mammals.

As I walked along, the stream broadened and I saw some fat amphibians hopping from rocks into the water. The occasional silver flash of a fish darted under the surface. I wondered if I dared drink some of the water from the stream. There was a risk that it was contaminated with alien bacteria that could kill me. I didn't have any purifying tablets handy. Starting a fire wasn't a problem, but I wasn't carrying a container in which to boil the water.

I was thirsty, but I wasn't at a point of desperation. Yet. I kept my eyes peeled for anything that looked like it might stand in for a camp pot. Melonlike fruits dangled from the high branches of a tree. I flew up to a branch and yanked one off, inspecting it. The shell didn't seem sturdy enough to withstand the heat of a fire, but the fruit inside might be edible. And if it was, I could probably take care of my hunger and my thirst in one shot.

I flew back to the ground, placing the heavy fruit on a flat rock covered in moss. I lifted the sword high and split open the fruit. The halves separated easily, revealing glistening yellow-orange flesh. Grabbing fruit by the handful and shoving it in my mouth would be stupid. The melons could be poisonous. I cut a tiny, mouse-sized bite off and put it in my mouth.

My intention was to eat it, wait a couple of hours, and then see whether it upset my stomach. But I didn't get that far. As soon as the fruit hit my tongue, I spit it out. It tasted like diesel fuel.

"Well, that's not going to work," I said, looking longingly at the stream again. I wanted to get the foul taste of the fruit out of my mouth. I would probably be safe if I just rinsed and spit the water. As long as I didn't swallow it, I would probably be okay. Probably.

I approached the water, knelt beside the stream. It was clear in the way water is when it's been untouched by man and pollution. I was sure I'd never seen water this perfect, this silver and crisp. I dipped my cupped hand in the stream and lifted it to my lips.

Sweetness exploded on my tongue, and it tasted so delicious that I swallowed involuntarily. The cool liquid slipped down my parched throat, and it felt so good that I couldn't help myself. I took another drink, and another, and another, until I was lapping at the stream like a dog. I wanted to take all my clothes off and crawl inside.

My hands were at the hem of my shirt before I realized what I was doing.

Wait. Think. This is not the way you would normally act, no matter how thirsty you are.

The thought was like a bolt of lightning, and it seemed to help me shake off the drunken haze caused by the water. I stood up and backed away, wiping the liquid from my mouth with the back of my hand. I'd been so worried about germs I hadn't even considered the possibility that the stream might be enchanted. Now, too late, I realized how foolish I'd been.

Little spots of light danced before my eyes. The trees and flowers and ferns suddenly seemed dusted with gold. All around me everything shimmered in the sunlight. Deep inside my belly, my son fluttered his wings faster and faster.

Was it too late to reverse the effects? The first sip hit my bloodstream, making me stagger. I shoved my finger in my throat, trying to make myself gag. Bile rose, but the enchantment fought back, resisting me. I coughed, choked, but I was unable to bring up the water I'd drunk.

I felt it coursing through me, freezing the fire in my blood. The world tilted to one side, and there was suddenly moss and dirt under my cheek. I pushed up to my hands and knees, shaking. The sun disappeared behind a cloud, or maybe my vision was just darkening. It was hard to tell.

Sweat broke out on my forehead. My baby beat his little wings, a frantic hummingbird inside me. I sat back on my haunches, wiped the sweat out of my eyes. I tried deep breathing but the extra oxygen only seemed to make the effects of the enchantment worse. I squinted into the trees. Shadows moved there, just out of the reach of the light.

The surface of the stream shifted, and figures rose from

the water. They were humanoid in shape, but carved from liquid instead of flesh and bone. I struggled to my feet as their arms reached for me. One watery hand enclosed my wrist. I tried to shake it off, but it clamped around me with surprising force.

"Get off," I slurred, and swatted at the thing's hand.

The water creature seemed to smile at me. At least, the topographical shape of its face changed. It was difficult to distinguish actual features. It was difficult to think.

The other creatures moved toward me. I had a sudden vision of being overwhelmed by these things and drawn down into the water.

"No," I said.

I put my free hand over the creature's, the one that was holding me tight, and blasted it with nightfire. The fire was swallowed immediately by the water.

Of course it was. I wasn't thinking clearly. In a battle between fire and water, fire loses. I suspected that the other tools in my arsenal—electricity, big giant sunbursts— wouldn't do me much good against a being made of water. So I fell back on my old standby—my sword.

I reached for it as the creature drew me closer. Its other arm went around my waist, wrapping me in its embrace. My fingers scrabbled at my back, feeling for a sword that wasn't there.

I looked around wildly. The metal gleamed dully in the dirt where I had dropped it on the side of the stream. The creature pulled its arms tighter, like a straitjacket around my body. Its face was pressed very close to mine. I turned my head to one side and tried to draw up my magic. Nothing.

The water I had drunk seemed to have slowly dampened my abilities, which were born of the sun. It would have been handy to have some of my uncle Alerian's power at that moment.

My wings beat against my back in desperation. My feet rose an inch or two off the ground. The creature's grip on me loosened a little, as if it were surprised.

I took advantage, wrenching my arms out and beating my wings harder. As I lifted off the ground, the creature and its fellows threw their arms around my legs, hissing. Fangs formed in their gelatinous faces.

Hoping for a miracle, or at least a successful Jedi mind trick, I held my hand out toward Lucifer's sword. Nothing happened. I couldn't be so lucky.

The weight of the water creature was pulling me down again. My legs felt like they were about to separate from my torso. I had no sword, no magic, only the force of my own will.

I would not be killed by a bunch of water demons. I would not die alone in this unknown place. My wings flapped. I pounded on the heads of the creatures with my fists. And then suddenly I was free, soaring above the stream.

The creatures spat and shook their fists at me. I went up just high enough to be safely out of reach. I still felt the effects of the water and didn't think it was a good idea to go flying all over the place at the moment. It seemed too likely that I would get tired or dizzy and come tumbling out of the sky. And there was no one here to catch me.

Plus, I wasn't going anywhere without my sword. I flew to a nearby tree and settled into the crook of a branch, my back pressed against the rough bark. The water creatures twisted and writhed on the surface of the stream like a mass of snakes. I heard them hissing their frustration. They obviously couldn't leave the water, so I was safe enough in the tree. For the moment.

I'd already had enough of running from the Retrievers. As soon as I could, I was going to hop out of the tree, grab the sword and make a portal to bring me back home. It seemed ridiculous for me to run around on an alien world encountering new things that wanted to kill me instead of just dealing with the thing that wanted to kill me in my own home.

I relaxed against the tree, ready to wait for the creatures to give up and disappear under the water again. I blinked, and it was night.

My body felt as through it had frozen in position. My eyes were gritty. I realized I had fallen asleep in the tree. I was lucky nothing had come along to eat me while I snoozed. I shifted on the branch, my legs dangling on either side of it, and waited for my eyes to adjust to the darkness.

You never fully realize how dark the night is when you live in a city. In Chicago there was always light coming from somewhere—a streetlamp, a traffic signal, the head-lights of passing cars. There are patches of deep night in a city, but there is always relief somewhere nearby. In a for-est, away from the artificial glow, there is no such relief. The sky had more stars in it than I could have imagined.

I was slowly able to distinguish the shapes of things in shadow. Here a tree, there a rock, there the glistening water of the stream reflecting the starlight. I flexed my fingers. The sleep had restored my magic as the enchantment had dissipated.

My stomach rumbled and I felt a powerful urge to pee. I was pregnant, and I had biological needs that had to be met. But I didn't want to jump down and potentially attract the water creatures' attention. If they woke up before I managed to get the sword back, I'd have to wait them out again, and who knew how long that would take?

I peered into the darkness, trying to catch a glimpse of the sword on the ground. I thought I saw a flash of the hilt, but I couldn't be sure it wasn't my imagination. The sword was on the far side of the stream. I'd been able to see it from my perch in the tree when the sun was up.

But the landscape seemed to have shifted in the dark. I wasn't sure exactly where the sword was now. There was nothing for it. I was going to have to get closer and hunt around. At least I would be able to fly above the surface. The water creatures would not have another opportunity to grab me.

I was about to lift off the branch when I heard something large moving through the brush. Something very large. It snorted, and I realized it was only a few feet from me. I froze. I couldn't tell what direction the sound came from.

The night was a place of deception, a place where predators thrived. It didn't seem like a very good idea to fly around attracting attention, especially as it wasn't safe to assume whatever was nearby didn't have wings. I'd been chased by plenty of monsters that flew.

And even if it didn't fly, it could have giant tentacles to snatch me out of the air. No, it was best just to stay still and wait. And hope that the creature passed by me in the dark without noticing my presence.

The creature snuffled around, knocking aside branches and brush. Heavy footsteps padded in the dirt. It felt like the air was getting hotter, getting heavier. It smelled smoky, like the remains of a charcoal barbecue that had burned out. The creature scraped against the tree that I sat in, and the whole thing trembled.

I grabbed the branch with both hands so I wouldn't fall on top of the thing's back. I could just make out a broad expanse topped with a ridge of triangular scales.

A stegosaur? I thought. *Nathaniel, just where in hell did you send me?*

The animal continued past the tree, and it seemed to go on forever. Whatever it was, it was a lot bigger than the skeleton of the stegosaur at the Field Museum.

I stayed still and tried to breathe quietly. I was up pretty high, at least twenty feet off the ground, but I could have reached out and touched the tip of the creature's scales. I didn't want to tangle with anything this size. I didn't want to engage in another battle if I didn't have to.

Truth be told, I was getting pretty damned sick of fighting. I wasn't the kind to run, but I was starting to feel like there had to be more to life than bludgeoning things. The gigantic creature's tail dragged in the dirt, and it was finally past me.

Unfortunately it headed directly for the stream. I wasn't getting my sword back as long as this thing was hanging around.

The gigantic animal stopped moving. Had it smelled me? I tensed, ready to fly away and come back for the sword later.

The night was lit by a burst of flame. Something squealed in pain, and the air filled with the acrid scent of burning flesh. I was deeply grateful that I hadn't tried to fly away when I heard the creature in the forest. The burst of flame had illuminated the creature's head, and I now knew that it would be able to catch me whether I was in the air or on land.

It was a dragon.

The dragon crunched noisily on its crispy prize. Bones cracked and muscle squished as it ate. Instead of making me sick, I was reminded of my own hunger, which had not yet been addressed.

The creature seemed to take forever to eat. I hoped that it wouldn't decide to nap there by the stream, because my bladder was starting to protest. After a very long while, the dragon finally lumbered to the stream and took a long drink.

I heard it slurping and wondered whether the water would enchant the dragon as it had me. Apparently not, because a few moments later the dragon beat its heavy wings and soared into the starry night.

I jumped down from the tree, using my wings to drift to the ground, and attended to my needs with great relief. Soon the baby would start pressing on my bladder all the time. I wondered how that would affect my ability to deal with the almost-daily threats to my life. I didn't think any of my mortal enemies would stop trying to kill me just because I said, "Hang on. I've got to pee."

And mortal enemies I had aplenty. Titania, the High Queen of Faerie, ranked number one right now, but Focalor was still lurking around somewhere waiting for his chance to strike. Focalor had gone to the trouble of helping my father, Azazel, rebel against Lucifer. He'd kidnapped and tortured Gabriel once and tried to sell my bodyguard to Amarantha as a stud. And he'd tried to have me killed many times over. There was no way he was going to just forget about me, not when I was instrumental in making sure he did not get what he wanted.

Amarantha had proved a tenacious foe despite the fact that I had already killed her once. And surely the vampires would be sending assassins my way soon in vengeance for the complete and utter destruction of their brethren at my hands—which had been caught on live television.

Then there was the pending problem of Lucifer's new progeny, conceived in death and currently growing inside Evangeline's belly. Now that Alerian had risen, it seemed the millenniums-old power struggle between Lucifer, Puck, Alerian and their mysterious fourth brother was starting anew.

You didn't need to be a seer to know that Evangeline's child was going to be a factor—or that Puck and Lucifer were going to do everything they could to drag Nathaniel and me into this mess.

All of that didn't even take the Retrievers into account, which were the reason why I was in the middle of a jungle on an alien world trying to avoid getting eaten by a dragon or drowned by malicious water sprites.

When I ran down the list like that, it was hard not to feel depressed. And my group of friends had shrunk rapidly. No matter how magically powerful I became, it was still a lot nicer to know that I had my super team at my back. Now I didn't have a team at all.

Well, hanging around here won't solve anything, I thought. I was going back. I'd take my chances with the Retrievers and the Agency. Maybe Lucifer would even show up and throw his weight around for a change. That would be nice.

I was hardly the helpless princess in a tower, but it would be refreshing if someone else rode to the rescue once in a while.

I realized I was standing under a tree in the dark, wool-gathering. It would be a fine thing if I was attacked because I was spacing out instead of getting on with my business.

I flapped my wings, ascending high enough to be out of the reach of the grasping water creatures. I flew over the stream, landing on the far side, looking for the glint of metal in the darkness. I didn't see it.

Maybe I'd miscalculated. Maybe the sword was a little farther up- or downstream. I was leery of getting too close to the water. I didn't know whether the sprites woke up only if you drank from the stream, or whether they lay in wait for anyone who approached. It didn't seem smart to risk it, but my memory told me the sword was pretty close to the water. If I wanted it, I'd have to get closer.

I crept cautiously toward the flowing water, and almost immediately felt an overwhelming urge to drink it again. I slid backward in the dirt, and the impulse passed. Interesting. The stream exerted a pull on anyone who had drunk from it before, so that if by chance the sprites' victim escaped, they would not be able to do so again. I hadn't experienced the same compulsion when I was flying, so the enchantment was probably limited to the ground close to the stream. I lifted up again and approached the stream as before. I felt like myself, no pull to drink water that would try to kill me.

Ha! I thought. At least I'd managed to outsmart at least one trap. A second later my elation faded. I'd seen the gleam of the sword in the darkness.

It was in the water.

2

I MUST HAVE BEEN BORN UNDER THE UNLUCKIEST star there ever was. I couldn't even drop a sword in the dirt without its retrieval turning into a minor saga. The blade flashed as the water ran over it, so tantalizingly close. But I knew as sure as I knew my own name that if I put one fingertip in there, the sprites would be upon me.

I floated back to the shore and settled down in the dirt, just out of reach of the spell. I wrapped my arms around my knees and stared hard at the stream, willing a solution to present itself.

Everything went blurry, and I wiped the tears out of my eyes. I figured I had a right to cry. I had been hounded out of my home. I was hungry, tired and pregnant. And I wanted my sword back.

That sword had saved my life in the Maze, and countless times after. And if I left it here, it would be gone forever, because I was most definitely not coming back to this place again.

There had to be a magical solution that didn't involve putting my hand in the water. I had already tried and failed to draw the blade toward me like Thor calling Mjolnir.

My skill as a firestarter was completely useless against water. The truth was I'd never learned to do much with my power except smash obstacles in my way.

Think like Lucifer would. There was both danger and wisdom in such a thought. Lucifer was a master of subtlety, a trait that I did not seem to possess. Subtle magic did seem to be required here.

On the other hand, thinking like Lucifer even for a moment opened a door that I wasn't sure I could close again later.

You could just leave the sword and go home. It's just a piece of metal. Maybe Lucifer will have another one made for you, this time with an auto-return feature.

That hardly seemed likely. Lucifer had put a bit of himself inside that sword, and he had done that for a reason. He certainly wouldn't give any part of his power away again, especially not with Evangeline leaning over his shoulder.

My many-greats-grandmother bore no love for me. She doubtless felt even less kindly toward me now that she had lost both her eyes and one arm as the price for passing from the dead back to the living. Despite the fact that the price had been set by the universe and not by me, I was sure to get blamed for this. I always get blamed for such things.

No, I couldn't leave the sword behind. It was more than a bit of metal. It was a powerful magical object. More than that, it was mine. I didn't easily give up anything that was mine.

And the idea of being defeated by a bunch of sneaky water monsters did not sit well with me at all.

Grabbing the sword out of the water was out of the question. But what if I moved the water? Could I even do that? The enchantment on the stream was very strong. If I tried to shift the water, it would probably fight back. Still, it wasn't as if I were trying to divert the whole body. I just wanted to move the water around the sword so I could safely grab it without being grabbed myself.

Trouble was, I'd never tried to do this kind of magic. I wasn't really sure where to start.

Think subtle. Think like you did when you exorcised Amarantha from J.B.

That had definitely been a delicate magic. I'd had to get Amarantha out without killing J.B. It had been difficult, but I'd been under pressure. So I hadn't really thought about how to do it. I just did it.

Now I was dawdling. I knew I was. I even knew why.

I'd honestly grown so accustomed to succeeding that I didn't know how to fail. I didn't know what other option I had except to leave the sword behind if this didn't work.

I stood up, took a deep breath and flew into the air. I positioned myself above the water, well out of the reach of any water creatures that might rise up. I hoped. There was always the possibility that the sprites could spray out of the surface like a giant fountain.

I reached for my power and it surged up, the way it always did, like a massive tidal wave. Except this time I didn't have a plan for it, or a place to go. My body was suffused with magic, magic that tingled on my skin and arced across my fingertips. I imagined that magic as an invisible force that poured steadily from my hands.

The moon had risen, drenching the sky and the landscape with blue-white light. I opened my palms, directing the spell at the water around the sword.

As soon as the magic hit the surface, the creatures exploded out of the water, hissing, their hands grasping for me. When they saw how high I was they gave off strange watery growls. I pushed the spell harder, into the face of the creature nearest to the sword. It flinched and covered its face for a moment with its hands, but this was not enough to make it leave. The spell didn't seem to do more than irritate it.

I wanted to just break the ground open and send the water into a chasm. That was more my style. But there were doubtless numerous animals that depended on the stream for water, and I didn't want to cause an ecological disaster. I just wanted to get my sword and go home.

I pushed the magic again, with more force, and a strange thing happened. I was aiming for the mass of creatures huddled around the sword. The magic bounced off the group, seemingly without affecting them at all. The spell spun sideways, hit the bank of the stream, and caused several clumps of dirt to tumble into the water.

The sprites gave a sharp cry as one, holding on to their heads. I was going about this the wrong way, apparently. The creatures must draw their power from the bank of the stream, not the stream itself. Or maybe they did draw power from the water, and the presence of dry land was like kryptonite. Either way, I could stop messing around with the water. Which was good, because I wasn't making much headway in that arena.

I shifted position so that I was closer to the shore, and sent a full blast of nightfire into the land that ran along the lip of the stream. It exploded in a very satisfying way, raining earth over the water creatures.

As soon as the dirt splattered over them, steam rose from the creatures' bodies at the points of impact. They screeched at me, the sounds horrible in my ears. Their voices were like pieces of broken glass grating together. I hit the bank with more nightfire, keeping up a continuous stream so that the creatures were pummeled over and over.

They screamed, they howled, they gnashed their watery jaws together, but they would not yield. These creatures didn't know me. I never gave up, not in an argument with Beezle or a battle against a more powerful foe. And I was pissed. And hungry. And thirsty.

All of those things were merging inside me as white-hot anger. I just wanted my sword back. It didn't have to be this difficult. How much more pain could these creatures take? When would they give up? When would they give in?

I was so busy working myself into a fury that I didn't notice that most of the creatures were gone. Only one remained, hovering over the sword like a possessive spirit, refusing to let go despite the fact that it was obviously in extreme pain.

Now it was really down to a battle of wills. But I would win. I could feel it. I could taste it.

The more dirt I blasted at the creature, the more of its body was eaten away. After a while it was a gross, distorted version of itself. It looked like a Dalí painting, its limbs elongated. Huge chunks were missing from its head and torso.

I dropped my arms for a moment, overwhelmed by a strange pity for this pathetic thing. It was like a broken insect, a daddy longlegs that had its legs pulled off by some cruel child and was left with nothing but its body, quivering and crippled on the ground.

"Let go," I said.

The creatures hissed at me in response.

"Let go," I repeated. My anger had faded, and I'd lost my appetite for punishment. I didn't want to hurt it anymore. I just wanted it to leave.

The creature rose up in response, showed me the full extent of the damage I'd done. It lifted its head in obvious pride, daring me to continue. But it would not leave, and I had started this, so I had to see it through.

"I'm sorry," I said, and let my power flow.

The creature kept its head up and its body straight even as the structure of it disintegrated around him. After a while I couldn't see it clearly anymore. My tears flowed too hard and too fast.

Finally, it was done. The creatures were gone. Whether I'd killed them or I'd frightened them away was irrelevant. I'd won. I flew down to the surface of the water, plunged my hand beneath it, and pulled out the sword.

"Yay for me," I said sadly.

I touched down on the ground well away from the stream and prepared to open a portal home. At least the Retrievers were a known quantity. Here I could end up fighting who knew what freaky thing.

And really, Lucifer *could* help for a change. Surely he wouldn't want his precious unborn grandchild to be taken by the Retrievers. Or maybe he did. Maybe it was part of some grand design of his. I wasn't going to pretend to understand Lucifer. If I started thinking Lucifer's actions made sense, then it was probably a bad sign.

I summoned up the energy necessary for a portal, concentrated on my destination and reached for the fabric of space and time.

When a portal is created, a seam is torn in that fabric. I'd never understood how to do this until I'd come completely into my powers. Now it seemed like a simple thing. Think of destination, carve a path home. Easy.

Except that when I tried to create that path, the world *resisted*. There was no other word for it. There was no space for me to cut a seam.

I exerted more power, more will, and all I succeeded in doing was making myself sweaty and frustrated.

"Just where in hell did you send me, Nathaniel?" I asked aloud.

So I couldn't create a portal. That didn't mean that there wasn't an existing portal somewhere on this world. Every world had an escape hatch. I just had to find it.

I could wander aimlessly until I bumped into it. Or I could use a tracking spell to zero in on its location. The only trouble was I had no idea how large this world was. I could expend a lot of energy on finding the portal and then discover that I was too weak to get there.

I was already past the point of extreme hunger and was moving into that place where I was so hungry I couldn't feel it. If I ate more than a couple of bites of anything at the moment, it would just make me feel sick. This was really bad, because I thought that my baby was eating up more than the usual amount of resources. My clothes weren't flapping on me yet, but it wouldn't be long before they were.

My priority was still to find edible food and water. But if

there was a portal nearby, I could go directly there and eat when I got home. After I defeated the Retrievers. Or not.

Hunger and sleep deprivation were making me scattered. I made a concerted effort to pull myself together. Find the nearest portal. Make an action plan after that.

Using the tracking spell was going to be pretty distracting, so I needed to find a semi-safe place to close my eyes. I flew back to the tree where I'd napped earlier. I'd slept there for several hours without disturbance, so it seemed my best option. I settled down in my perch and tried to ignore my growling stomach.

Once, when Gabriel and Beezle had gone missing, I'd thrown a net of power over an alley and found a permanent portal in the middle of Chicago. I wanted to do something like that now, but given the potential size of this world, I needed to start small and expand slowly.

I visualized the net in my mind, imagined it settling over everything I could see. Once I felt I had a good grasp on it I expanded the net out slowly. I deliberately limited the parameters of the spell to a portal. If I expanded it to include anything with a magical signature, I'd end up getting a lot of signals. Anything with even a touch of magic, including the dragon, the water creatures, and the enchanted stream bank, would show up.

As the spell spread its fingers slowly outward, I could "see" the shape of the land underneath it. This jungle seemed to go on forever with nothing to interrupt it except the occasional body of water. There were streams, rivers, lakes, waterfalls. The ground undulated with softly rolling hills, and far in the distance, across the forest, were high, rocky peaks.

All of that water had to go somewhere, so I expected—and found—a huge body that could only be an ocean.

And still there was no portal.

For the first time I felt a little twinge like despair. It seemed impossible that I had survived such insane odds over and over again only to die of thirst or starvation on a lonely planet far from home.

Keep looking, I told myself. *Keep going. If you're not going to fight, you might as well have allowed the water creatures to take you.*

My spell expanded outward, crossing the ocean. I sensed the movement of gigantic animals under the surface, and couldn't help but think of Alerian. Lucifer's brother. The water god.

He'd first appeared as something that looked a lot like a giant squid. I wondered whether Lucifer and Puck had managed to find out what Alerian wanted, why he had woken after such a long time. I wondered whether Chicago would still be there when I managed to get out of here, or if I would return to a smoking ruin.

Who cared enough to protect it in my absence? Nathaniel? Maybe. But he had sent me to a place that I couldn't easily leave. He may have done that in order to guarantee my safety, since he knew me well enough to realize I would have second thoughts about running from the Retrievers.

Or, if I wanted to be suspicious, it was also possible that he had sent me here to get me out of the way without killing me and therefore drawing the wrath of Lucifer down on his head.

I didn't want to think of Nathaniel that way. But he belonged to Puck now, and Puck and Lucifer hated each other. If it came down to me or Puck, would Nathaniel choose his reluctant almost-lover, or his father?

I shook my head to refocus. I couldn't worry about Nathaniel right now. I had a plan and I needed to stick to it. Find a portal. Find water. Find food. Get the hell out of here ASAP.

My spell stretched ever outward. The ocean finally ended, and on the other side were more mountains, young ones, with high, jagged peaks unworn by time. Past the mountains, in the foothills, I finally discovered what I was searching for. My escape hatch. The portal.

I opened my eyes. It was hundreds of miles away, maybe thousands, and past a series of mountains that were probably loaded with peril. How would I ever get there? The flight across the ocean could kill me. On a good day I didn't have that kind of stamina.

Well, I had to get there. I would just have to figure out a way. Casting the tracking spell had nearly exhausted me again, but I thought I should try to make some progress in the right direction. I knew there was no food or water for me here, so I decided to fly toward the nearest lake. I just hoped that they weren't all under the same enchantment as the stream.

I rose above the trees and headed off in the direction where I'd detected a largish body of water. More time had passed than I'd realized. The moon was already setting, so low in the sky that it appeared to brush the tops of the trees.

In the distance, off to my left, something huge spread its wings and soared into the sky. The dragon. Or rather, *a* dragon. There was no guarantee that there was only one dragon in this forest.

The gigantic animal flew away from me. It seemed not

to have noticed me at all. Thank goodness. Maybe my luck was changing. I'd managed to avoid a dragon twice.

I flew low, just above the tree line. I was keeping a sharp eye below, looking for the lake or a good place to forage for food. I didn't see any movement or any evidence of creatures beyond the dragon.

Soon enough I realized I was too tired to keep going. I lowered into a tree, found a comfy-looking branch, and was asleep before I knew it.

My dreams were tangled things, images of Gabriel and Nathaniel twisted into one body; the dark, lurking menace of the Retrievers; the sight of Alerian rising from Lake Michigan; the feeling that I was drowning when I touched his hand.

Then Lucifer was there, and behind him Evangeline. He smiled at me as Evangeline rose up, growing taller and taller, her belly huge with child, her shadow threatening to smother the world. I was just an insect to her, something to be smashed.

I ran and ran, my own belly unwieldy, swollen with my son, but I could never run far enough or fast enough. She was coming for me.

I woke to a searing pain, and the sensation of falling. There was an arrow embedded in my upper right thigh, and whoever had shot it had knocked me out of the tree. I flapped my wings so I wouldn't smash into the ground. But they got tangled in something.

A net.

I hit the dirt hard and all the breath went out of my lungs. I rolled over, the net twisting in my wings and covering my face. My thigh burned from the arrow embedded in it. I grabbed the net with my hands and tried to set fire to it, but it was made of some kind of flexible metal and all I succeeded in doing was burning myself.

There was a flurry of movement all around me, soft footsteps in the dirt, voices whispering in some musical language. I struggled inside the net, flopping around, unable to make any headway because of my wings.

Tall, slim shadows crowded around me, their faces hooded. They all held bows with nocked arrows pointing straight at me.

I stopped flailing around. I was only tiring myself out anyway. There were six of the figures surrounding me, all of them perfectly still. I knew that if I tried throwing magic, those arrows would fill me up like a pincushion.

I hate feeling trapped, and I hate thinking I have no choices. I had enough obstacles in my way without being kidnapped by some hostile species.

"What do you want?" I asked, trying to sound like I wasn't as insanely ticked off as I actually was.

The hooded figures did not respond.

"What do you *want*?" I repeated. I confess that I sounded a lot meaner the second time around.

Which may have been why one of the figures stepped forward and hit me in the head with his bow.

Everything faded to black again.

Someone was calling me.

Madeline?

Gabriel? Was that Gabriel's voice?

Madeline, be careful. They are not what they seem.

"Gabriel!" I shouted, or rather, tried to shout.

My mouth was gagged with a piece of cloth. I was in a low hut that appeared to be constructed of large leaves and long strips of tree branches. The floor was dirt, making the structure little more than a glorified tent.

My hands and ankles were bound with something cold and metallic. I tested the strength of the bonds to see whether I could pull them apart. I am a lot stronger than an ordinary human, but the bracelets around my wrists had no give. In fact, they seemed to get tighter. My skin chafed against the metal, and I ceased before I tore my wrists up.

I lay on my right side facing a wall, so I rolled myself to the other side so that I could see the rest of the room. This was not as easy as it seemed, especially when one's ab muscles were—*ahem*—underdeveloped. After spending several moments doing an excellent imitation of a fish out of water, I managed to heave myself to my left side.

The view from this side was less than inspiring. The hut was small and round and just one room. In the center were a fire pit and a small opening at the top of the hut to vent smoke.

There were no other objects in the room. Several leaves cut into long strips hung over the doorway in a kind of makeshift curtain. I was alone in the hut, but there were surely guards posted outside. Well, I wasn't going to lie here and wait for them to come for me.

I still had my wings. I tested them out to see whether my captors had restrained them. Unfortunately, they had. I felt some kind of cord pulling on them. There was no way I'd be able to fly like that. I was trussed up like a Sunday turkey, and I couldn't move at all unless I flipped over and did an impression of an inchworm.

Crawling on my belly hardly seemed like an efficient method of escape. But if that was the only option available to me, then that was what I would do. Nobody had ever taken me prisoner before, and I was a little insulted.

Plus, I had pretty much been spinning my wheels since I'd landed on this stupid planet. Now that I knew where the portal was, I wanted to get to it.

The first order of business was to get out of these bonds. If I had endless time and energy, I could probably figure out a way to pick the bracelets apart at the molecular level. But I did not have endless time or energy. So I did what I do best.

I set the hut on fire.

My palms faced outward even though they were bound behind my back. So all I had to do was call up some fireballs and make sure my hands pointed at the walls.

Soon the hut was smoking. Very quickly the flames spread, and in a short time the whole hut was ablaze. The heat of the flames got uncomfortably close pretty quickly, and I rolled toward the exit.

A guard rushed in, his face set in lines of surprise. His hood was pushed back against his neck, and I could see the pointed tips of his ears. *Faerie,* I thought.

He looked from the flaming wall to me. I widened my eyes and tried to look helpless. I flopped my feet up and down a couple of times so that he would know what I wanted. He seemed torn for a moment, unsure whether he should douse the fire or save the prisoner.

I heard shouts and cries outside as the fire spread. The guard seemed to make a decision. He knelt beside me, hovered his hands over the bracelets that bound my ankles and said something in that musical language I'd heard earlier. The bracelets clicked apart, and the guard put his hands under my shoulders to help me to my feet.

He wasn't stupid enough to release my hands or my wings, but that was okay. I could work with this. I stumbled as he dragged me out the door, both of us coughing from the smoke that now billowed out of the hut.

Several faerie were running toward the blazing structure carrying containers of water that sloshed onto the ground. The guard pushed me to one side so that I fell to the ground again. I rolled over and sat up, glaring at him.

He pointed his finger at me and said something in a firm voice that was likely some variation on, "Stay here. Don't move." Then he ran in the direction the other faeries had come from, probably to help with the fire dousing.

The faeries trying to put out the flames took very little notice of me except to shoot me a quick glance and get on with their business. That suited me fine.

The hut was isolated from the rest of the village, which appeared to be made up of several structures considerably more elaborate than my prison. The village was set in a large clearing, and my hut was right on the edge of the forest. That also suited me fine.

I scooted backward on my bottom toward the underbrush. Leaves scraped against my back. I waited until I thought everyone was engaged with the blazing hut, then went a little farther, until I was against a tree. I used the tree as a brace so I could rise to my feet. The wound in my right thigh burned like hell as I put weight on it.

Then I turned and ran. My hands were bound painfully against my back, and it made running extremely awkward. But I needed to get away. I would figure out how to break the manacles on my wrists later.

The forest was so thick and dense that the sound of activity in the village was quickly muffled by the foliage.

31

I could hear my own desperate, frantic breathing and my unsubtle crashing through the bush, but no sounds of pursuit.

The scent of smoke drifted along behind me, clinging to my clothes and burrowing inside my nostrils. I don't think I ran for very long, but after a while I was wiped out. My body was losing energy fast. I just couldn't keep up with the constant exhaustion and hunger and fear anymore. With every day that passed, my baby got bigger, using more and more of my resources. I was supposed to be eating chips and dip on the couch, not running for my life from creatures that intended me harm—again.

I wasn't really paying attention to where I was going. I was just trying to get as far away from the faerie as possible.

So, naturally, I stumbled into the dragon.

3

I BARRELED THROUGH A PARTICULARLY ROUGH PATCH of brush that was full of tangled pricker branches. I fought my way through the thorns tearing at my face and arms, and finally I was out.

And there he was.

The dragon was sleeping, curled up like a cat in a small clearing. His tail was wrapped around the front of his body, which was so much more massive than I'd realized. He was the size of three city buses lined up with three more stacked on top. And that didn't even count the length of the coiled tail, or the triangular spike that protruded from his back.

His face was long, the bones beneath the scaled skin sharply defined. The closed eyes were huge, easily the size of my head. I already knew it could fly, and breathe fire. I wondered what else it could do.

It was a plain miracle that I hadn't woken it up by crashing through the bushes like that. Maybe it was confident enough in its superiority as the dominant predator in the forest that it didn't need to stir just because it heard a little human noise.

I didn't want to go backward into the thorns, so I'd have to go around the dragon. I crept slowly to the right, toward the base of the tail. I figured if the dragon woke up and attacked, I'd be farther away from its mouth and the inevitable fire, and hopefully more likely to survive.

I kept well away from the creature, leaving several feet between it and me. I just had to get through this clearing. And then get my hands and wings unbound. And then fly thousands of miles to the portal. No problem.

The dragon's tail shifted, uncoiled and landed in front of me. I turned my head slowly, and met the orange eyes of the dragon.

I went perfectly still.

The dragon bumped me with its tail in the back of my legs, herding me closer to its head and its immense jaws.

My mind was a mass of gibbering terror. Everything had finally caught up with me—the stress, the fear, the physical wear and tear. Even if my hands were free, I don't know whether I could have summoned a spell. I just didn't have the wherewithal to hold it together anymore. Given the amount of stress I'd been under, it was only surprising that it hadn't happened sooner.

I stumbled closer to the dragon, unable to go anywhere else. The animal seemed more curious than anything, but maybe I was just projecting human emotion on a monster in hopes that I wasn't about to be barbecued. The dragon drew me closer and closer, until my face was level with one eye.

The pupil was slit and long, like a snake's. It exhaled

noisily, smoke rising from its nostrils. I couldn't think. I didn't have a plan, or even a half-assed idea. I couldn't fly away. I couldn't do anything except breathe, and hope each breath wasn't my last.

The dragon peered at me for a long time. I stared back, mostly because I didn't know what else to do. And as I stared I felt like I was sinking, sinking into flame, flame hot enough to kill, but it didn't hurt me.

The fire was everywhere, dancing on my skin and over my fingers. It consumed me, and it didn't feel like death. It felt like life.

I came back to myself, to the dragon's eye, which now seemed speculative. I leaned toward his face, yearning for something I didn't understand. The dragon turned its muzzle toward me, nudged me with its nose. Its scales were rough and hot against my skin.

"I know you," I whispered. "I know you."

The dragon huffed out a smoky breath in response. Then it jerked away from me, bellowing. An arrow was embedded in its neck.

I spun around, trying not to fall over. My coordination had pretty much gone out the window with my hands bound.

The dragon roared, spitting fire at the platoon of armed faerie that surrounded us. I noticed several of them carried long shields in addition to bows and arrows. As my dragon blew flame at them, the faerie held up the shields, which were made of a shiny hammered metal and deflected the fire away.

Other faerie continued to shoot arrows at the dragon, who knocked the intruders away with his tail if they approached too close. Why would the faerie risk death at the mouth of a dragon just to retrieve me? Why was I so important?

"Go," I said to the dragon. I couldn't bear it if they killed him because of me. I didn't know why, but I wouldn't be able to bear it. "Go. It's me they want."

The faerie were grim-faced and obviously determined. More and more of them appeared, streaming silently out of the trees, more than I'd thought possible.

The dragon huffed out a sound that might have been refusal.

"Go!" I shouted, my eyes full of tears. I didn't want them to hurt him anymore. Whatever they wanted from me didn't even matter. I was tired of fighting. I was sick of death.

And if I died, I could be with Gabriel. There was a lot of peace in that thought.

"Go," I said to the dragon for the third time. I turned my back on the faerie closing in around us so I could meet his eyes. The dragon roared, blasted fire at the faerie.

"Please."

He narrowed his eyes at me, then flapped his wings and lifted off. I followed him with my eyes as he rose above the forest. He paused for a moment, high above me. I heard a low voice in my head, almost a growl.

Be careful, Madeline. They are not what they seem. Do not give in.

Then rough hands were on me, dragging me down, binding my ankles again, lashing my arms to my sides. I jerked my head around, trying to see him, trying to catch one more glimpse of my dragon.

But by the time the faerie had trussed me up again and backed away, the sky was empty. The dragon was gone.

I felt a strange mixture of relief and despair. I was glad the dragon was safe, but now I was alone again—and back where I'd started.

Two faerie came forward carrying a long strip of the same silver netting they'd used to capture me in the first place. I was unceremoniously hoisted into it and the two faerie were joined by two others who held me in it like four posts holding a hammock. All of this was done without speaking, and I wondered who was in charge. The faerie seemed to know instinctively what their job was, moving seamlessly like insects in a hive.

My captors fell into line and began moving back toward the village. It was rough going for me. I rolled around inside the net, unable to control my movements as all of my limbs were immobilized. The fae that carried me weren't deliberately trying to harm me, but they weren't taking any special precautions, either. If they bumped into a tree or a rock, they weren't concerned. And I didn't hear anything that sounded like an apology.

The sky and the roof of the forest whirled dizzyingly above me. After a while I started to feel sick and closed my eyes. I didn't think I had run that far, but the journey back seemed to take forever.

I fell asleep again despite the uncomfortable ride. The pregnancy book I'd purchased (a hundred years ago, in another life, it seemed) had mentioned a constant state of tiredness, particularly in the first trimester. It hadn't mentioned anything about supernatural offspring, although I could extrapolate that my child might be especially exhausting.

I was shaken roughly awake when I was unceremoniously dumped in another dwelling. This one was a lot less primitive than the last. There was an actual floor, made of smooth planks of light wood. The floor was scattered with shiny green leaves.

The faerie that had carried me silently left the room. They probably figured I couldn't do too much damage as tightly bound as I was. Which meant they hadn't realized I was the one who had set the other hut on fire. That was good. It meant I could still surprise them. And the way things were going so far, I would need all the surprises I could get.

I rolled onto my back so I could get a good look at the rest of the room. This position was not even remotely comfortable. My wings and hands were bound behind me so I had to lie on top of them. Still, by lifting my head up I could get a better view without flopping from one side to another.

There were a few pieces of furniture—some chairs, a low table—all of which looked as if they'd been formed from the branches of trees. There were no paintings or photographs on the wall, but a large shrine was given pride of place on one side of the room.

The top of the shrine was decorated with several carved figures. Candles were set at five separate points around the top. I wondered who these faerie worshiped. They were like no fae I had seen before.

Two doorways covered in leaf curtains stood at either end of the room. I suspected that I was about to meet some kind of leader, and I was right.

A tall man who could have been anywhere from thirty to fifty years old entered. Faeries age differently than humans do, at least in my time and place, so he was probably well older than he appeared. The man's face was grim, his eyes were blue, and he had the lean, sinewy look of someone who spent a lot of time outdoors. He was flanked by two younger men who walked a step or two behind him in obvious deference to his status.

He strode in with the air of a person about to lay down the law. I figured I'd better throw him off balance before he went all "Off with her head" on me.

"I'm hungry," I announced.

The three men stopped at the sound of my voice. The leader spoke to the man on his left. This faerie was also tall, with caramel-brown hair streaked with yellow, and very golden brown eyes. The third man had blond hair and green eyes, and a strange quality that seemed to make him fade into the background.

All of the faerie wore a sleeveless brown tunic with leggings, which made them look like escapees from Middle Earth. The man on the right, the disappearing blond, held my sword in his hand. I breathed an inward sigh. I thought I'd lost it.

The leader and the brown-haired man had a short exchange in their own language before the second man spoke. In English. That was a surprise.

"My lord Batarian requires information of you. If you answer honest and true, your bonds will be released and you will be given nourishment."

"If not, then death and/or dismemberment will follow, et cetera, et cetera?" I asked, watching Batarian carefully as I said this. His face did not move a muscle, but his eyes flickered.

The second man spoke again. "I do not know what this 'et cetera' is, but I assure you that you will suffer if you do not cooperate."

"I'm suffering now," I said, making my voice as whiny

and annoying as possible. "I'm hungry. I'm thirsty. My hands are going numb. I was dragged out of a tree when I wasn't bothering anyone."

"I think you misunderstand your position," the man said icily. "You are a prisoner, not a guest."

"Well, at least that clarifies my status," I said. "I thought this was the way you invited people over for dinner."

"My lord has—" the man began again, but I cut him off.

"In my country, prisoners have certain rights," I said. I was going to make this guy snap if it was the last thing I did. I didn't have a lot of power while tied up and lying on the floor, but as long as I wasn't gagged, I could drive some-body crazy.

"You are not *in* your country," the translator said through gritted teeth.

"Yeah, and speaking of that, just where in the hell am I?" *Because when I get back home I want to thank Nathaniel for sending me here—before I smack him in the head several times.*

"I will be the one to ask the questions!" the man thundered.

"No," I said, gesturing toward Batarian. "He will."

The translator looked uncertain for a moment, then gathered his dignity. "Of course, Lord Batarian is the ultimate authority here, but he will ask his questions through me."

I shook my head. "I don't think so."

"Are you saying you refuse to cooperate?"

"No," I said. "I'm saying Batarian can stop pretending he doesn't speak my language."

I had to give Batarian credit. His expression never changed.

"Lord Batarian has entrusted me to . . ."

I glared at Batarian. "Stop. Pretending."

The translator made a move like he was going to strike me.

"Stop!" Batarian said in English.

I raised an eyebrow at him. He gave me a slight nod of acknowledgment. "How did you know?"

"All the time that I was going back and forth with this guy, you never asked what I was saying," I said. "In my experience, a ruler likes to know everything, especially when a conversation is occurring in his presence. You weren't interrupting constantly to ask what I was saying, and he wasn't translating everything I said as a matter of course. He's a failure, too, actually. Neither of you played your parts very well."

"Perhaps that is because duplicity does not come as easily to us as to one of your kind," the translator said.

"And what do you know of my kind?" I said. "We seem to be thin on the ground around here."

"Enough to know that one of Lucifer's cannot be trusted," he shot back.

I stilled. What did they know of Lucifer here, and how did they know about me?

"Sakarian!" Batarian snapped. He looked furious. The younger man had given away information that his lord was not yet ready to share.

Sakarian, looking chastened, bent his head toward Batarian and said something in their native language, sounding apologetic.

Batarian responded, his tone clipped. I looked from one to the other. They did not physically resemble each other except for their height, but still . . .

"Is he your kid?" I asked, jerking my head toward

Sakarian. This gesturing-with-my-head thing was getting old. My neck was sore.

"I do not understand 'kid,'" Batarian said, his brow furrowing.

"Your son," I said. "Is he your son?"

The two of them exchanged glances with the third man, who had thus far remained silent and still.

"How did you know that?" Batarian asked.

"Are you some kind of witch?" Sakarian asked suspiciously.

I shrugged—or, at least, tried to. I could barely move my shoulders a millimeter with the way I was tied up. "It's just the way you act with each other. There's a familiarity, despite all of the 'my lord'–ing."

Batarian looked troubled. "It appears we have revealed far more than we have concealed. Perhaps Sakarian is right. We are not practiced in the ways of duplicity."

His face darkened. It seemed he was dwelling on some bad memory. I didn't want to get persecuted just because he was remembering someone who had tricked him before. Someone like, say, Lucifer.

"Listen," I said. "You want to talk, let's talk. But I need to eat. It won't do you any good if your prisoner passes out in the middle of the interrogation."

Sakarian shook his head. "We cannot trust her. She will flee as soon as we loose her bonds."

"What do you want to keep me for, anyway?" I asked. "You don't trust me, but I didn't attack you. You attacked me. Twice. You're acting pretty self-righteous for a people who initiated the conflict."

Sakarian started to speak again, but Batarian held up

his hand. I could see him weighing his options, trying to determine the best tack to take with me.

"Release the bonds on her arms and legs but keep her wings tied," Batarian said.

"You know," I said conversationally. "Once my hands are free it's nothing for me to get my wings unbound. So you might as well save me the trouble and take care of that as well."

Batarian gave a short laugh. "You would not be able to release yourself. These cords can be undone only by the voice of our people."

I remembered the guard holding his hand over the knots tied around my ankles, how he had spoken words in his own language before they had released.

"Okay," I said. "But it would still be polite to untie my wings. They're not just accessories, you know. It hurts when they're bound up like this."

"I think it is not a bad thing for you to suffer some discomfort," Batarian said. "It will remind you of your place."

Sakarian came forward to release my ankles and wrists. He unknotted the cords that had been wrapped around my body until all that remained were, as promised, the bindings around my wings.

His eyes dared me to try anything as I sat up, rubbing my limbs to get feeling back into them.

If I wanted to, I could have done a lot of damage now that my hands were free. I could have killed all three of them and escaped on foot before anyone realized what was going on. Three things stopped me from doing just that.

One, I didn't really have a grievance with them despite the fact that they had captured me for no apparent reason.

43

No one here was my enemy, and my life was not in immediate danger. So it didn't seem very sporting to kill them just because they were holding me up.

Two, I was never going to reach the portal on foot. I needed my wings to fly over the ocean, and according to Batarian, only one of his kind could release them. I needed to ingratiate myself to my hosts so that they would trust me enough to unbind my wings.

Three, I was hungry. Really, really, really hungry. And I'd had no luck finding anything edible on this world so far. So I might as well let them refuel me before I went tripping through the wilderness again.

I stood up carefully, wanting to get the blood flowing again, but my knees buckled. All three of the faerie started at my sudden movement and three knives appeared from nowhere.

The third man, whose name I still did not know, brandished a dagger in one hand and my sword in the other. It was more than a little insulting to be threatened with my own blade. I wanted to rip it from his hands and knock him in the head with the hilt, just to show that I could.

But it didn't seem like a productive way to achieve my ends, and I would probably wind up wrapped in knots again so I held my temper. Beezle would be proud of me. If I ever saw Beezle again.

I held up my hands to indicate that I meant no harm. The three faerie relaxed, the knives disappearing into the secret pockets from which they had emerged. Batarian spoke to Sakarian for a moment. The younger man went to the door and called to someone. There was a brief conference, and then Sakarian returned. I hoped he was arranging for food to be brought; otherwise I was going to start chewing on the furniture.

Batarian indicated that I should sit on one of the tree-branch chairs. I eyed the seat dubiously, but it didn't seem wise to refuse. When I settled in one, I realized I was right. It was like sitting on wicker furniture, only two thousand times less comfortable.

The lashed branches were bumpy and round and didn't evenly remotely conform to the shape of the human body. My bound wings made it impossible to lean comfortably against the backrest. The other three settled easily into the other chairs and appeared perfectly at ease, so it must have been comfortable to them. Me, I could have gone for a nice down-stuffed cushion and some synthetic fabric.

I also realized my injured leg was puffy and tender. I needed to heal it, but revealing such a power in front of Batarian seemed the height of stupidity.

Batarian followed my gaze to the arrow wound. "You need a poultice for that. Litarian."

The third man placed my sword next to Batarian and went out of the room. I wondered vaguely why all their names ended in "-rian." I looked at my sword, just sitting there, leaning against the chair.

I could grab it right then and hold it to Batarian's throat, force them to release my wings. Except that I still had not eaten. I was starting to feel like Beezle. I didn't really care what happened next so long as someone gave me a meal.

"What are you called?" Batarian asked.

"Maddy," I said. "Maddy Black."

No one called me Madeline except fallen angels. They liked the formality of it, I supposed.

"Maddy Black," Batarian said, rolling my name around in his mouth like an exotic food. "And what is it you are doing here, Maddy Black?"

"Trying to get home," I said honestly. "I've got no interest in staying here."

"But how is it that you have come to our land in the first place? We have had no visitors for thousands of years. This world was closed off in honor of the accord between our people and Lucifer."

"I kind of ended up here by accident," I said. No need to go into the whole business with the Retrievers. "But I want to leave, believe me. And the longer you hold me prisoner, the longer it's going to take me to get out of here."

"But we cannot trust that you are simply an accidental traveler and that you mean us no harm," Batarian said. "We have only your word of this."

"Well, it's not like I can prove it," I said. "I'm a stranger here. No one is going to vouch for me."

"Yes, you are a stranger. A very strange stranger, I might add," Batarian said. "One with wings."

"You've got pointy ears and a bow," I said. "In my town that would be considered strange in itself, pal."

"You will not speak so disrespectfully to Lord Batarian," Sakarian said.

Ah. Here was familiar ground. "I speak disrespectfully to everyone. You'd better get used to it."

"Everyone?" Batarian raised an eyebrow. "Including Lucifer?"

"Especially him," I said without thinking.

Sakarian pounced. "So you are an associate of Lucifer's, then."

" 'Associate' is too strong a term," I said, trying to back-pedal. Damn me and my stupid mouth.

"Father, Lucifer has broken the ancient accord," Sakarian said. "He sent this spy upon us. We should exe-cute her immediately and assemble an army against him."

"Whoa, whoa, whoa," I said, holding my hands up in front of me in a "calm down" gesture. "Way to jump to conclusions."

"I do not know why you speak of jumping, spy," Sakarian said.

So they spoke English but their dialect wasn't up-to-date. Interesting.

"I mean you've made a decision without knowing all the facts," I said. "I'm not a spy for Lucifer."

"Then why do you have his mark upon your palm?" Sakarian challenged.

I wondered why Batarian seemed content to sit back and let his hotheaded kid take the reins of the conversation. Was it because he wanted to observe my responses? What-ever the reason, now was not the time for telling the truth. If I said I was Lucifer's descendant, they would definitely think the worst.

"It was kind of an accident," I said. This was true. I'd used Lucifer's sword in the Maze and against Baraqiel. Somewhere along the way it had marked me.

"You certainly seem to have a great number of acci-dents," Sakarian sneered.

"Hang around me long enough and you'll see that's true," I said. "How is it that you know of Lucifer, anyway?"

"We will ask the questions," Batarian said.

Just then Litarian reentered the room carrying a small

woven bag. Behind him were several other faerie. The first two held a table between them, which they set before me. The other faerie silently placed dishes of food on the table.

There were several plates of vegetables, one with some kind of meat and one that appeared to be roasted insects in sauce. I was not so hungry that I was going to eat bugs, especially if other options were available.

I glanced at Batarian to make sure it was okay for me to eat before I dove in. He nodded, and I grabbed a plate of something that looked like a salad. There were no utensils so I used my fingers to pick up bits of some peppery greens. There were also berries, round and red like cranberries, but when I bit into one, it had none of the tartness of a cranberry. The sweet juice burst over my tongue. It tasted so delicious it was hard for me to hold back.

My stomach twisted as the food hit it, reminding me to take it slow. If I gobbled down too much at once, I was just going to make myself sick.

Litarian silently handed me the bag he was holding. It was filled with bitter-smelling herbs.

"Place it on your wound," Batarian said.

I put the bag through the hole in my jeans and onto the swollen wound beneath. I doubted very much that this little sack of smelly stuff was going to help me, but holding the poultice against my leg allowed me to send a healing spell through it without being noticed by the others. I hoped.

I shoveled food into my mouth with one hand and pressed the poultice against my wound with the other. I could feel the three faerie watching me like I was an alien from another planet. Which I was. I certainly was not on the Earth I knew anymore.

I cleared the plate of greens and berries and pulled

something toward me that looked like a potato. It might have been a giant bug, though, so I asked first.

"Is this a vegetable?"

Sakarian looked confused. "Vegetable?"

"Is it a plant? Something that grows out of the ground?" There were some interesting gaps in their language. I could understand them not knowing modern American vernacular, but "vegetable"?

He nodded. "That is the root of the halalia plant."

"Like a potato, then," I said, digging in. It actually tasted more like a turnip, but at least it wasn't a giant mealworm.

"You do not eat the flesh of animals?" Batarian asked, tilting his head to one side. It was like he was trying to assemble the puzzle of me in his head.

"I do. But I prefer when it's cut and wrapped at the grocery store. Never mind." All three of them had the same confused look. "Ask your questions."

"Will you answer honestly?" Batarian said, his gaze piercing me. He had disconcertingly blue eyes—very light, like the way Nathaniel's used to be before he'd been changed by Puck's legacy. I felt a little pang like homesickness.

I chewed and swallowed a bite of the turnip-thing before answering Batarian. I wanted to get out of here, and practicing duplicity was not the best way to get them to trust me so I could achieve that. However, there was no reason to agree to answer every single thing they wanted to know. Certain information could and would be misinterpreted, especially by Sakarian, who seemed particularly suspicious of me.

"I'll answer as honestly as I can," I finally said.

"You will reveal your intentions to my lord, or else you will pay the price," Sakarian said.

"I would be a fool if I told you everything about me," I said. "As you would be if you were in my position and you did so."

"You—" Sakarian began, but Batarian cut him off.

"She is correct. Were I in her place, I would not reveal all. Omission is not necessarily a sin. But I expect the courtesy of truth," Batarian said.

"I can work with that," I said.

"You have admitted you are an associate of Lucifer's," Batarian said.

"I told you, I'm not an associate," I said.

"That is difficult to believe. You carry his mark upon your body."

I could tell them a little, if I was careful. I wasn't about to explain that I was a blood relative of Lucifer's. Part of me was amazed that he'd managed to piss off a bunch of creatures in an entirely different dimension. Another part of me was not shocked in the least. Making enemies seemed to be what Lucifer did best.

"The sword gave me the mark," I said, pointing to the blade that still rested against the chair.

I had a very strong impulse to snatch up the sword and swing it at somebody's head. That was a worrisome thought. I'd had these dark impulses before, but they usually emerged in the heat of battle, when I was under stress.

At the moment I was sitting peacefully, having a somewhat civilized conversation with three faerie. I wasn't under any particular stress, but I was feeling frustrated. I didn't have to tolerate these creatures. They were beneath me. I could destroy their whole village as I had destroyed the plague of vampires upon Chicago.

I realized what I was thinking and made a conscious decision to rein it in.

This must be the way Lucifer feels all the time, I thought with sudden insight. What must it be like to be a creature of such immense power, always under tightly wrapped control?

I became aware that the room was silent, and that I had not been interrogated further after I'd admitted to being marked by the sword. The other three were staring at me.

Litarian looked stoic. He seemed to be the best at concealing his thoughts. Batarian appeared intrigued. Sakarian looked like he couldn't decide whether to be amazed or furious.

"What?" I asked.

"You were . . . glowing," Batarian said.

"And there was a crackling in the air," Sakarian said. "Like the wind before lightning strikes."

Not good. All I'd been doing was *thinking* about destroying everything in sight and my power had risen up without my consent. If I wasn't careful, I would turn into the monster that Beezle feared I was becoming.

4

"WHAT ARE YOU, MADDY BLACK?" BATARIAN ASKED.

"I'm human," I said.

"No human has ever had wings," Sakarian said.

"I haven't seen very many humans around here, so you'll forgive me if I consider you an unqualified observer," I said.

"I have seen humans before," Sakarian answered. "No human has ever looked like you."

I wondered whether there were people in this place, or if he was speaking of a time that had already passed.

"Whatever you might have seen before, I am human," I repeated.

"One of your parents was. I suspect your father was Lucifer," Batarian said.

"Wouldn't he love that?" I muttered. "Nope, you're off base there. I'm not Lucifer's daughter."

"Then who was your father?" Batarian persisted.

"What do you care?" I said. "I don't see what my parentage has to do with anything."

"I wish to determine what you are so that I can decide if you are a threat to us. If you are of Lucifer's kind, then Lucifer is in violation of the treaty, and you are a threat," Batarian said.

"There is no one of Lucifer's kind," I said. "I don't belong to him. I don't represent him. I told you. I just want to go home."

"She will tell us nothing, Father," Sakarian announced. "She will not betray her master."

"No one is master of me," I said coldly.

Batarian gave me a long look. "Every creature has a lord."

"Not me, pal. I'm an American."

"What is an 'American'?" Sakarian asked.

"Do you want the long version or the short version?" I asked.

The three of them blinked at me, looking confused.

"Never mind," I said, peering into a cup of something that smelled sweet with a whiff of alcohol. "Got any water?"

"We do not drink the water here," Sakarian answered. "It is disrespectful to the gods that live there."

"Gods, huh? I thought they were nothing but a bunch of mean-ass water sprites," I said.

There was a cry of alarm from outside, and the sound of running feet.

All three men stood abruptly. Batarian and Sakarian started toward the door. The king barked orders in his native language to Litarian.

The third man silently stood and indicated that I should

go with him. I stuffed something that looked and tasted roughly like bread in my mouth and followed him out of the room.

He held my sword loosely grasped in his left hand. I could knock him out, take the sword, and get away in the chaos. There were people running everywhere, carrying weapons. Even looking the way I did, it would be easy to take advantage of the confusion.

"I would not attempt what you are considering," Litarian said, his English heavily accented. He seemed to have a lot more trouble with the language than either Sakarian or Batarian.

"What am I considering?" I asked as we continued down a passageway. The walls were uniformly bland—plain wood with no decoration. Several rooms emptied off the hall, all of them with leaves hanging over the entranceway.

"You are considering escape, as I would if I were you," Litarian said. "However, if you run, you will be captured again, and Lord Batarian will not be so kind to you a second time."

"Who says I'll be captured?" I said under my breath, but I knew Litarian was right.

I couldn't run far or fast enough to get away from the fae. I needed my wings, and to get my wings back, one of them had to unknot the bindings. So I was stuck playing along for the time being.

We reached the end of a passage, and Litarian politely held the hanging leaves aside so that I could pass through. I ducked under his arm and found that we stood on a balcony. I stared down. And down, and down.

I hadn't realized we were in a tree house several dozen

feet off the ground. My fingers curled around the railing as I twisted around to get a sense of the size of the place.

The structure continued up for three stories, laced with a series of stairs and outer walkways. The trunk of the tree was enormous, larger than anything I'd ever seen, and its height would easily rival that of a sequoia.

Far below, I could see the remaining buildings of the village neatly laid out. They appeared to be similar in construction to the building I'd burned down—simple, one-room huts.

Warriors carrying weapons disappeared into the forest. Several women holding children converged upon the tree. I couldn't see whether there was some kind of walkway below, but I assumed they were fleeing to the safety of the tree house. Despite its lofty position, I couldn't see much of the surrounding area. The forest was too thick.

Litarian's hand closed around my upper arm, gently but firmly pulling me away.

"It is not safe to be outdoors at this time," he said.

"What's going on?" I asked. "Are you under attack?"

"Yes," Litarian said briefly.

"Another band of faerie?" I persisted. It would be useful to know more about the situation here.

"No," Litarian replied without elaboration. "How do you know that we are fae?"

"I've seen faeries before, in my world," I said.

Litarian did not reply, but his forehead wrinkled slightly.

Something about him reminded me of Gabriel. Gabriel never said two words when one would do.

Inside my belly, my baby fluttered its wings, as if he felt the same sadness I did whenever I thought of Gabriel. My memories of my husband were getting further and further away from me. I never seemed to have time to dwell on the past. The present always required too much of my attention.

Litarian led me to an external staircase that wrapped around the tree until it reached the next level. We followed the stairs up and then crossed the length of the building. I thought we would reenter, as the main body of the house didn't appear to go any higher, but Litarian followed the balcony to its end and then pointed up.

A rope ladder hung there, leading up to what looked like a small, covered platform.

"You want me to go up there?" I asked.

The platform didn't appear very large or very stable. Without my wings, it didn't seem very safe either.

He nodded. "Someone will return for you later."

I was nearly overwhelmed by the desire to punch Litarian in the gut. It really burned to have to submit to someone else. But there was nothing much I could do about it at the moment. I needed my wings. I'd never escape—or make it to the portal—without them. So I gritted my teeth, grabbed one of the rungs of the ladder, and climbed.

The platform was farther away than it looked. Sweat beaded on my forehead. I couldn't believe how tired I felt. About halfway up I paused and glanced down. Litarian watched me impassively. Lucifer's sword glinted in the sun.

I continued up, trying not to think about how far I would fall if I slipped. Litarian didn't seem like the sort who would catch me unless he was ordered to do so.

I finally reached the top of the ladder, bumping the crown of my head on the platform. There was a trapdoor just above the ladder. I pushed it open and pulled myself through, slamming the trapdoor behind me.

The space was small. Frighteningly small.

The platform was perhaps five feet by five feet, which meant that even with my less-than-impressive height I would not be able to stretch out. There were four beams holding up a little roof, but no walls.

I pressed my back against the tree, feeling dangerously exposed. I'd never been afraid of heights before—how could I be, having spent so much of my life in the air? But my wings were bound and the ground below was much farther away than I liked.

I discovered I was not immune to vertigo.

My leg had healed completely, and my stomach was full. Sleep was what I needed now, but the idea of sleeping on this platform was terrifying. What if I rolled off the side in my sleep? The best-case scenario would be that I'd land on the roof of the tree house below, which would break my fall.

Or, quite probably, my neck.

The sounds of frantic activity below had ceased, and there was no noise from the forest. Even the birds and insects had gone quiet. The air was heavy, hushed with waiting. I folded my hands over my belly. My eyes drifted closed.

I heard Gabriel's voice in my head saying, "Things are not as they seem."

"Where are you?" I called, groping in the shadows. "I don't want to be alone."

"You are not alone," another voice said.

A figure rose out of the darkness, sheathed in flame, its eyes two pools of exploding stars. "You will never be alone again."

The figure reached for me, hands drenched in fire. I was drawn to the flame, even as I shrank from it in terror. There was a keening cry, something metallic and alien, and my eyes opened.

My clothes were soaked with sweat, and my face felt as though it had been singed by flame. My son beat a rapid tattoo in my belly. It was full dark.

The moon had risen over the trees and shafts of white light filtered through the branches. I was surprised that I had gone to sleep. I thought my fear of falling was greater than my exhaustion.

The alien cry echoed through the forest again. I realized it had not been part of my dream as I'd thought but had woken me from sleep. The sound was vaguely familiar. It fluttered at the corner of my brain, just out of reach. I knew what made that sound. I just couldn't remember.

A flock of birds suddenly rose into the air from their roost nearby, several of them flying straight at me in their panic. I flattened myself on my belly against the platform, not wanting my eyes to be pecked out by some crazed bird. The crown of my head stuck out over the edge.

My own wings were cramping from being tied together for so long. I pressed uncomfortably into the wood, waiting for the birds to pass by, burning with jealousy at their freedom. My personality is really not well suited to being a prisoner.

After a while the flapping and the chirping stopped. I eased forward an inch or so until I could peek over the edge. Far below, I could see the shadows moving, the silent warriors returning.

A glad cry was raised, and torches were lit in greeting. It was difficult to tell from that distance, but several of the faeries seem to be covered in blood. None of them seemed to be seriously wounded, and no one was carrying the dead home. Either they had left the corpses behind or the attack had just been a skirmish.

I wondered what had panicked the birds, though. The faerie seemed to slip through the woods unobtrusively. There must be another predator out there. I stared hard into the foliage, but couldn't see anything. The forest kept its secrets.

Now that I was awake, I was hungry again. And thirsty. No one was going to send room service to me in the middle of the night, so I was just going to have to deal with the discomfort. I pushed up to a kneeling position and carefully eased back against the tree.

My mind buzzed with questions. What had happened in this place between Lucifer and these fae? Why was the world closed to others but I had been able to arrive? How far was I from my own home? And most important—had Nathaniel known where he was sending me, and if he did, why here? If he didn't, then how did I end up in another dimension where Lucifer was not only known, but despised? Was it nothing but bad luck, or was I a magnet for Lucifer's enemies? Did my blood draw me to them, ensuring that I would never have any peace?

I couldn't do much about philosophical questions regarding my unlucky bloodline. There was no way to determine Nathaniel's trustworthiness from here. What I could do was find out what had happened between these fae and Lucifer. And I had to gain their trust so that my wings could be released, but I couldn't wait forever for that to happen.

When I'd left Chicago, Puck, Alerian and Lucifer had met for the first time in centuries. I didn't think it was a good idea for the three of them to run around unsupervised for long. And twice since coming here I'd dreamed of Gabriel warning me that "they" were not to be trusted.

Did he mean the fae, or was he warning me of others I had not yet met? Was I actually hearing Gabriel speaking to me from beyond the dead, or was it all just a projection of my anxieties?

Usually when I had this many questions, I took action. I tracked somebody down. I followed clues. I smashed and burned things. I smote my enemies. At the moment there was nothing for me to do except cool my heels.

Unless I wanted to use my power to terrorize the fae, burn down their village and slaughter them one by one until they gave me what I wanted—my wings. But that seemed like the sort of thing a bad person would do. Someone like Lucifer. A monster.

I was still trying hard to be a good guy. According to Beezle, the jury was out on whether or not I was succeeding. Killing a bunch of innocents just so I could get my way would definitely cross a line.

So I waited. The moon set. The sun rose. My eyes remained open. As the first rays of sunlight touched the tops of the trees, I thought I saw a figure moving among the branches. Aside from my physical discomfort, the sensation of being watched made it impossible for me to fall back asleep.

Whatever was making the back of my neck prickle was probably the same creature that had disturbed the birds earlier. It was just a flash of something green. It might have been nothing but a branch moving. Or it might have been yet another creature that wished me harm.

My throat was scratchy from lack of water. The fae

clearly thought it was fine to live on mead or whatever had been in my cup yesterday, but I was having elaborate fantasies about a truckload of iced bottled water falling from the sky.

Barring that, I'd settle for some rain. Surely the water gods wouldn't have dominion over flying drops from the clouds. But the sky was clear and cloudless, and no relief was coming from there. So I waited. And waited.

The sun rose higher. I got more hungry, more thirsty, and a headache built behind my eyes. There was very little movement from below.

The whole village seemed subdued. I started contemplating doing something stupid, like climbing down through the porthole, blasting nightfire at whoever stood guard and then taking Batarian hostage until he released my wings.

I heard movement on the walkway below and leaned carefully out over the edge to see.

Litarian was crossing underneath the platform, carrying a bowl and a cup. I was trying to figure out how he would get up the ladder with that stuff when a rope flew up from beneath, wrapped around one of the poles holding up the roof, and returned to Litarian's waiting hands.

He placed the bowl and cup inside a sack and tied the sack to the rope.

"Won't that spill everything?" I muttered, but the sack was already on its way up to me.

The bag was made of soft, aged leather. I unknotted the tie at the top, expecting to see the contents slathered all over the inside. But the bowl and cup rested neatly on the bottom, almost as if Litarian had placed them on a tray and carried them to me.

I took out the bowl, which had something oatmeal-porridgy in it. The cup was filled with the same honey-colored mead drink I'd had the day before.

Once I'd emptied the bag, Litarian yanked on the rope until the sack returned to him. He coiled up the rope and continued without so much as a nod.

"Well, good morning to you, too," I said loudly.

I tipped the bowl toward my mouth—Litarian hadn't bothered to provide a spoon—and tentatively tasted what was inside.

The porridge was good, kind of nutty, and seemed to have been cooked in milk. I gulped down the mead, though it was very unsatisfactory and left me feeling more thirsty than before.

The silence of the forest was broken by another of the eerie, metallic cries that had interrupted my sleep. This time another voice joined in, and then another, and another.

The sound seemed to worm inside my ear and permeate my brain. I threw myself on my belly and covered my head with my arms, trying to block out the noise. It grew louder and louder as more voices joined the chorus. Below, the faerie were running to and fro again, as they had the day before.

However, the warriors did not enter the forest. They set up a perimeter around the village and waited, watchful and still. The alien song grew louder, more persistent, and I knew that whatever made that noise approached the village. It was an army, and the fae were ready for war.

The pain in my head made my eyes squint. Just as the song reached a crescendo, it suddenly stopped. I raised my head, my breath held. The first creatures leapt from the forest, a poison green blur.

The fae fired arrows, and when the creatures were close enough the warriors pulled out daggers for hand-to-hand fighting. Both the fae and their enemies moved so quickly that I couldn't easily identify the creatures.

After a few moments I realized what they were, and why their cries were so familiar to me.

Just before I had given up my Agent's status forever, I had lost a soul named Jayne Wiskowski. She had been killed by one of these monsters, which looked like giant preying mantises. When I'd fought with the overgrown insect, it had threatened me, told me it was the vanguard of a vast army to come.

I'd never discovered who had sent the thing. Shortly after that I'd killed my father and defeated a city full of vampires, so I never gave the bug another thought.

At the time I'd assumed it had been sent by Azazel or Titania, and I had not seen another one since. Until now.

But how had a creature from this world wound up in Chicago? One of my enemies had to have a way into and out of this place, despite Batarian's insistence that the borders of the world were closed, even despite the evidence of my own magic, which would not create a portal for me to leave.

There was a way, but who controlled it? Whoever it was would not be friendly to me, for sure. The mantis I had killed had told me that Jayne Wiskowski's death had simply been a way to get to me. That girl had died for nothing, just another casualty in an ongoing war.

The revelation of my blood ties to Lucifer had caused me to accrue more enemies than any one person should have, and they were here even in this strange place.

Why, why, why had Nathaniel sent me here? It was

disturbing to think that I had shared intimacies with him and that he had still managed to trick me, to betray me.

Of course, it was possible that he hadn't betrayed me at all, that this was all just a coincidence. It was hard for me to buy that, though. Coincidence didn't play a huge role in my life. Pretty much everything that happened to me was by somebody's design.

I didn't know whether the collection of mantises below was their entire population or just a small portion of it, but there seemed to be a lot of them. And the fae did not appear to be doing very well.

I remembered fighting the mantis myself, remembered the tough carapace that resisted the blade of my sword. The only part of the insect that was vulnerable was its joints.

The fae bowmen were excellent shots. I saw more than one mantis fall after a perfectly placed arrow pierced its neck. But the trouble was that there were a lot of mantises, and it took time for even a preternaturally fast archer to nock the arrow, draw the bow, and let it fly.

The end result was that the faerie were falling as fast as the insects. I didn't know whether the fae here were my enemies or my friends. The only faerie I'd ever met who hadn't tried to kill me was J.B. But I knew the insects were definitely not the good guys.

So I could help the fae, if they would let me. I scrambled back to the trapdoor, opened it, and peered down the ladder. As I expected, no one was guarding me. They had their hands full with the insect attack.

I climbed down the ladder to the balcony on the third level. There was no one on this floor as far as I could see. They were all down below, fighting, protecting their children, building fortifications to prevent the insects from climbing into the tree.

I'd never tried this spell from a distance. Usually I was in a hand-to-hand situation when I decided to set something on fire. I didn't want to accidentally hit any of the faerie, so instead of targeting the insects in the fray, I aimed for a group of mantis that were just emerging from the forest.

I took a deep breath, felt the power of the Morningstar flow through me, and let the lightning fly. Electricity crackled through the air, leaving behind the scent of ozone. It slammed into the knot of mantis, which screeched and fell to the ground, their flesh smoking. The air filled with the scent of burning insect.

Several of the mantis screamed and pointed upward at me, and a number of the fae turned to look as well. From this distance, I couldn't tell whether they were scared or grateful. I almost didn't care which it was so long as they realized I was not to be trifled with.

Besides, it felt so good to release some of the magic that had built up inside me. I hadn't realized it was like bottled tension, that the breadth and depth of the Morningstar's power was so huge that it needed to be released at regular intervals. Normally I was fighting bad guys on a regular basis, so I had more than enough opportunities to blow off some steam.

Even before I'd come into my legacy from Lucifer I'd had an Agency pickup at least once a day. I'd always been able to release my magic before it got too dangerous. I hadn't even known it *was* dangerous.

I wondered how Lucifer dealt with this. Maybe after so

many millennia it didn't bother him anymore. Or maybe he had some secret outlet for his magic. It was slightly amusing to think of Lucifer hanging out in space somewhere, smashing planets just to get rid of his pent-up energy.

Amusing, and more than a little frightening.

I continued blasting at the insects for a few more moments, taking down several of the creatures and evening up the odds for the fae.

Finally, one of the creatures gave out a call, and the remaining mantis—the ones fighting hand to hand with the fae—retreated into the forest.

The exhausted warriors below turned as one body to look up at me. They did not seem grateful. They looked frightened, or angry, but none of them looked ready to thank me.

I curled my fingers around the banister, magic still humming under the surface of my skin. The urge to take off, to disappear into the sky, was tremendous. My wings strained against the tether that bound them. As it had when my wrists were tied, the cord seem to grow tighter with my struggles, to squeeze more painfully.

My palms were smoking against the wood of the railing. It didn't hurt, but when I lifted them away I could see the imprint of my hand charred into the surface.

There was a pounding of feet from both sides of the walkway as fae poured up the stairs. They were coming for me.

I stood still and waited. I didn't have a choice. I couldn't fly away. All I could hope was that Batarian would interpret my actions as trustworthy.

The fae appeared on either side of me, Sakarian leading one group and Litarian the other. Sakarian looked wary, but defiant. Litarian appeared unruffled as always. He held a coil of rope in his hands.

"You're not tying me up again," I said.

"Lord Batarian has ordered you bound and brought before him," Sakarian snarled.

"I will kill all of you and burn this place to the ground before I will submit any further," I said.

As I said it, I knew it was true. I didn't have to tolerate them.

"You cannot kill us all without incurring harm to yourself," Sakarian said.

"Oh, yeah?" I said softly. A ball of flame appeared above my palm. "Who wants to try me?"

All of the fae stared in reluctant fascination at the fire floating above my hand. They had their own magic here, to be sure, but there was nothing like this that I had seen.

"How about you?" I asked Sakarian. "Do you think you can loose one of those arrows before I turn you into Korean barbecue?"

I was sure my reference went over his head, but my meaning was clear. I really hoped Litarian wouldn't try to lasso me. I'd have to hurt him if he did, and if I had to hurt him, it would bother me. Something about him reminded me very strongly of Gabriel. But I would do it if I had to. I'd made the threat, and I would follow through.

The fae were frozen in place, obviously unsure what to do. I stepped back slightly so I could keep an eye on both Litarian and Sakarian.

"I will go with you to Batarian," I said. "But you will not bind me."

"You cannot be trusted," Sakarian said. "Now that we

know what you are capable of, we cannot allow you to appear before our lord unbound."

"You're afraid I'm going to kill him," I said. "I could have done that already."

There was a little flicker in Litarian's eyes, as if he were acknowledging the truth of this.

"I could kill Batarian even if my hands were bound. And you, and anybody else I wanted."

As I spoke, the flames rose higher, and with it, my temper. The air was filled with light, and it came from me. Forget trying to be the nice guy. They needed to know who they were dealing with.

"I will come, but it will be on my terms, not yours."

The eyes of every fae were on me, and the majority appeared terrified. Sakarian was scared but trying very hard not to show it.

Something predatory awoke in me, something that recognized Sakarian was a weak link. It was a dark feeling, one that frightened me. I wanted to crush Sakarian because I could. I turned toward him. His eyes widened. Before I could find out what I would have done, I heard, "Wait."

I looked over my shoulder at Litarian. He held my gaze, tossed the rope over the edge. Sakarian spoke to him in their own language, his voice furious. Litarian ignored him, focusing on me.

"There are children here," he said.

I felt my fury dim a little, the light inside me easing down. "Then keep them safe."

He nodded, then spoke loudly to the assembled warriors. The other fae left—most eagerly, a few reluctantly, but they all left—until I stood alone with Litarian and Sakarian.

Litarian held out his hand to me. "My lady," he said.

I raised my eyebrows at him.

"Only a queen would have the strength you have," he said in reply to my look.

Technically I was a queen. I was heir to Azazel's court, and the fact that I had killed my father and blown my court to smithereens was neither here nor there. I might be monarch of a fallen court, but Litarian was correct. I was a queen.

I nodded at him, and allowed him to approach.

"Would you extinguish the flame? I will not attempt to harm you," he said.

Sakarian spoke to Litarian again in their own language. I didn't need a translator to know Sakarian wanted to know what the hell Litarian was doing. I doused the ball of fire, allowed Litarian to take my hand.

He spoke to Sakarian in a firm voice, and the other fae cursed angrily in response. I looked from one to the other, and realized something I should have sooner. As with Sakarian and Batarian, there was no physical resemblance, but still . . .

"You're brothers."

This time even Litarian's face registered shock.

"Only a witch could know that," Sakarian hissed. "We should kill her now."

"Brothers," I continued. "With different mothers."

"How could you know such a thing?" Litarian said.

"The way you act toward one another gives you away. You're older," I said to Litarian. "But illegitimate."

"Perhaps you are a witch," Litarian said faintly.

For some reason Litarian was in the stronger power position. Sakarian, despite his protests, had been forced to submit to his brother's decision regarding me. I wondered what family drama was at work here. It was clearly not widely known, if at all, that Litarian was Batarian's son.

In my initial encounter with the king, the power dynamic seemed to indicate that Litarian was below Sakarian. Perhaps this was simply a performance, something that was used to deflect attention away from Litarian. No matter what, the information was obviously useful—and probably dangerous.

Litarian spoke in a low voice to Sakarian, then gave my hand a tug. "Lord Batarian awaits us," he said.

As Litarian led me away, I was abruptly aware of my stinky, smelly clothes, my torn and bloodied jeans, my knotted hair. I thought of Amarantha on her throne, dressed and coiffed like a supermodel. I might be a queen, but I most definitely did not look like one.

Litarian led me into the main building. I expected to return to the room where I'd met the king earlier. Instead of going down two flights of stairs, we stayed on the present level.

At the end of the hallway was a large room, much more lushly appointed than the one I'd been in previously. There was more furniture, and all of it of a higher quality. Rugs and blankets woven of some soft- and fluffy-looking material were scattered on the floor or draped over the backs of chairs. The end of the room opened to a private verandah.

Batarian was there, his back to us, his shoulders hunched and tensed. As we entered, he turned on us, his face drawn in lines of fury. He strode toward me, his hands outstretched like he would strangle me.

I dropped Litarian's hand and curled my fists. "Don't even think about it. You'll never get a chance to lay a finger on me," I warned.

"Do not threaten the king unless you wish to meet an immediate death," Sakarian barked.

Batarian stopped a few feet from me, his hands frozen, fingers curled into claws. He made a visible effort to calm himself, drawing air noisily through his flared nostrils.

"Just what in the name of all the gods that are and ever will be do you think you are doing?" Batarian said through gritted teeth. "And I thought I said she was to be brought here bound and under guard."

"Litarian permitted her to come before you in this fashion," Sakarian said snidely.

"It seemed wise to prevent further loss of life," Litarian said, ignoring Sakarian's tone.

"Did you threaten my men? After I showed you hospitality?" Batarian said.

"Hospitality?" I snorted. "Is that what you call it? Leaving me on that platform, ignored, exposed to the elements? Keeping my wings bound and forcing me to stay here when I have told you repeatedly I mean you no harm, that I only wish to leave? I've killed your enemies for you, for crying out loud. You would have lost that battle were it not for me."

"We have lost the battle anyway," Batarian said grimly. "You have no idea of the damage you have done."

"Then why don't you tell me," I said. "I'd expected a little more gratitude, frankly."

Batarian seemed to crumple suddenly. The anger that held him upright dissipated, leaving behind a bone-deep weariness. He looked much older than he had a moment before, the weight of his cares hanging heavy upon him.

This is a true king, I thought. He obviously cared more for his people than for himself. That definitely made him a rarity in my book. Every other monarch I'd met thus far had been concerned only with their own whims, their own comforts.

"I do not know how to make you understand," Batarian said.

"Try me," I said.

5

"START WITH THOSE CREATURES," I SAID. "WHAT ARE they, and where do they come from?"

"They are known among us as the Cimice. I do not know what they call themselves. As for where they came from, we do not know. Our people have lived in this place for thousands of years, in harmony with our surroundings, since Lucifer left this place and our borders were closed . . ."

Batarian trailed off, like he was lost in memory, and Litarian took up the story.

"Then, one day about a year ago, the creatures appeared in the forest. We kept our distance from them, as we did not know how they had arrived here, and if they were friend or foe."

"Could they have arrived by boat, from across the ocean?" I asked.

The three of them stared at me blankly.

"You know, from the continent on the other side of the big water?" I said, gesturing to indicate a large body.

"There is no such thing," Sakarian said derisively. "Ours is the only land on this world."

"Uh, no," I said. "I saw it with my magic when I was trying to find a way out of this place. There's another land far across the ocean. If the Cimice suddenly appeared one day, they could have come from there."

Batarian appeared stunned at this news, Litarian thoughtful, Sakarian disbelieving.

"We had assumed the borders were broken somehow," Litarian said. "Especially after you arrived."

"Yes," Batarian said, frowning. "But if they come from this other place, that puts a different face on things."

"It does not change the simple truth that she does not belong here," Sakarian said. "Nor does it change the fact that she has done more harm than good by her actions."

"But you still haven't told me why," I said, looking at them expectantly.

"Yes," Litarian said when it became apparent that the king would not continue the narrative. Their leader appeared lost in thought. "As I was saying, when the Cimice first appeared, we avoided them and they avoided us. There did not seem to be many of them, and we were content to live in peace."

"We did not realize they were such prolific breeders. If we had, we would have killed them on sight," Sakarian said bitterly.

"What happened?" I asked.

Litarian continued. "The Cimice established a colony in the mountains on the other side of the forest. Our scouts told us that there were only about twenty or thirty of the creatures. After a month, there were a hundred. Within three months, three or four times that. Now there are thousands of them, a massive teeming horde, spilling forth from the mountain like an infection."

Litarian's description reminded me very strongly of the way I'd seen the vampires that had invaded Chicago. They, too, seemed like an infection, a disease that had spread so quickly there was no hope of stopping it. But I had stopped it. Maybe I could help the fae with their problem, too, and then they would see that I could be trusted. Then I could be given what I wanted most—my freedom.

"So you were all living in peace, even if there were a lot of these Cimice," I prompted. "What changed?"

"Perhaps the Cimice realized they were too many for their resources and decided not to share the forest with us any longer. Perhaps they had intended to destroy us all along, but were simply waiting for superiority of numbers. In any event, it started as a series of small raids in which the Cimice would attack our hunters in the forest."

"Those first attacks took us unawares," Batarian said.

I didn't need him to draw me a picture to know that they had suffered heavy losses.

Batarian continued. "After that, we were more cautious. However, we were also forced to be more daring. Meat was becoming very scarce. The Cimice, it seems, will eat anything. The area of the forest where they live is completely stripped."

"Like locusts," I murmured.

Litarian looked at me questioningly.

"They're these little insects that descend on crops in massive hordes. They strip everything clean and then fly away to do it again somewhere else."

"That sounds like the Cimice," he said. "Except that they did not fly away. They stayed. And as time passed, they grew more aggressive. They began to attack the village, always in small numbers."

"They were testing our defenses," Sakarian said. "To see how much risk would be required to defeat us."

"We have always managed to hold them off, to make them pay for these excursions," Batarian said. "Enough to make them doubtful of their success if they attempted a full-scale attack."

I stared at the king. "You've got to be kidding. If their numbers are as great as you say, then they could have overwhelmed you at any time. You are under a serious delusion if you think your fighting abilities affected them in any way. They're feinting and retreating for some reason of their own."

Realization and chagrin dawned in the eyes of all three. The arrogance of every fae I had ever met on any world was astounding. These guys had actually believed they had held off an enemy that outnumbered them simply by virtue of their skill.

"What reason would they have for doing such a thing?" Sakarian asked.

"Maybe they're practicing for some other foe, and they're using you to season their soldiers," I said.

"They're killing our people as part of some game?" Batarian asked, disgust showing on his face.

"Well, I don't know for sure," I said, backpedaling. Batarian seemed like he might shoot the messenger. "I'm just guessing."

"But what other foe could they prepare for?" Litarian

asked. "There are no other fae in this land, nor any other creatures like the Cimice."

"Maybe they don't plan on staying here," I said. "Maybe they're planning an assault somewhere else."

And as I said this, my heart froze. I had killed a Cimice in Chicago, one who had warned me that it was merely one of many, one who said it was the advance of an assault that would cover the city. My legs wobbled a little.

"Not again," I said. "Not again."

"What is it?" Litarian asked.

"I know where they are going," I said. "To my world, to my city."

Maybe Nathaniel hadn't meant me harm in sending me to this place, after all. But how could he have known that the Cimice were here? Was it really just a horrible coincidence?

I needed to stop worrying about Nathaniel and his motivations and deal with what was in front of me. I knew the Cimice were here. I knew they intended to attack Chicago. There was no reason for these monsters from another world to choose my home unless they were being directed by one of my enemies.

Which meant that 1) despite all evidence to the contrary, there must be a way to get on and off this world without going to that permanent portal on the other side of the ocean, and 2) while determining the identity of the Cimice's puppet master was important, it wasn't nearly as important as stopping the Cimice from descending on my city.

The people of Chicago had just survived an infestation of vampires. They could not survive another large-scale attack so soon. As it was, I was certain many people would not return. I couldn't blame them. Once you knew the monster under the bed was real, it was hard to go back to your old life.

I became aware that Litarian was speaking to me but I didn't register any of the words.

"Huh?" I said.

"Why do you believe the Cimice's ultimate goal is your world?" Litarian asked.

Might as well put my cards on the table, I thought. It looked as though these fae and I had a common enemy.

"This isn't the first time I've seen these creatures," I said.

I quickly explained that I'd encountered one while acting in my capacity as an Agent, which of course they didn't understand. Then I had to explain the purpose of the Agency.

"You collect dead souls?" Sakarian asked. "That is the province of Lucifer. You have lied to us about your connection with him."

"Wow, you really haven't seen Lucifer for a long time," I said, deftly avoiding the accusation of lying. "He hasn't collected a soul since before the fall."

"What fall?" Sakarian asked.

"I am not going to get into the history of the fallen angels," I said. "Suffice it to say that Lucifer had a disagreement with his previous employer and they don't work together anymore. But you're really missing the point here. The point is that we both have reason to want the Cimice gone. I can help you. I think I've proven that. Although you never did explain why my killing the Cimice was a bad thing."

Batarian looked slightly embarrassed. "I believed that

your display of power would frighten the surviving Cimice, and that they would return to their leader with tales of wonder. I thought that their fright would cause them to descend upon us with their full strength. However, in light of your belief that they could have done such a thing at any time, my anger with you seems foolish."

I didn't rub his face in it, although I was sorely tempted. I had been raised by Beezle, after all.

"Look," I said. "I can't let the Cimice attack Chicago. And your people are going to be wiped out sooner or later if you don't take serious action."

"Serious action?" Batarian repeated. "You mean attack the colony. No. I will not risk my people."

"You don't have to," I said. "You can risk me."

"You will eliminate the entirety of the Cimice alone?" Batarian looked incredulous. "Even with powers such as yours, you could not do such a thing."

I remembered rising above Soldier Field, filled to bursting with the feeling of vampires who had come at my call. I remembered the power of the Morningstar moving through me, exploding outward, eliminating the vampires so thoroughly that nothing remained, not even ash.

"Yes, I can."

Sakarian and Batarian continued to look doubtful. Litarian, as always, appeared thoughtful.

Sakarian better watch his back, I thought. Litarian was smart, way smarter than his brother. For now Litarian seemed content in the role he had, but I doubted it would stay that way. Fae lived a long time, and there was a limit to what a smart person would tolerate from a stupid one.

"Why not allow her to go?" Litarian said. "We have nothing to lose and everything to gain."

"Because if we allow her to leave this place, she will try to escape," Batarian said. "She will not continue to aid her captors. It is only logical."

"Except that I told you that I, too, need to defeat the Cimice," I said.

"I am not certain I believe this tale of the creatures in your world," Sakarian announced. "It all seems too convenient. And impossible. Our borders are closed."

"For the love of the Morningstar," I swore. "You are being deliberately obstinate. The fact that I am here is proof positive that your borders are not as secure as they seem."

Batarian's face took on that brooding look again. "I must think on this. Litarian, return her to the platform and guard the ladder until I make my decision."

"No," I said. "I'm not going back up there."

"You are still a prisoner here," Batarian said.

"Let's be real for a second," I said. "As of this moment I'm only a prisoner because I don't feel like destroying your whole village. So don't act like you have some kind of dominion over me."

"I am the ruler in my own kingdom," Batarian said through gritted teeth.

"Sure you are," I said. "But I am not a member of your kingdom. I'll go in some other room, and you don't need to waste a man guarding me. I'm not going to run away. My proposal is this—you let me kill the Cimice. And then you release my wings and I go home."

"You will return to the platform. That is where the prisoners go," Batarian said.

I could tell he was trying to reestablish his sense of authority when his world had been turned upside down.

But I wasn't going to spend another minute on that platform. I sighed.

"Don't make me prove a point," I said. It would be nothing for me to set this place on fire. But I didn't want to burn down the whole tree house unless I had to.

"You are a prisoner," Batarian said.

"Father, I don't think that—" Litarian began.

I shot nightfire at Sakarian. I didn't like him anyway.

The bolt deliberately missed any vital organs. The blue flame struck the fae's upper arm, then danced along his limb and down to his wrist, stripping away the flesh as it went.

Sakarian screeched in pain and fell to his knees. Batarian and Litarian stared at me in shock. Neither of them made any move to help Sakarian, who was whimpering.

"Quit that noise," I said. "I didn't even give you the benefit of my full strength."

Batarian moved toward me. I don't know what he intended to do. Litarian grabbed him by the shoulder, pulling the king away from me.

"I am not going to the platform," I repeated. "Think all you want on my offer. I'm going to wait in another room."

Litarian stepped forward, his hands up to show that he was no threat. "I will show you," he said.

We left the room without another word from anyone.

It was possible, even probable, that I'd misplayed this. I'd bruised Batarian's pride by demonstrating I did not have to do as he wished. I'd quite literally harmed Sakarian by using him as a demonstration. He hadn't liked me to begin with, and he doubtless hated me now.

On the positive side of the balance book, maybe Batarian would conclude that I was more of a threat to him as a prisoner and would just let me go, which was all I'd wanted in the first place.

Litarian led me to a much smaller room across the hall that looked like a little parlor. He nodded and then left me there—unguarded.

Regardless of the outcome of their meeting, I was going to find a way to get to the Cimice and destroy them. If I had to sneak away in the middle of the night, then I would.

At this point killing the creatures before they arrived in Chicago was my priority. If Batarian never released my wings, then I could probably find another way to do so. Surely Lucifer—or one of his brothers—could overcome the magic binding the ropes.

It would be annoyingly inconvenient in the meantime, but I couldn't wait here much longer for Batarian to get his head on straight. I'd already been more than polite.

There was a long sort of sofalike thing made of branches that stretched out against a wall. I lay down on it. My mind was racing, and I was still pumped full of energy from using my magic during the battle with the Cimice. I didn't think I would be able to sleep, but almost immediately I drifted off. My body knew what it needed even if I didn't.

My baby fluttered inside me. My son. The last tangible evidence that I had of my beloved. In my mind were Gabriel's eyes, Gabriel's mouth, Gabriel's touch. Gabriel's voice whispering in my ear. For now and forever they would only be in my mind, only in my memory. Since he had died, I'd had only fleeting moments to remember.

I chased monsters. I battled demons. I felt the shadow on my heart growing larger and larger with each passing day. But the grief was always there, the pain that was unyielding and unending. Even when I tried to hide from it, to find solace where I could, my sadness chased me down and overtook me.

I woke with the wetness of my tears on my cheeks, salt in my mouth, and Litarian standing above me, an indefinable expression on his face. He held my sword in one hand.

I sat up quickly, scrubbing my cheeks. "What did Batarian decide?"

"Despite my arguments to the contrary, my lord feels you cannot be trusted," Litarian said. "He has ordered me to bind all your limbs, heedless of any possible harm to myself, and remove you as far from the village as possible so you can do no damage here in retribution."

"Under normal circumstances I would consider that a threat," I said, studying him carefully. "But I don't think you're going to carry it out."

"No," he said. "I am not."

"You don't agree that I am a threat to your village?" I asked.

"I believe that you could harm us all greatly if you so chose," Litarian said. "However, I also believe you would not choose to do so unless necessary."

"I don't want to hurt you at all," I said. "I just want to be free."

Litarian nodded and indicated I should turn around. I did so, hoping he was going to release my wings and not slit my throat with my own sword when my back was turned.

He murmured low in his native language, and the bonds were released. My wings stretched, unfurled—and immediately cramped from being held in a fixed position for so long.

I eased them out slowly, until they were at their fullest extension, arching my back like a cat as the blood flowed though the tight muscles. I felt a touch on the silver feathers and closed my wings, turning to Litarian in surprise.

He drew his hand back, his cheeks coloring. "I'm sorry," he said. He handed my sword to me to cover his embarrassment. "They are just so beautiful. It must be an incredible feeling, to soar above the trees."

"It is," I said, thinking of how free I felt when flying. "Well, listen, thanks for letting me go."

"You go to destroy the Cimice," he said. It wasn't a question.

"Yes," I said. "I can't let them get to my city."

"I will go with you," he said.

"Um," I said. I could travel a lot faster without him, especially now that I had my wings back.

"I can show you precisely where the colony is located," Litarian said. "My life is forfeit, in any event. My lord will certainly take it hard that I released you."

"I could knock you out," I offered. "Make it look like you tried to hold me here but I escaped."

Litarian shook his head. "Batarian would see through such a fiction. I argued too ferociously in your favor."

I didn't want to bring Litarian with me. But it seemed a poor repayment for my freedom to leave him here to be executed.

"All right," I said finally, although I had no idea what I would do with him once I'd taken care of the Cimice. "Take my hand."

Litarian hesitated.

"If you want to come with me, you're going to have to trust me," I said impatiently. "If I wanted to hurt you, I could have done so a hundred times over."

Litarian nodded and took my hand. There was a supple strength in his fingers, honed from years of pulling a bow-string. I spoke the words of the veil that would cover us, and heard him gasp.

"You disappeared," he said, his voice full of wonder.

"Yes," I said. "And so have you. We're more or less invisible now."

I kept a firm grip on his hand so he wouldn't go wandering off.

"What is 'more or less invisible'?" Litarian whispered.

"Most things can't see us. Some can," I said. "It kind of depends on how magical the being is that's looking."

I didn't know whether the spell would actually hide us from the fae on this world. I figured if it didn't, I could always fall back on my usual crash-and-burn routine.

"Lead the way," I said. "And remember, you're invisible but people will still be able to feel you if you bump into them."

"I will be cautious," Litarian said.

I put my hand on his shoulder so we would stay close together, and followed him out of the room. There was no one in the hallway, which was a surprise. Either Batarian completely trusted that Litarian would follow through on his orders without question, or else he didn't care about the possibility that his son might be killed by me.

It seemed foolish to have sent Litarian without a guard to back him up. The whole settlement seemed unusually quiet. I must have slept longer than I realized. Still, why was Batarian not more vigilant? He was so concerned that the Cimice would send the horde down on their heads.

There was something strange going on here. The more I

considered it, the more I realized that Batarian's response to my aid during the battle didn't make any sense. I'd just been too tired and out of sorts myself to realize it.

We moved out of the hall and onto the walkway. Some guards were posted at intervals, but not nearly as many as I thought there would be. I wanted to ask Litarian about it, but first we needed to get away. The guards would still be able to hear us even if they couldn't see us.

Litarian led me to a staircase that went to the ground. The stairs were narrow, and I hoped that we wouldn't encounter anyone on the way down. I would be able to fly out of the way, but I didn't think I would be able to lift Litarian. I was stronger than an ordinary human, but not strong enough to lift a man twice my size. But there was no one on the staircase, and only a few guards posted at the perimeter at ground level. The guards seemed preternaturally still, almost like dolls or statues.

We slipped easily out of the village and into the dense forest. Once we were out of sight I dropped my hand from Litarian's shoulder and lifted the veil.

"Something isn't right," I said, keeping my voice low in case it carried back to the village.

The light was faint under the trees but I could easily read Litarian's troubled expression. "I agree," he said.

I sensed the tug that pulled him back toward the village, toward his people, but he seemed to shake it off.

"First, the Cimice," he said.

He started through the forest, moving with the smooth stride of an experienced woodsman. I grimaced and followed as quietly as I could.

Litarian looked askance at me when he heard me clomping through the woods like a team of horses, but he didn't say anything.

We walked in (relative) silence for some time. "How far is the colony from the village?" I asked.

"Several hours' walk," Litarian said.

"Do you think Batarian will raise the alarm and send men after us?"

"Perhaps," Litarian said. "Perhaps he will not consider my safety a priority."

"Your relationship with your family is more confusing than mine," I said. "It seemed like Sakarian had to obey you when you came to arrest me. Batarian seems to have given you a lot of power, as well. But you're saying he wouldn't come after you if he thought you'd been kidnapped or thought you'd disobeyed him."

Litarian was silent for a while after this. We continued moving through the forest. I figured Litarian wasn't going to comment, and I wasn't going to push it. I didn't need to get involved in anyone else's weird family dynamics.

Finally, Litarian said, "My father has mixed feelings about me."

I could sympathize. "Yeah, so did my father."

"Did?" Litarian asked. "What happened to him?"

"I, uh, blew him up," I said.

Litarian paused, his gaze assessing. I could almost hear the calculations in his head, his rapid reconsidering of both my ruthlessness and my abilities. "I will be very cautious around you."

"He was gathering an army to destroy humanity at the time," I said. "Also, he was really, really mean to me."

As in trying-to-kill-me-multiple-times kind of mean.

"I will certainly make every effort not to be 'mean' to you," he said seriously.

I laughed, but it was without mirth. People who were mean to me had an unfortunate tendency to die in horrible ways. Chloe had said something to that effect once, when we were arguing about my methods. I'd told her I wasn't a monster.

But then I'd destroyed every vampire in the city in one fell swoop. I'd tortured Bryson. I'd condoned and acted on morally questionable impulses. And Beezle had left, because I was changing.

Maybe if Gabriel still lived, it would be different. But he was gone, and I was left to fend for myself, to muddle through, to do whatever was necessary to preserve my life so that I could keep my child safe. So first I would destroy the Cimice, even though they hadn't invaded my city yet. But before that . . .

"Someone's directing the Cimice," I told Litarian. "If we can, I'd like to find out who."

"Why do you think that?"

"It's too much of a coincidence that they're here and that one of them came through to Chicago. One of my enemies is giving them pointers."

"You make it sound as though you have many enemies," Litarian said.

"Probably more than I can count," I said.

"Then how will you determine who is leading the Cimice?" Litarian asked. "They do not speak our language. They do not feel pain the same way that we do. You will not be able to bargain with them, or torture them."

"They speak my language," I said, remembering the metallic voice telling me that its brethren would descend upon me, destroy everything I loved.

"They have never indicated such to us," said Litarian, sounding vaguely insulted.

"Maybe that's because they don't want to converse with you," I said. "They want to kill you."

"Still," he said. "If we had known they could speak with us, we would have tried to negotiate, to save—"

"You couldn't save them," I said, cutting him off. "There is nothing you could have done. Just as no amount of fae fighting ability would have defeated the Cimice if they had chosen to advance. Your people are nothing but pawns in some larger game."

Litarian said nothing to this. I knew it was a bitter pill for him to swallow, to think that there was never anything that could be done to save his people.

We passed through a particularly dense patch of trees and into a clearing. The moon had risen high while we walked, and the light danced on the surface of a sparkling stream. I pulled up short.

"I'll be flying over that, thank you," I said. "Come on, I can hold you up for a few seconds."

Litarian turned toward me, a question in his eyes. "Why would I need to do such a thing?"

"Because of the creepy, grabby water creatures that live in there," I said.

Litarian shook his head. "The gods in the water will not harm you if you show them respect."

To demonstrate, he walked to the water's edge and knelt there. He spoke what sounded like a prayer in his own language, then stood and offered me his hand. "Come. It is safe to cross now."

"I think I'll just stay and watch," I said, waving him away.

Litarian shrugged and stepped into the water. I tensed, expecting the creatures to rise up and grab at his legs. But he crossed without incident. When he was done, he turned back and gave me an expectant look.

I rose up into the air, muttering to myself. "Of course. I should have thought to say a prayer in a language I don't know. How stupid of me."

I didn't care what Litarian said. I'd destroyed one of the water "gods." I didn't think any amount of respect from me would let them allow me to pass unharmed.

Sure enough, as soon as my feet crossed high above, the surface of the water broke, filling with hissing faces.

I landed beside Litarian, who goggled at me. "What did you do to them?" he asked.

"It's not worth getting into," I said briskly. "Let's go."

Litarian didn't press. That wasn't his way. I'd figured that out pretty quickly. I was again strongly reminded of Gabriel. Gabriel was never one to press, either. He just waited, with his infinite store of patience.

I swiped at the tears that had risen to the surface, the unwanted proof of a grief that seemed to creep up on me more frequently since my arrival here. I was glad Litarian walked in front of me. He wouldn't press, but I didn't want to feel obligated to explain anything to him. Gabriel belonged to me. He had nothing to do with this place.

Litarian suddenly held up a hand to halt me. "What is it?" I whispered.

"The dragon approaches," he said, very still.

I didn't see or hear anything. "How do you know?" I asked, moving up to his side. His eyes were closed.

"Can you not feel him?" Litarian said, and his voice didn't sound like his own.

I looked at him sharply. For a moment, I thought I'd heard . . .

But the thought faded as the presence of the dragon filled my mind. Litarian was right. I could feel him approaching, like a flame-lit shadow that covered the night.

"I know you," I said into the darkness. I felt that inexorable pull that I had experienced in the dragon's presence before, felt something buried deep in my blood that drew me toward the creature. I took a step forward.

6

LITARIAN GRABBED MY ARM, HIS VOICE ANGRY. "WHAT are you doing? Do not draw it to us. I told you to halt so that we would not attract its attention."

"It won't hurt me," I murmured, my head full of fire and darkness.

I yearned for something, something elemental and just out of reach.

Litarian came around to grab both my shoulders, to shake me. The jolt snapped the connection between the dragon and me. Litarian and I stared at each other. Something shifted behind his eyes, and just for a moment I thought the color of the iris changed.

It must have been a trick of the light. Then he was speaking, more harshly than I had heard him speak before.

"Are you mad?" he asked through his teeth. "That creature would destroy both of us in an instant. What were you thinking?"

He punctuated this with another little shake, which made me angry. I slapped his hands away from my shoulders.

A headache was brewing behind my eyes as the darkness in my mind retreated. It felt like this when I was first coming into my power, my legacy from Lucifer. There had been the same sense of a door opening just a crack before it slammed shut again. And because the door hadn't opened all the way, pain streamed in its wake.

There was a mystery here to be solved, something else I needed to discover before I left this place. And Litarian was keeping me from that discovery. He was preventing me from finding the source of fire deep inside me.

"I told you, he wouldn't hurt me," I said.

"But he would hurt me," Litarian said. "He despises all of us."

"He wouldn't if I asked him not to," I said, still angry, still longing for the thing that was just out of reach.

"Can you communicate with the dragon?" Litarian asked suspiciously. "I thought you said you had not been here before."

"I haven't," I said, now feeling defensive. "It's just . . . a feeling I have when I see him."

"A feeling," Litarian said flatly.

"Look, I don't have to explain to you," I said, pushing past him.

"I think you do," Litarian said, following me. "I have a right to know if you're going to draw the dragon down on my head."

"Don't be stupid," I said. "Look, just forget it, okay? The dragon isn't coming anywhere near us right now. Let's just focus on the Cimice."

He wanted to pursue it. There was a quality of expectation

in his silence. But he didn't. Maybe he'd decided to trust me. Maybe he'd decided not to pursue the issue so long as he wasn't in immediate danger. All I know is that we did not speak another word to each other for all of that long night.

The fae from the village did not pursue us; nor did we encounter any animals in the wood.

I don't know what was in Litarian's head, but I was brooding on my seeming connection to the dragon. Had the dragon been left here by Lucifer, created by Lucifer's magic long ago? Was that why I was drawn to him, and him to me?

As the moonlight began to fade and the first rays of sunlight showed pink in the sky, I noticed the forest had changed. We were no longer surrounded by lush vegetation. Everywhere I looked the trees were stripped of their leaves, the underbrush similarly denuded. The back of my neck itched. I felt exposed.

"I suppose we're getting closer to the colony," I said.

"Yes, we are very near now," replied Litarian. "We must proceed with caution."

"Let's get under a veil," I suggested. "We're too easy to see here."

Litarian hesitated, like he wasn't certain he wanted to be that close to me.

"I won't attract the dragon while we're under a veil," I said impatiently. "That doesn't even make any sense."

He stepped closer, his expression embarrassed. I summoned my magic, settled the veil over us.

"Stay close to me," I warned.

"I remember," Litarian said.

We moved forward again, proceeding more cautiously.

Neither of us wanted to be surprised by the Cimice. The landscape grew bleaker, more barren, as we walked.

"They've completely destroyed this part of the forest," I said. "I wonder if it will ever even grow back."

"We cannot allow them to encroach any further on our village," Litarian said.

I agreed, but I wasn't thinking of the fae. I was thinking of Chicago, and what would happen if these creatures appeared in my city. They would destroy every thing, every person in their path. And when they were done they would move on to the next city, and the next. All the while they would breed, until their numbers were impossible to comprehend.

Once they had wiped every last trace of life from Earth, they would move to another world, presumably through the power of whatever architect had brought them here in the first place.

I gradually became aware of a buzzing sound that filled the air. It was like the persistent hum of cicadas, only a lot louder and after a while a *lot* more irritating. The headache behind my eyes spread. I found myself growing angry. I was hot, tired, thirsty. I hadn't showered in a couple of days and I was desperate to get out of my clothes and wash.

And my head hurt. And that sound was so pervasive, so damned annoying. It wasn't just in my ears. It was in my teeth, and the sockets of my eyes. It vibrated up and down my spine, crawled over my nerve endings, made me madder and madder until I felt like I would explode.

"Stop," Litarian said, his hand going around my upper arm.

"Quit manhandling me!" I shouted.

The veil had fallen away at some point. I'd lost track of the magic, become preoccupied with the noise.

"You need to stop. You need to breathe," Litarian said soothingly, the kind of tone that you use on a child throwing a temper tantrum.

"No," I said angrily, wiping my face with my sleeve. I was covered in sweat. It poured from me like I'd just run a very long distance. "I don't need to breathe. I need for this damned noise to stop. I need it to stop."

I scrunched up my eyes, covered my ears, but it was still there, inside me.

"Stop. Stop. Stop. Stop," I said.

Litarian closed his arms around me. "*You* stop," he said insistently. "Relax. Breathe. The Cimice will make you insane if you allow them to do so."

I kicked at him, flailed, but he was strong, much stronger than he seemed, and he held me fast.

"Breathe," he repeated. "Breathe with me."

The low, steady insistence of his voice was finally breaking through the haze of madness. I tried to push away the noise, to focus on the steady rhythm of his inhalations and exhalations. I let my breath go, let it fall into the same pattern as his.

The buzzing of the Cimice continued, but it receded from my body. My nerves felt scraped raw. I was a hollow thing, ready to be born anew.

I opened my eyes and looked into Litarian's—and saw what he had tried to hide.

"You!" I said, wrenching myself from his embrace as Litarian's green eyes bled blue—the merry sapphire blue of Puck.

"Are you not pleased to see me?" he said, grinning.

I punched him in the face.

Last time I'd hit Puck, he had tried to strangle me to death. This time he was so pleased with his trick that he just shook off my blow, still smiling.

"I'd have thought you'd be pleased to see a family member in this strange place."

"What the hell are you doing here pretending to be a faerie?" I demanded. "Aren't you supposed to be in Chicago with Alerian and Lucifer?"

I had a sudden thought that chilled me to the bone. "Oh, gods above and below. You didn't let him take over the city, did you?"

"So many questions. Which to answer first?" Puck said, tapping his finger on his chin.

"I don't care which you answer first so long as you do answer," I growled. "Are you the reason I'm here in this thrice-forsaken place?"

"I may have given dear Nathaniel a little nudge," Puck acknowledged. "Although when I did so I didn't realize the dragon was here."

"What's the dragon got to do with anything?" I said, my mind generating more questions before he could answer the first ones. "Have you been here all along, playing the part of Litarian? Or is that just something new for me? Does Batarian know who you really are?"

Puck held up his hands. "I will tell you all."

"I doubt that very much," I muttered. "But you will answer my questions."

"Or what?" Puck asked, raising an eyebrow in challenge. "We both know you can't kill me."

"I won't," I said. "I'll call the dragon to me."

It was a calculated risk. I was pretty sure that the panic

I'd seen in Puck's eyes was real when we had sensed the presence of the dragon.

It was very satisfying to see him pale a little, even though he was careful to maintain his expression of merriment. "Ah, well, it suits me to satisfy your curiosity in any case," he said offhandedly.

But I had seen, and I knew. Puck was afraid of the dragon. I would find out why. But not yet. First I wanted to know why I was here, and why he was here, and what web he was spinning.

"So start talking," I said.

"And where shall I begin?" he asked.

"Tell me why you pushed Nathaniel into sending me here," I said. *I'm sorry for doubting you, Nathaniel.*

Puck feigned a look of surprise. "Why, to protect you from the Retrievers, of course. I knew they had no dominion here."

"Where is *here*, anyway?"

"A planet that is light-years from yours, in time and space. Long ago a war was waged here between Lucifer's armies and the fae that live here. Lucifer won, but he did not particularly care to keep the spoils. He simply wished to prove that he could win, that he was stronger than his opponent."

This last was said with no small amount of bitterness. I sensed that Puck had been on the losing end of more than a few conflicts with his brother.

"After the war, Lucifer graciously agreed to leave this land to those he had defeated. He told them that as punishment for their defiance against him, they would not be able to pass freely from world to world, that they would be confined to this place always. He also told them that he closed all the portals between this and other worlds, so that none may enter or leave."

"But he lied," I said, thinking of the portal across the ocean.

"Yes, he does that," Puck said. "He wanted to ensure that he had a way in and out if he needed it."

"But why?" I asked. "What could he possibly want from such an out-of-the-way place, from a people he'd already defeated?"

"As you might say, do not ask me to explain what he is thinking," Puck said. "And it was of no concern to me if he chose to have a bolt-hole on this planet. At least, it was of no concern until Titania chose this place as the launchpad for her invasion of Earth."

"Titania," I said. "I should have known."

"Yes, you probably should have," Puck agreed. "At any rate, once Titania chose this world, I felt it was a good idea if I were on the spot, as it were. Monitoring the situation. Since Lucifer closed the borders of this world, he might take Titania's decision to open a portal here as an act of aggression."

"So you—what? Presented yourself to Batarian as his long-lost son?"

Puck's eyes twinkled. "Not exactly."

Mine narrowed. "How was it, exactly, then?"

Puck shrugged. "I gave Batarian and all of his people a memory of Litarian. A memory that told them he was always here."

"And how do you explain your absences to Batarian when you must attend to Titania?"

"I don't have to. When I am here, they remember me as though I were always here. When I am gone, the memory of Litarian fades without a trace. I established the spell as such so that if I am unable to return, Batarian would not be haunted by the memory of a lost son."

"Very thoughtful of you," I said sourly.

I was very disturbed by the depth and breadth of Puck's power. That kind of spell took more than strength. It took subtlety. It would also need safeguards built in so that the magic would continue even if Puck were not there to maintain it. I knew Lucifer and his brothers were strong, that their power was almost beyond comprehension. But it was one thing to know that, and quite another to be confronted with the proof of it.

"Yes, I am thoughtful," Puck said in response to my comment. He sounded perfectly sincere.

"Does Titania know you're here?" I asked.

Puck shook his head. "My queen does not monitor my every move."

"Are you sure about that? If I were Titania, I would definitely keep a close eye on you."

"I am certain," Puck replied with a touch of arrogance. "Powerful the faerie queen may be, but she is not yet as powerful as I."

And yet you pretend to be her inferior. Why? I had always wondered about this, but now was not the time to try to get the answer.

"Okay," I said. "Titania is using the Cimice to do what? Take over Chicago? Claim dominion over the Earth?"

"Those are side benefits. If she releases an army on your planet, it would be tantamount to declaring war on Lucifer, as my brother believes that world belongs to him."

"Then why do it? Does she think she can defeat Lucifer with the Cimice?"

"Yes, she does," Puck said.

I stared at him. "But she's wrong."

"I know," Puck said.

"And if she brings her armies against Lucifer and he chooses to retaliate—"

"He will," Puck interjected.

"Then there will be nothing left of the planet," I said.

"Precisely," Puck said. "Which is exactly why I brought you here."

"And what am I supposed to do?" I said.

"Just what you intended to do when you thought I was Litarian," Puck said. "Destroy the Cimice."

"First of all, if you're here, why can't you do it yourself?" I asked. "And second of all, won't Titania be pissed if she finds out you screwed up her plans? And finally, since when do you care if humanity is destroyed?"

"I like people," Puck said lightly. "Existence was so much more fun once you came along."

"That's only part of an answer," I said.

Puck sighed theatrically. "Oh, Madeline, you know me so well."

"Why?" I repeated.

Puck tapped the tip of my nose with his finger. "What if I said it doesn't suit my purpose to have the two of them at war just yet?"

"That, I would believe," I said, although I didn't like to think about what would happen once he did decide it would suit his purpose. Puck might think the world was more fun with humans in it, but if he could harm his brother, then people had just better watch out for the cross fire. Puck would certainly not be looking out for them.

No, that's your job. It was a little startling to think of myself in those terms, to consider that I might really be all that was standing between the monsters and civilized society. Especially since the civilized society seemed perfectly willing to throw me to the wolves to protect themselves, as was demonstrated when a bunch of kids had tried to turn me in to Therion's vampire authority.

I realized Puck was watching me with a knowing look. I wondered how much of my thoughts he could read on my face. Then I decided I was better off not knowing. It would be nice to at least have the illusion of privacy in my own mind, especially since Lucifer and Puck and all of their brethren had infected every other corner of my life.

"So?" I said. "How come you need me to hammer the Cimice when you have more than enough power to do it yourself?"

"It's better if I don't make grand gestures," Puck said. "It tends to draw unwanted attention."

"And it doesn't draw unwanted attention when I do it?" I asked.

"Well, yes, it might," Puck admitted. "But when you do it, ancient beings don't construe your actions as an act of war. They just think you're flying off the handle—again."

"So lovely to know my reputation precedes me," I said.

Puck grinned. "It does. It really, really does."

"And what will happen to you if Titania finds out you've thwarted her?" I asked.

"She won't find out," Puck said.

I didn't know whether it was extreme arrogance or that he had a fail-safe in place, but he seemed supremely confident that Titania would not discover his machinations. Fine. It had nothing to do with me, anyway. It was none of my business what happened to Puck, and I had no desire to make it my business. I had enough on my plate.

"Will you continue on with me now and eliminate the threat posed by the Cimice?" Puck asked.

I was angry that Puck had manipulated both Nathaniel and me, but I was going to help him anyway and Puck knew it. There was no way I could allow Titania to set the Cimice on my city.

"Let's go," I said, and started forward again. And stopped.

The buzzing of the Cimice had ceased. Good for my sanity, sure, but possibly bad news otherwise. I dropped a veil over myself. Beside me, Puck did the same.

"Can you see me even when I'm veiled?" I whispered.

"Yes," he said.

"Fine," I said. "Stay close to me, because I can't see you."

"Will do," he said.

It sounded so strange to hear modern phrases coming out of the mouth of such an old creature, but both Puck and Lucifer were much more attuned to the modern world than most ancient things. All the faerie pretty much seemed trapped in the fifth century.

I continued moving through the forest in the direction the noise had come from. I assumed Puck would put me right if I strayed too far in the wrong direction. That was, if he hadn't just decided to trip off somewhere and leave me for his own amusement.

I wanted to ask whether he was nearby, but I didn't want him to think I was needy.

"I'm right here," Puck said, touching my right shoulder.

"Can you read my mind?" I asked suspiciously.

"No," Puck said, laughter in his voice. "But in some ways you are very predictable."

I didn't respond to that. On one hand, it was definitely good news that Puck was not a mind reader. On the other hand, it stung my pride a little to think that anything I ever did was predictable.

The barren forest slowly gave way to tumbled boulders as a series of high, rocky peaks rose before us. I had not seen or even detected any sign of life since our brief encounter with the dragon.

"How much farther?" I asked as we started to climb. "Can't we fly?"

"It's better if we don't," Puck said.

"Because of the Cimice?" I asked. "I didn't think they could fly."

"They can't," Puck said briefly, and then he did not elaborate any further.

Which made me think of the dragon, and wonder again why my uncle was so determinedly hiding from this creature.

The climb fatigued me very quickly. I had yet again traveled very far with little sustenance, and my body was devoting all its resources to my growing baby. I was sure now that I was getting thin despite the swelling in my abdomen. My pants were getting looser almost by the minute.

After a while I stopped, leaning against a large rock and panting, my face soaked with sweat. "Look, I can't take much more of this without food. We're going to have to take our chances in the air."

"We can't," Puck said. "It's too dangerous."

I felt his arm go around me, lifting me up so I could lean against him.

"It's just a little farther," he said.

"Yeah, but what kind of shape am I going to be in when I get there? What if I can't destroy them all?"

"You will have the strength to do what is necessary when the time comes," Puck said. "You always do."

We were both silent for a few moments. I focused on just putting one foot in front of the other, trying to conserve my energy for what lay ahead.

"You're so like him, you know," Puck said, and there was a mixture of tenderness and bitterness in his voice. I knew that the "him" Puck referred to was Lucifer. "Are you sure he's not your father?"

"Don't even joke about it," I said fervently. "Besides, don't you think he would have laid claim to me if he were my father?"

"Probably," Puck said. "He does brag about you with annoying regularity. It's quite sickening, actually. I'm sure he would love to be able to claim you were his child instead of his granddaughter."

"When is Lucifer talking about me with you?" I asked. "I thought the two of you could barely stand to be in the same room together."

"We can barely stand to be in the same galaxy together, to tell the truth," Puck said. "And despite all that, we do communicate regularly."

He said this with all of the relish of a person describing a trip to the dentist. I gave a short laugh.

"At least I'm not the only one who doesn't cherish my family ties."

"The truth is, the only being who has ever actively desired my brother's company is Evangeline," Puck said. "Which is probably why he was unable to let her go, even in death."

"What about all of the other women who bore him children?" I asked.

"Oh, he can—and does—seduce. And those women will want him, at least for a little while. But sooner or later my brother's true nature will reveal itself. And once it does, his conquests usually flee screaming. That is, if they haven't already been killed for some minor slight against his lord and majesty. But only after the baby is born, of course. He always makes sure to take the children."

It was sickening to think of Lucifer using and abusing scores of women as nothing more than broodmares. And I knew that if given sufficient opportunity, he would lay claim to all life on Earth, would declare himself emperor and demand fealty from all.

But a part of me, a very small part of me, felt sorry for him. No one had ever loved him except one lone, crazy girl. Even his own family couldn't stand the sight of him. Had lack of affection created the monster, or had his monstrosity ensured he would never be loved?

Of course, Puck and Alerian weren't exactly lovable, either. There was a warmth and charm present in Puck that wasn't in the other two, but I knew there were hidden depths in Puck. I'd seen just a hint of them, but they were there. I would no more trifle with Puck than I would with Lucifer. And my brief encounter with Alerian had terrified me. I didn't even want to meet brother number four, who was apparently so frightening that the other three left him to his own devices as much as possible.

I was so busy thinking of all of this that I didn't notice I was feeling better until Puck dropped his arm, saying, "You should be able to walk under your own steam now."

I was suddenly aware of the fact that I felt warm and well rested, like I'd just had a nap and a big cup of hot chocolate.

"What did you do?" I asked.

"No need to sound so accusing," Puck said mildly. "All I did was give you a little boost, so that you would not feel quite so tired. I can do that because we share blood."

"You didn't do anything permanent?"

"Like what?" Puck said.

My mind conjured up a lot of possibilities, starting with his magic harming my unborn son and finishing with Puck planting some kind of time bomb inside me that would force me to do his will at some later date. But I didn't say any of that out loud. I didn't want to give him any ideas. Instead, I zeroed in on his non-answer.

"I noticed you didn't actually say 'yes' or 'no.' Did you leave a permanent mark on me?"

"Not in the way you are thinking," Puck said after a long pause. "I cannot force you to do anything you do not wish to do. Lucifer's power over you as Hound of the Hunt is too strong, and would take precedence. Likewise would I be unable to harm your child."

"I'm sensing a big 'but' here," I said, growing angry.

"But all magic leaves a trace. And that trace of my magic left in you may be enough to keep you from harming me should the day ever come when you should wish to do such a thing."

"That day is now," I growled. "I'm not some toy for you—or Lucifer—to play with."

"I only meant to help," Puck said. I could not see his eyes because of the veil, but I was sure they were twinkling.

He may have intended to help, but he couldn't resist the chance to help himself, as well.

"Next time you feel the urge to aid me, resist," I said. "I don't need any more assistance from you."

"If you say so," Puck said.

"I do," I said, and stomped away with much more energy than I'd had before Puck's boost.

7

BECAUSE I WAS ANGRY, AND MY ANGER OFTEN MADE me blind and deaf to everything around me, I blundered over the crest of a hill and nearly walked into a troop of patrolling Cimice.

I skidded to a stop, the loose gravel shifting beneath my boots. The lead insect called a halt just a few feet away, its mantislike head twisting this way and that. I stayed perfectly still, pulling my veil tighter around me, and hoped the Cimice would not be able to sniff me out. My veil would never have fooled a werewolf, but I knew nothing about an insect's ability to smell. I had no idea where Puck was, but presumably he had more sense than I did and hadn't practically walked into the Cimice's arms.

After a few long and tense minutes in which the little band of six crawled all over the immediate area looking for signs of intruders, they finally decided to continue on their way.

I exhaled the breath I'd been holding and waited for Puck to reveal himself. His voice at my ear almost startled a little scream out of me, but I swallowed it. I did not want to draw the Cimice back to me.

"We must proceed with caution from here," he said. "No more temper tantrums."

I wanted to say that a temper tantrum implied my anger was unjustified, and that was definitely not the case. I wanted to say that I would not have been angry at all were it not for his behavior. But I did neither of those things. I did not feel like being drawn any further into Puck's logic. Plus, even when I was right, I always had the vague sense that I was losing when I argued with him.

That happened a lot with Lucifer, too.

We continued in silence for a while, passing two more small Cimice patrols. The cicada-like buzzing had started up again, but this time I was able to block out the noise by concentrating on my will and my magic.

We went farther into the mountain, surrounded by rock and the noise of the Cimice. Every so often Puck would put his hand on my shoulder so I would know he was still present. And then, suddenly, we were there.

It looked like a hive because it was a hive. There was a great gash torn in the mountain, and from it the Cimice spilled forth. The giant insects crawled all over the side of the mountain.

We drew off behind a series of large rocks and dropped the veil so we could counsel.

I wasn't sure what the Cimice were doing, but the place hummed with activity. All of the creatures moved with a purpose in and out of the cave. I could see the problem immediately.

"How do we kill them all?" I murmured.

According to the fae, the Cimice bred like city rats. One or two breeding pairs could replace the whole population within a few months. So the only way to do the job thoroughly was to make sure every last Cimice was eliminated. But how could I possibly do that?

"How did you kill all the vampires?" Puck asked.

"The vampires had all taken Azazel's serum in order to walk in daylight. Azazel had infused the serum with his magic, and his magic was also in me, since I was his daughter. So I called the vampires to me using that link, and once the magic was activated and we were bound, I sent a spell of destruction out through them."

"Blood," Puck said. "So mundane and yet so powerful. I suppose that does mean that you are, in fact, Azazel's daughter and not Lucifer's."

"Off topic," I said. "We already covered that. So how do I make sure to get all of the Cimice?"

"You've already presented the answer," Puck said.

"Blood?" I asked. "How will that work? I don't have the blood of the Cimice inside me."

"So crude," Puck chided. "You just need some of the Cimice's blood to direct the spell. Since only a few of the creatures settled here, all of the subsequent generations will share genes from the first group."

"So I just need to catch one of them, take its blood, and then use the blood to push the spell through?" I asked skeptically. "I'm not sure about that. I don't know if I can do that kind of magic. All of the spells I've used thus far have been internally motivated—you know what I mean?"

"Just because you have not done something like this before does not mean you cannot," Puck said. "Madeline, now that you have fully opened yourself to Lucifer's legacy, you have a vast, untapped store of power. You have not even begun to plumb the depths of that power."

"If you say so," I said.

It was extremely scary to think that I was sitting on a massive well of power. What if I lost control? I could go off like a nuclear bomb. More than once I'd suspected that I'd barely skimmed the surface of my magic, but I didn't like to think that I had unlimited abilities sitting at my fingertips. That would make me like Lucifer, and I did not want to be like Lucifer.

Even if I had crossed a few lines in defense of my life, I still believed I was on the side of good. I was still trying to be something better than my grandfather wanted me to be. But every time I went deeper into that pool, every time I drew a little bit more of that power and made it my own, I was also drawn a little deeper into Lucifer's web. Puck may have known, or at least suspected, most of my feelings on that count.

He wouldn't want me belonging to Lucifer any more than I already did, unless it served his purpose. And Puck's purpose was just as opaque as that of his brother. If I used my magic in this new way, I would get rid of the Cimice, thereby eliminating a threat to my city and thwarting Titania at the same time. But it was also possible—even probable—that I would play myself right into the middle of some scheme of Puck's.

Could I avoid being trapped by Lucifer's brother? Was the risk worth it if I could save innocent lives? If I wanted to stay on the side of good, then the answer had to be yes. But maybe I could clear myself of an obligation at the same time.

"If I do this, I want one of the favors I owe you wiped off my ledger," I said.

Puck shook his head, tut-tutting. "Oh, no, no, no. A favor from Lucifer's best beloved is far too valuable a quantity to give up for something such as this. Besides, you would go after the Cimice whether I were here or not. You were going to do it when you thought I was Litarian."

"Yes, but it also benefits you if I do your dirty work. So I want one of my favors cleared."

Puck continued to shake his head. "Are you telling me you would really allow innocent humans to die just because you didn't get what you want? I don't believe that of you. If you did behave that way, I would say you were more like Lucifer than I thought."

"Of course I won't allow anyone to die because I didn't get my way," I said.

Puck spread his hands wide. "Then I rest my case."

"But if you don't clear me of my obligation, then I'll call the dragon here, and you can take your chances."

Puck stared, his jewel-blue eyes carefully blank. "You wouldn't," he said.

"I would," I said, and made sure he could see the conviction on my face.

I was definitely taking a gamble. If Puck became angry that he had been boxed into a corner, he'd find a way to pay me back later—and I was certain I wouldn't like the payback. It was always possible that he wasn't actually scared of the dragon. Maybe he'd feigned fear just to see what I would do.

I was giving myself a headache, thinking in circles like this. How did Puck and Lucifer and Titania do it—weigh all the angles, contemplate all the possibilities?

Beezle had once compared me to the Hulk, and it was an apt description. I liked to crash and bash and worry about the consequences later. The trouble was that everyone around me was playing the long game, and if I continued the way I had before, I was always going to be on the losing end of the stick.

I watched Puck, and waited for his decision. I didn't have a hint of what he was thinking.

Finally, he said, "Deal."

I couldn't conceal my shock. "Deal?"

"You don't want it?" Puck asked craftily.

"Of course I do," I said. "I want your word, by the blood we share, that you forfeit your right to one favor from me if I kill all the Cimice present on this world."

I was careful to add that last qualifier. If there were Cimice alive on other worlds, Puck could easily claim that I had not adhered to the letter of our agreement. He would then absolutely use that as a loophole to put my favor back in his ledger.

"I give you my word, by the blood we share, that I forfeit the right to one favor from you if you kill all the Cimice present on this world," Puck said solemnly, but his eyes twinkled.

Had he thought of something that I hadn't? It was very likely he had, but my brain was pretty much done with exhausting the options. I'd have to accept that I wasn't as well equipped in that department as my relatives.

"So now we've just got to catch one of these suckers so I can use its blood to direct the spell."

"We?" Puck said.

"Aren't you going to help me?" I asked.

Puck shook his head. "You are fulfilling an obligation to me. You must perform the task on your own."

I bit my tongue so that I wouldn't give him the satisfaction of listening to me curse him out. "Enjoy the show, then," I said.

I veiled myself and stalked away, Puck chuckling softly behind me.

I surveyed the situation. The Cimice were all pretty centrally located around the cavern. Even if I was under a veil, the Cimice would notice if I grabbed one of them. Then an alarm would be raised, and I would lose the element of surprise, and this whole enterprise would quickly become more annoying than it already was.

If I had known I'd need the blood of one of the creatures, I would have taken out one of the patrols we had passed earlier. They were nice and isolated from the rest of the population. Now it would be too time-consuming to double back. I was just going to have to take my chances here. That was pretty much the default of my life, so at least I was in familiar territory.

I crept carefully over the ground between me and the colony, mindful of any place where there was loose rock or dirt that I might dislodge beneath my boots. I skirted around the entrance to the cavern and took up a spot several feet away from the epicenter of activity.

The Cimice were carrying rocks of various sizes inside the cavern. They were obviously building something, and I was really not interested in what. Understanding them was not going to help me get rid of them.

After several moments, a Cimice drifted close to my location. First, I quickly dropped a veil over the creature. I could still see the Cimice underneath, but it seemed see-through, like a ghost. I wondered why I could see it when I couldn't see Puck under my veil before. Was it a product of my will? Or because I hadn't expected to see Puck then, but needed to see the Cimice now?

There was a lot I still didn't understand about my powers. Regardless, the insect did not seem to be aware of the veil. The creature went about its business, busily collecting rocks and loading them into the sack it had slung around its neck.

The Cimice were well armored, with shiny green cara-paces everywhere except at the soft joints. I remembered killing one before, in Chicago, under the Southport El. That creature had known I was coming, had fought me to the point of exhaustion. But I had managed to kill it by shooting electricity through it at the vulnerable exposed flesh just under its head. Using electricity now would attract a lot of attention. In any case, I needed the creature's blood, and frying it wasn't the best way to achieve blood loss.

What I needed to do was use the sword to slit the thing's neck. There were a couple of logistical issues I needed to work out first, though.

For one, the Cimice were tall—like, NBA-player tall. I am decidedly un-tall. I could fly up behind the insect in order to reach its neck, but it's a lot harder to be stealthy that way. The Cimice might sense my presence behind it—feel the breeze from my wings or something like that. It seemed better to do it from the front, especially if the insect was distracted into looking up. Which gave me an idea.

Sheer rock rose above the Cimice's cavern, and above the place where I stood. If I very carefully caused a small piece of rock to break off and tumble down . . . Yes, that could work.

I moved into position. I was close enough to where the Cimice worked to lunge forward and slice its neck. It was kind enough to help me in this regard by suddenly deciding to work on all fours, which made it a lot easier for me to reach the soft throat with my blade.

Now the tricky part. I needed to hold the veil over myself and over the Cimice while using a very small, focused amount of power to dislodge an eensy bit of the rock wall above. I didn't want to start an avalanche, although that would have been better suited to my skill set.

I took a deep breath, focused my magic and my will to hold the veils steady, and then shot a tiny amount of night-fire at the rock wall. A chunk the size of a potato was dislodged, and it tumbled down in front of the Cimice. It then immediately did the logical thing and looked up.

And when it did, I pounced. The blade sliced through the Cimice's neck. I put a lot of force into it, nearly taking the thing's head off entirely. As it was, the creature's head flapped backward, bending the remains of its neck in an unpleasant way and exposing the cut muscle and veins.

Blood spurted, covering my sword. And my arm and chest and face and hair. This thing had a lot of blood. But at least I had what I hoped was enough of the stuff to perform the necessary spell.

I was congratulating myself on a job well-done when a nearby Cimice let out a high-pitched cry of alarm. And then pointed one of its pincers right at me.

The veils still held steady, so I couldn't figure out what had given me away. Then I noticed the blood spatter all over the rock. Ah. Yes. That would attract some attention, wouldn't it?

I raised the sword up, ready to take down any Cimice

that came for me. But the creature who had raised the alarm wasn't actually pointing at me.

It was pointing at the splattered blood, which was behind me. My veils were holding. The insects gathering now could see neither me nor their fallen brethren. They saw the blood, and didn't understand where it came from. It frightened them.

Good, let them be scared, I thought. It was such an un-Maddy-like thought, such a dark-side impulse that I shook my head immediately. No, I was not going to enjoy their fear. I was going to get the job done and then make sure Puck got me out of this place.

Puck had been adamant that flying was a bad idea, but it was the fastest way for me to get out of the corner I was boxed in. More Cimice were gathering, pointing at the spattered blood and chittering among themselves. I really needed to get away before they approached the wall. They would bump right into me, veil or no veil.

I lifted off, debating whether or not I should drop the veil on the dead Cimice's body. There were already on to the fact that something was amiss. I would have an easier time with the blood spell if I could focus all of my attention on it. That settled the question.

I dropped the veil on the dead one and flew away. Behind me was an explosion of noise and activity as the body was revealed.

I went straight to the spot where Puck waited, still hidden behind the rock. He laughed out loud when he saw me.

"I told you to get blood, Madeline," he said, his eyes crinkling with merriment. "I didn't tell you to roll in it."

"Shut it," I said. The Cimice's blood was drying stickily all over me. I felt like I'd been dipped in a vat of caramel sauce. Except I didn't smell that good. "Okay, obviously I've got the thing's blood. Now what?"

"I'm sure if you think about it, a solution will come to you," Puck said.

"You . . . are . . . useless," I said.

"We could renegotiate our deal," Puck said.

"No way," I said. "I'll sort it out without you."

"Just as I thought," he said, but he looked a little disappointed that I hadn't changed my mind.

I studied the grayish-green substance clinging to the blade of the sword. When I had called the vampires to me I'd used the magic in their blood, the traces of magic Azazel had left on the serum the vamps had swallowed.

But there was no magic for me to latch on to here. All the Cimice had in common were their genes.

Although creating life is its own kind of magic, isn't it? I thought. And magic always leaves a trace of itself behind.

I touched the tip of my finger to the blade, brushed some of the blood onto it. Then I sent my power through that drop of blood, just a little questing thread looking for a spark of magic. And I found it.

Deep inside the blood of the Cimice was a minuscule remnant of magic, the magic that was life itself. And this magic bound all of the Cimice together. I knew it with the same certainty that I knew my own name. My power welled up inside me, knowing instinctively what to do.

It surged through the magical spark in the Cimice's blood, searching for the next connection, the next link in the chain.

It touched that Cimice, and sped through its bloodstream. And then it stopped the insect's heart.

Once my power had done that, it looked for the next link, and the next. And the next. And so on and on.

119

The Cimice's voices rose as one as they screamed their anguish to the sky. The spell plowed forward, knocking the Cimice down one by one, squeezing their hearts until they stopped.

I felt them die, their agony in their final throes, and the pain brought me to my knees. I hadn't calculated this. I hadn't considered the possibility that I might feel sorry for the monsters. But there was no stopping it now, and in any case my purpose was still clear. They meant to kill innocent humans at the behest of the Faerie Queen. I couldn't let that happen.

This was preventive medicine. It was necessary.

The spell went deep into the heart of the cavern, to where the vast majority of the Cimice were. I gasped as I felt the presence of all of them. There were not hundreds, or thousands. There were *millions*, stacked up on one another in a vast hive.

My spell was killing them all, and I could feel every one. I closed my eyes, covered my ears, tried to drown them out. But I couldn't drown them out. They were inside me, their screams and their pain. I couldn't escape the truth of what I had done.

I believed I had done this for the right reasons. But there was no disguising this darkness. This was a shadow on my soul, and it would stay there forever.

I thought it couldn't get any worse. I thought my body was numb to what was happening. Then the spell hit the hatchlings.

They were just little monsters, I told myself. They weren't children screaming.

If I hadn't done this, there would be children screaming—

human children. The Cimice hatchlings would grow up to be just as ruthless as their parents.

"They're just monsters," I said over and over. "Monsters."

But what are you? a voice in my head asked, and that voice sounded a lot like Beezle's. *You keep justifying what you do, but when do you draw the line that's not supposed to be crossed?*

"I'm still myself," I said as the spell ravaged the Cimice, worked its destruction on them. It seemed to take a long time, but then, there were a lot of the creatures.

I don't know how long I knelt in the dirt, muttering to myself, hands over my ears, tears running down my face.

Eventually the spell found the last of them, every last insect out on patrol, every creature hidden in a cavern in the darkness. I opened my eyes and dropped my hands.

The spell was over, but I could still hear them screaming in my head. I could still feel them in my heart.

I felt weary in a way that I had never been before. I had pushed my body to the limit on countless occasions, gone past the point of pain and exhaustion. I had suffered in my body and soul—when Gabriel died, when Ramuell had torn my heart out, in the Maze. But this was worse than any of that.

This was not the weight of my own pain. You can carry your own suffering, learn to adapt, learn to live with it. But this was not my suffering. This was the hurt of another, of many, many others, and I was the one who had deliberately done them harm.

The burden was tremendous, almost incomprehensibly huge. I felt broken inside.

I stood slowly, like an old woman. Puck sat on top of a

large boulder, his legs dangling down. He looked like a child who had just seen a wonderful show.

"That was excellent," he said, clapping his hands together. "They never knew what hit them."

"No, they didn't," I said wearily.

"Are you not pleased?" Puck asked. "You have done what you set out to do. You have destroyed the Cimice utterly."

"Yeah," I said, looking out over the place where the creatures had built their colony.

Everywhere I looked there was death. Death, my constant companion, the truest friend I had ever had. There was no point in denying my true nature any longer. I was now, and always had been, an instrument of Death. As I thought this, something shifted inside me. The mantle of darkness settled more comfortably on my shoulders.

I opened my arms wide, and rose up into the air.

"What are you doing?" Puck called, and there was real alarm in his voice.

"Burying them," I said. "If you don't want to be buried yourself, you'd better get the hell out of the way."

I threw my head back, let the power flow through me, the power of the sun tempered by shadow, the power of Lucifer that I had tried for so long to suppress, to deny. Now that I was no longer holding it back, it burst forth in a great array of light.

The ground beneath began to shake, and I rose up, higher and higher. Puck shot into the air as the rock he perched on began to crumble.

He did not have a visible pair of wings, but I'd long suspected he could fly anyway.

Puck came to my side as my power hit the mountain before us and the whole thing started to fall. First rock sheared off the sides and crashed hundreds of feet below. Then the mountain seemed to cave in, collapsing inward upon itself.

I rose higher in the air as giant clouds of dust billowed upward. The sound was tremendous, like the earth itself was being rent to pieces. And in a way, it was.

Puck said nothing as the final resting place of the Cimice was covered with the remains of the mountain. Then we both turned in the direction of the forest, because we could feel him coming.

The dragon.

"I told you it was dangerous to fly," Puck said, cursing. "You've attracted his attention."

I shook my head, closing my eyes. I felt his approach like fire in the blood, a blaze that spread throughout my body, all-consuming. "That's not what draws him here. He felt my power when I brought down the mountain. It pulls him to me."

"Great," Puck said, obviously disgusted. "The two of you are *connected*."

I opened my eyes again, looked toward the forest. The dragon was coming for me with all speed. Smoke and flame trailed behind it.

"Who is he?" I asked Puck. "I know you know. Don't pretend otherwise."

Puck appeared more annoyed than I'd ever seen him. "You know yourself. You do not need me to give the knowledge to you."

And just like that, I did know. My heart had known him from the moment I'd see him.

"Daharan," I breathed.

"Yes," Puck said. "My brother."

Beneath us the ground shifted and settled as the last of the mountain crumbled to pieces. I flew away from the Cimice's graveyard, toward the dragon. Toward Daharan and the strange pull I could not deny. Inside my body, my son fluttered his wings in welcome.

I had never felt this way about Lucifer or Puck or Alerian. With them there was always dread and repulsion and annoyance and fear on a sliding scale, depending on which brother I was dealing with. But Daharan—he was the one the others feared the most, yet from the moment I'd met him I'd felt a sense of safety, of coming home.

"Daharan," I said.

The dragon curved its body as I approached. I landed on its neck, on the smooth expanse in front of the ridges that covered his back. I laid my head there. The dragon snorted in response and flew off in a different direction.

My mental map of this world told me we were heading toward the ocean. I wondered what Batarian and the other fae would make of the collapse of the mountain and the destruction of the Cimice. Maybe Batarian would finally realize he'd dodged a major bullet, and that he should never have messed with me in the first place.

I settled more comfortably on Daharan's neck, glancing behind only to see what had become of Puck. He followed several feet behind. If a person could fly resentfully, then Puck was definitely doing it. He obviously didn't want anything to do with Daharan, and he was glaring at his brother like he'd just taken Puck's favorite toy.

I turned back, smiling to myself. I have to admit that it was enjoyable to see Puck being thwarted.

Daharan flew over the forest. It was even wider and longer than I had thought. Even when I'd done the tracking spell to find the portal, I hadn't fully conceived of the size of this place. It made me realize just how difficult it would have been for me to reach the portal, even with my wings.

I was so warm and comfortable. I didn't feel like I could fall, even though I wasn't holding that tight to Daharan's neck. My exhaustion caught up with me again, and I drifted off to sleep, waking only when Daharan nudged me with his nose.

The sound of waves rolling to the shore filled my ears. I could taste the salt in the air. I opened my eyes and slid off Daharan's back to the sand below. Daharan took off flying again, and I covered my eyes to watch him circling above, expelling flame.

"He wants to change to his human form, but he's got to get rid of some of the fire first," Puck said behind me.

He'd done some kind of magical quick-change act with his clothes and was wearing a pair of leather pants with a black T-shirt. His hands were stuck in the pockets and he was glaring at Daharan, his jewel-blue eyes bright with anger.

"What are you so pissed about?" I said. "Aren't you happy to see your brother?"

"We don't get along," Puck growled.

"So why don't you just leave, then?" I said.

"I can't," Puck said, and there was a wealth of frustration in his voice. "I cannot show such disrespect to the eldest."

I looked thoughtfully up at Daharan. "He's the eldest, huh? Who's second?"

"Alerian, then Lucifer, then me," Puck said.

"That explains a lot," I said. "Lucifer seems like he has middle-child syndrome."

Puck snorted out a laugh. "Yeah, that's his problem. Middle-child syndrome."

"Wait—you told me that Lucifer was the firstborn," I said. "You told me that in my apartment, when you revealed yourself as Nathaniel's father."

"He is the firstborn of his kind. But Daharan is the eldest," Puck said.

"Aren't you all the same kind, from the same parents?" I asked.

"Not exactly," Puck said, grinning. He was enjoying my confusion.

His smile disappeared as Daharan slowly descended in lazy spirals until he landed farther down the beach. I'd never seen Puck look so genuinely unhappy as he did now, not even when he'd discovered that I'd accidentally undone the spell he'd put on Nathaniel at birth.

Daharan's claws touched the sand, and for a second he looked blurry. Then the dragon was gone, and in his place stood a man made of fire.

He walked down the beach toward us, and the flame gradually receded until he looked like an ordinary man. He was dressed in jeans and a T-shirt and work boots, and he looked a lot like a guy headed to a construction job. His hair was as black as mine, a little shaggy and overlong.

But when he reached me I realized he would never look normal. He would never be able to disguise those eyes. They blazed with the fire that he could not bank completely.

"Madeline," he said, and he took my shoulders in his hands. He kissed both of my cheeks very gently, like I was something precious to him, and tears came to my eyes.

This is what it feels like to have a father, I thought. *This is why he makes me feel so safe.*

Then he turned from me to look at Puck, standing with his hands still shoved in the pockets of his pants.

"Brother," Daharan said. "Will you not greet me?"

Puck gave Daharan the barest of nods, then dropped his hands to his sides and approached his eldest sibling. The two of them embraced, with much stiffness on Puck's side and, I think, amusement on Daharan's. It was very apparent that Daharan was the more powerful of the two, and they both knew it.

"I was surprised to find you here, in this place," Puck said when they parted.

"As I was surprised to find you, and Madeline," Daharan said.

Some unspoken undercurrent passed between them, and they stared intently at each other. I wondered whether they were communicating telepathically, or whether they were just trying to stare each other down.

After a few long moments Puck looked away.

"Now, my niece," Daharan said, turning to me. "I believe you wish to return to your world, and have had some difficulty doing so."

I nodded, and Puck glanced at me in surprise.

"You want to go back to Chicago? To the Retrievers? But I brought you here to keep you away from them," Puck said.

"No, you brought me here to manipulate me into doing something for you that you were too cowardly to do yourself," I said. "The fact that I needed to escape the Retrievers was just a happy coincidence for you."

"You always think the worst of me," Puck said, the twinkle back in his eye.

"That's because you always prove me right," I said.

I addressed Daharan. "So, do you think you can help me get out of here? I tried to open a portal myself but the world wouldn't let me. The fae told me that Lucifer had closed all the ways out of this place, but I found a permanent portal across the ocean."

"The fae told you that, hmmm?" Daharan said, looking significantly at Puck again. "Yes, Lucifer did close all the ways to and from here, save that one. It is just possible, with the right manipulation of magic, to come into this world. But the only way to leave it is that permanent portal."

My heart sank. "So I've got to cross the ocean."

Daharan nodded. "Yes. But I will help you. It will take less time for my dragon form to take you there. However, there is a catch."

"There always is," I muttered.

"The portal does not lead directly to your world. You must pass through it to another place, and then you can go on," Daharan said.

"And where does the portal lead?" I asked, dreading the answer.

Daharan looked at me, and the flames in his eyes burned more brightly than before.

"The land of the dead."

8

"THE LAND OF THE DEAD," I SAID. "OF COURSE IT DOES. Because I'm already in trouble with the Agency and I need to be in even more hot water."

Daharan frowned. "Why does Lucifer not clear your way with the Agency? Particularly since you collected Evangeline at his behest."

"You know about that?" I asked.

"I know much more than you think I do. Either of you," Daharan said, with a pointed look at his brother. Puck shifted uncomfortably in the sand.

"Well, anyway," I said. "Lucifer likes to see me get out of my own jams. That's why he wouldn't do anything about the Retrievers coming after me. And it wouldn't matter, anyway. They've got it in for me—Sokolov and Bryson and probably some faceless members of the board. Bryson's got a personal problem with me because I, um, might have physically harmed him at one point or another."

Daharan raised an eyebrow at me.

I wasn't going to go into detail about how I'd let Nathaniel torture Bryson. I hurried on. "But mostly they don't like that I managed to squeeze out of my eternal contract with them. Nobody at the Agency ever thought it would be possible."

"Yes, they believe you could incite rebellion amongst the Agents, cause them to give up their duty," Daharan said. "It is foolish. None of the other Agents has your powers or your bloodlines. Were you not one of us, you would have been entirely unable to throw off the mantle of death."

"I'm not sure it will help my case if they know that," I said. "They're already afraid of me as it is. And a lot of bad stuff has happened to Agents because of me."

Ramuell and Antares breaking into the Agency with a horde of demons, killing indiscriminately. Agents being taken and used for Azazel's experiments. Yes, the Agency had a lot of grief it could lay at my door, even if most of it was indirect.

It wasn't really my fault that my enemies used innocents in their quest to get to me. But I carried the burden of those deaths anyway.

My stomach grumbled loudly, breaking the tension and the silence. I grinned in an embarrassed way. "Sorry. Can't remember the last time I ate."

To my surprise, Daharan turned to Puck with an angry look. "Did you not think to feed the girl before you put her through her paces? She is with child. She needs nourishment."

He muttered something to himself, and a picnic blanket appeared on the sand. And on the picnic blanket there were . . .

"Pancakes!" I said. I'm not ashamed to admit that I dove for that plate like Beezle going for the popcorn bowl.

There was a whole spread, with orange juice and a bowl of brightly colored, cut-up fruit, and every kind of pancake topping I liked—butter and syrup and fruit jams. There was even bacon, and it smelled so heavenly that I almost fainted in ecstasy.

"Slowly," Daharan said. "You will make yourself sick."

I nodded, and carefully cut up one pancake on my plate after drowning it in butter and syrup. I ate slowly, letting my shriveled stomach adjust to the idea of food again.

While I shoveled food in my mouth—in a careful, measured way, of course—Daharan indicated to Puck that he should follow him. The two of them wandered down the beach.

I was definitely curious about what they were discussing, but I was probably better off not knowing. The less I knew of the plans of Lucifer's brothers, the better.

I was sure I could trust Daharan, but that didn't mean that he wasn't also harboring a secret plan for world domination, or some desire to see one or more of his brothers destroyed. I didn't want any part of that. I sincerely hoped that Daharan wouldn't help me get to the portal and then ask for some unnamed favor later.

It's pretty likely, though, isn't it? I thought. I'd never had dealings with any supernatural creature that didn't want something in return.

Down the beach, Puck turned to Daharan, his face angry. He was gesturing wildly, obviously furious. Daharan faced him with crossed arms, and he seemed unmoved by Puck's performance.

I ate until I couldn't eat anymore, and the little guy

inside my belly beat his wings happily. Now that I was full, I felt sleepy again. It seemed like all I'd done in the last couple of days was deal with insanely stressful situations and then pass out as soon as they were over. But I could feel my eyes closing, my mind drifting.

I was warm and I was safe, and so was my child. I had no fear.

When I woke it was night, and I was no longer on the beach. Daharan cradled me in a kind of sling that hung from his front claws. The ocean rolled away beneath us, and the wind blew in my hair. It should have been uncomfortable, but the heat emanating from Daharan's body kept me warm, and I wasn't worried that he would drop me. I drifted off again.

The next time I opened my eyes the sun was blazing, and the ocean was gone. Below us were the spiky peaks of mountains. I felt wide-awake and refreshed for the first time in days. I felt like I could take on anything—the Retrievers, the Agency, Evangeline, even Alerian. Well, maybe not Alerian. But I felt a lot better than I had for a while.

I reached up and put my hand on Daharan's claw so that he would know I was awake. He snorted in response, and kept flying. We were close to the portal now. I wondered how long I'd been asleep, and how long we'd been flying.

It is a much different experience to be carried by a flying dragon than to fly yourself. The dragon moves a lot faster, for one. I'd never been in an airplane—I'd never had any need to be in one—but I imagine that dragon flight is not unlike jet flight. The ground was much farther away than it would have been if I had been flying myself, and it seemed like we were passing slowly over it, though I knew we were covering dozens of miles every minute.

I relaxed in the sling that Daharan had made for me, and made a concerted effort not to worry about what consequences might be in store for me if I passed through the land of the dead again. There honestly wasn't much worse that the Agency could do to me that they hadn't already done, but my actions would probably inflame Sokolov and his gang further.

On the other hand, I couldn't control what the Agency decided to do. Or Lucifer and Evangeline. Or Alerian or Daharan or Puck. I could only respond to what they chose to do.

I realized that had become a way of life for me. At some point I had ceased taking the initiative. I'd become a person who responded to what happened instead of making things happen. But could I do any different? I wasn't going to sit back and let my family members run roughshod over innocent people.

Daharan pointed his nose down, releasing flame as he descended. The mountains had morphed into smaller foothills, and the portal was near us. We dropped slowly, but I was still forced to crack my jaw to make my ears pop.

Daharan landed softly in the grass in front of the portal. Most portals exerted a strong, vacuumlike pull on their immediate vicinity. Some of them created temporary cyclones so strong that they sucked in small objects from several feet away. This portal wasn't like that. It hung in space like a mirror, quiet and still. It blended in to the landscape in such a way that you would not know it was there if you weren't looking for it.

Unlike most of the other portals I'd seen, the world on the other side was not obscured by mist. I could see the scorched earth of the land of the dead, the place that I'd taken Evangeline from.

Daharan transformed into construction-worker-guy next to me. I turned to him.

"Thanks," I said simply. "Thanks for feeding me, and bringing me here. If you hadn't, I probably would have had to ask for Puck's help, and he would have demanded another favor in return."

"Madeline," Daharan said. His face was very serious. That seemed to be his default emotion. I bet there wasn't a lot of levity when Daharan was around. "Be wary of any deals you make with Puck. He is as changeable as the air."

"Yeah, I know," I said. "But sometimes I don't have a choice."

"There is always a choice," Daharan said.

"Not always," I said, thinking of the first time I'd indebted myself to Puck. He'd given me a jewel to escape Titania and Oberon's court, and hadn't bothered to mention that I would owe him a boon in return. Apparently you didn't have to actually verbally agree to anything in order to make a contract with Puck.

Daharan gave me a brooding look. I sensed that there was something else he wanted to say to me, that there was something Puck had done that upset him. But he just gave a small sigh and said, "Shall we go?"

I looked at him in surprise. "Wait—you're going to go with me?"

"Of course," Daharan said. "I would not be able to leave this world otherwise. And I will not leave you to the tender mercies of the Retrievers as my brother would."

I blinked away the tears that sprang up. "Thank you," I said.

"He should do this himself," Daharan said, and the flames in his eyes blazed higher for a moment.

"We both know that Lucifer only does what Lucifer wants to do," I said.

"He has always been like that," Daharan muttered. "From the cradle."

I had a very strange vision of the four brothers as children. It looked a lot like a chibi-anime cartoon in my head, all soft edges and big eyes. Alerian was a tiny cute squid in a baby pool. Puck a troublesome toddler with chocolate on his face and a stash of cookies behind the couch. Daharan was a teensy dragon blowing puffs of smoke. And Lucifer rose up on little wings before falling to the ground, unable to stay aloft.

I shook my head. My brain seemed to enjoy delivering me these non sequiturs from time to time. A thought occurred to me.

"Who are your parents?" I said. I'd always assumed the four brothers had sprung fully formed from the dust of the universe or whatever. "If you were children, you had parents."

Daharan shook his head. "This is not for you to know."

"Why not?" I said. "They're related to me, too."

"Our parents are very ancient beings, and they have slept for millennia," Daharan said. "To speak of them would be to wake them, to draw their attention."

"Isn't that a good thing?" I said. "Maybe Lucifer and Puck would calm down if Mommy and Daddy put them in a time-out."

"They would not put them in a 'time-out,'" Daharan

said. "When we were children, if Lucifer and Puck fought over a toy, my parents would simply break the toy."

"Oh," I said, getting the picture. "So if they thought that Lucifer and Puck were fighting for, say, dominion over the Earth . . ."

"They would wipe out the Earth and everything on it," Daharan said.

"Okay, let's not wake up Great-Grandpa and -Grandma," I said.

Daharan gave me a very small, very brief smile. "Yes, let's not."

In silent agreement we both turned toward the portal.

"I will go first," Daharan said.

A cold, unreasoning fear gripped my heart. Gabriel had always wanted to go first, and that was why Azazel's sword had killed him instead of me.

"Do not worry," Daharan said. "It would take a great deal to kill me."

"Of course," I said, and watched Daharan step into the portal. A moment later, I followed.

9

THE PASSAGE THROUGH THE PORTAL WAS RELATIVELY placid. It felt like floating through water, and then I was out on the other side. Daharan caught me easily and placed me on my feet. I shaded my eyes from the burning sun and looked around.

The land of the dead was just as crappy and desolate as it had been the last time I'd been here. The sun beat down on a bleached landscape that was broken only by the occasional rock or tree.

"Do we have to walk?" I asked.

Daharan shook his head. "No, we are not souls that are supposed to be here. We can pass through without penalty."

"Penalty from this world, maybe," I said. "The Agency will probably have something else to say about that."

"The Agency has become too narrow-minded and rigid in its focus," Daharan said as we took to the air. Like Puck, he didn't have visible wings, but glided along as easily as Superman.

We didn't speak as we flew. Daharan didn't seem like the type for casual chitchat, and I had a lot to contemplate. The existence of Lucifer's parents had given rise to other questions, but I didn't think Daharan would give me the answers. Where had the angels come from? Had they been created by Lucifer? By his parents? What did Puck mean when he said that Lucifer was the firstborn of his kind? What about humans? Were we some kind of grand experiment, or just an accident of chemistry and biology?

I guess these were the questions that most people had about their existence. But most people didn't have access to the answers through their relation to some of the oldest creatures in the universe.

When Evangeline and I had crossed the desert, it had taken us less than a day on foot to find the portal. Daharan and I were flying, so I'd assumed it would take less time. But after a couple of hours we still hadn't come across the place where I'd helped Evangeline's soul cross over.

Everything in the desert sort of looked the same, so it was possible we were going in the wrong direction.

"Hey, shouldn't we have found the portal by now?" I said to Daharan. "The one I used with Evangeline wasn't that far away."

Daharan shook his head. "That portal was only present by your will and Lucifer's, a tool of the Hound of the Hunt. The real portal is much farther."

"Right, because nothing can ever be simple or straightforward," I said.

"Madeline," Daharan said. "You need to stop thinking

that the universe is tossing obstacles in your way for its own amusement. You are just a tiny thing in the grand scheme."

"Well, nothing like having your uncle put you in your place and remind you how insignificant you are," I muttered.

"You have a part to play," he said calmly. "And it is an important one. But the gears of the galaxy are many, and they grind exceedingly small."

"Does that mean I can take a break from saving the world, then?" I said.

"No, you may not," Daharan said. "Unless you are willing to let the innocent die."

"You know that I'm not going to let that happen."

"Then this conversation is pointless," Daharan said. He didn't sound irritated, but there was a finality in the way he spoke that told me the subject was closed.

I was annoyed and I didn't really know why. I'd resisted taking on this role. I didn't want to be a hero, but I felt it had been thrust upon me over and over. I'd repeatedly said I just wanted an ordinary life, but that life had been sacrificed at the altar of the greater good. And because of that I'd gotten a little arrogant, I guess. I'd thought that I was important, that the world couldn't do without me.

Now Daharan was telling me that I was just a little piece of a grand jigsaw. A very little piece. And that made me wonder whether all the sacrifice was worth it.

It's worth it if you save one life, I thought. Hadn't I said that to Nathaniel once? He'd questioned why I struggled, why I threw myself in front of the bus over and over for people who would never know or care about me. And I'd told him that it was worth it if I saved one person. No one deserved to be mowed down in the street just because they had gotten in the way of something huge and horrible and incomprehensible.

I sank into my own thoughts, brooding. I didn't really pay attention to where we were going or how long it took. I just kept close to Daharan, who seemed to know what he was doing. So I was surprised when we suddenly started to descend.

I was equally surprised when I saw that the landscape had changed significantly. The parched desert was gone, replaced by lush and rolling hills dotted with trees and flowers. But I didn't sense the presence of the portal.

"The portal isn't here," I said. "Why are we going down?"

"Do you not need to rest?" Daharan asked, but he avoided my eyes as he said it.

Daharan had been extremely straightforward in my dealings with him thus far. I had to wonder why he was keeping his gaze from mine. And if I should be worried that this was the double-cross I'd been half expecting ever since Daharan had agreed to help me.

"What's down there?" I demanded, stopping in the sky.

Daharan paused, turned to face me. His eyes were sad, the fire in them banked. "Not what. Who."

There could be only one person he meant.

"Is he here?" I said, my heart leaping with a joy that I hadn't felt since the day I'd lost him.

Daharan nodded. "You have a short time. I will return for you."

My whole being flooded with anticipation. I dropped to the ground as rapidly as I could, turning in a circle, looking for the one face that I'd been searching for ever since he'd been taken from me.

And he was there, coming to his feet beneath a tree, his expression a mixture of astonishment and wonder.

"Gabriel," I breathed.

I ran to him, ran like I'd never run before, tears blinding me. I leapt into his arms and kissed him like I would never kiss him again. Because I wouldn't. I knew that this was the last time, the last chance. And Daharan had given it to me.

"Madeline," he said, over and over, his hands on my face, in my hair, like he couldn't believe I was real.

Inside my belly, my son fluttered his happiness. He knew his father was near.

Gabriel sank to his knees, pushed my shirt up so my stomach was revealed. He put his hand there, and his head next to it, turning his ear to my skin.

A pulse of magic passed through his fingers and shot through me, into the place where our son was cradled. Incredibly, the baby gave a tiny little pulse back, his magic meeting Gabriel's.

I looked at Gabriel in wonder and amazement, through eyes blurred by tears, and saw that he had the same expression on his face.

"How can he be so strong already?" I whispered.

"He is growing quickly," Gabriel said. "You will show soon."

He stood then, and gave me an assessing look. "You are not eating enough. You look pale. And thin."

"Really?" I said, shaking my head at him. "We're reunited after death, and you're worried about how much I'm eating?"

He gave me a brief smile, his dark eyes dancing. "I'm sure I can think of something else to do, if you only have the time."

"We have time for that," I said, reaching for him, but he drew back. I stopped, confused. "What's the problem?"

"Madeline, I do adore you, but . . . perhaps a bath is in order first?"

I looked down at my clothes, which were covered in dirt and sand and Cimice blood. My boots were coated in some unidentifiable goop. My hair felt greasy, and I probably smelled bad. But . . .

"Okay, you have a point," I said. "But it's not exactly tactful to point it out."

"I would like to make love to my wife when she is not covered in bug organs," Gabriel said, taking my hand and leading me to the sparkling lake.

"You're so romantic. How can I resist?" I said.

The lake was so blue and perfect it didn't seem real. The whole place seemed like a faerie illusion, something out of a dream. I put my sword on the ground and sat to pull off my boots. Even my socks were disgusting.

"The problem is," I said as I undressed, "that once I'm clean, I'm going to have to put these yucky things back on again."

Gabriel shook his head. "No, you will not. This place has a way of providing what is needed."

I paused, still in my bra and underpants. "Why is it so different here, compared to the way it is where Evangeline was? And why are you the only one around?"

He looked thoughtful. "I think it is because we see what we expect to see."

"So if you think you're going to sit on white fluffy clouds and all your loved ones are going to be there, that's what will happen?" I asked.

"I do not have all the answers," Gabriel said. "I have never seen another soul in all my time spent here."

"Isn't that lonely?" I asked.

"Not right now," he said, and his eyes were full of heat. "Madeline. Take the rest off."

I felt suddenly shy with him looking at me like that. He was still clothed, and I was just about bare-assed naked with the sun shining down on me. But there was also longing, and need, and so my underthings fell to the ground. I stood before him, and he just looked. Heat spread over me, soft and languid.

"Gabriel," I said, and it came out breathless.

He reached for me, took my hand, and led me to the lake. The water was warm as it lapped against my bare feet. I stepped in up to my ankles, and turned to him.

"You're still wearing your clothes," I said.

"I know," he said, his hands going to the top button of his shirt. Even here, in the afterlife, he dressed like a young professional in a button-down and slacks. "Let me wash your hair."

Just like that, there was shampoo and soap and soft towels on the bank of the lake. I waded in deeper, folding my wings against my back, ducking under the water, letting it run over my body. My shyness was diminishing rapidly. I felt so free and easy, naked in the water, with no one near to stumble upon us.

I kicked back to the surface and found Gabriel standing in the water up to his waist.

"Come here," he said, and there was nothing else I could have done. I was drawn to him, the way I had been from the first moment I saw him.

I walked to him, aware of what was revealed as the water became shallower.

"Turn around," he said, and I had the satisfaction of hearing the need in his voice.

I turned, conscious of my body and my power over him in a way I had never been before. He trailed one finger down the curve of my spine, stopping just before he went anyplace interesting. I shivered, and he gave a low chuckle.

Then his hands were in my hair, massaging through something that smelled sweet and herbal. He rinsed my hair clean, and then started on the rest of me. He took his time, and also took the time to touch and to kiss when he wanted, turning me in the water, building anticipation until I thought I would explode.

Then he lifted me to him, meteors shooting across the dark expanse of his eyes.

"I love you," he said, and then he was inside me, taking my breath away.

His magic flowed through me, and mine through him. I could feel Gabriel in my blood and in my bones, in the very beat of my heart. I was a part of him, and he was a part of me, and it would be this way forever.

The tension between us rose, our magic and our bodies winding around each other until they reached a fever pitch, until the stars in his eyes and mine exploded and light poured from inside us.

After there were soft towels on the beach, and a blanket for us to lie upon in the sun. We faced each other on the blanket, lying on our sides, hands intertwined. It felt so good to let the sun dance over my bare skin, to feel happy and content for a change. I never wanted to leave.

Gabriel must have sensed the direction of my thoughts.

He leaned toward me, kissed me once again, softly and gently. Then he said, "This cannot last. You cannot stay."

My afterglow receded like a balloon that had been pierced by a pin. The grief was bubbling up again, the broken parts of my heart tearing anew.

"I know that," I said.

"But you considered it," Gabriel said.

I couldn't lie to him, but I didn't want to admit it, either. "Don't you want me to stay with you?"

"You are not part of this world, Madeline," Gabriel said. "You are not dead."

I pulled away from him, and sat up, drawing my knees to my chest. "It's only a matter of time."

"Do not say that," Gabriel said. "Do not make me think that you wish for this."

"I'm so tired, Gabriel," I said. "I'm tired of fighting, of trying to do the right thing over and over when no one else bothers to."

"That is exactly why you must," Gabriel said. "Who will stop those in power, those who would abuse it, if you are not there?"

"I don't know. But I don't know why it always has to be me. Surely there are others with powers like mine," I said, coming to my feet.

I felt self-conscious again, and wished for something to cover my nakedness, to hide my vulnerability. As soon as the thought occurred to me, there was a neatly folded pile of clothing beside the blanket.

There was a set of plain cotton underwear in light blue, and a bra to match. The jeans and black T-shirt could have come from my own closet, and they were warm to the touch, like someone had just taken them from the dryer.

There was even a pair of new boots, just like my old ones. The leather was stiff as I slid my foot inside. I had the brief but strange thought that magic shoes shouldn't cause blisters. It seemed like that would violate some sacred law of the universe. I felt better once I was clothed, like I'd put my armor on. I slung my sword over my shoulder.

"There are others like you, but that does not mean they wish to expose themselves to harm," Gabriel said, standing as well. His own clothes appeared and he silently began to dress.

"I didn't wish to expose myself to harm, either," I said angrily. "And I certainly don't wish to expose our baby to harm. But you know that as soon as he's born, every enemy Lucifer has ever made is going to come for him."

Gabriel buttoned his shirt, his face brooding. He seemed to come to some kind of decision. "You should take your gargoyle's advice, and go to Lord Lucifer. He would be able to keep the child safe."

My mouth dropped open. "Are you crazy? Lucifer will take our child from me. He'll mold him in his own image, make our son a monster. I could never go to Lucifer. And I don't know how up on current events you are here in dreamland, but Evangeline is back and she's pregnant. She's going to see any child of mine as a threat to her progeny. The first thing she would do is try to strangle our baby in his crib."

"I am well versed in current events," Gabriel said. "I know everything that has happened to you since my death."

He looked pointedly at my wings. Only then did it occur to me that he had never asked why my wings were silver instead of black, and why they were visible instead of hidden.

"Oh," I said, feeling small. "So you know . . ."

"About Nathaniel, yes," Gabriel said.

There was nothing to say to that. We stared at each other, the silence between us lengthening. What do you say to the man that you married about the new man in your life? The fact that Gabriel had died seemed hardly relevant now that I was facing him.

"Gabriel, I—" I began, but he cut me off.

"I cannot be angry with you," he said. "I would like to. I would like to rage, to say you betrayed me. But you are alive, and so is he. And I am not. I cannot blame you for wanting comfort."

My whole body was filled with pain, the pain that only love can bring. Not only was I standing here about to lose Gabriel again, but he knew that I had been with another man. I scrubbed my hands over my face, but nothing could stop the tears now.

"Madeline," he said gently, and enfolded me in his embrace. I felt his love and his forgiveness flow over me, and I wept into his shoulder.

Gabriel, always so patient, so gentle, so understanding. A better human than I could ever be, and he had only the smallest drop of human blood in him. How could I do this again? How could I leave him?

He kissed my cheeks and my lips, kissed me until my crying ceased. We stood with our arms around each other, holding on, neither of us speaking. There was nothing left to say, and we both knew we didn't have much time.

Then the voice I'd expected to hear was behind me.

"Madeline," Daharan said.

I clung more tightly to Gabriel, breathing him in, wanting a few more moments, wanting to keep him with me forever.

He pulled away first, always the stronger one, always more practical than I.

"It is time," he said.

I nodded. I couldn't speak. I couldn't say good-bye.

"You must not return again," Gabriel said, stroking his fingers over my cheek. "You must give up your dreams of death."

"I don't dream of death," I said. "I dream of you."

"Then you must let me go," he said softly.

"I thought I did," I said. "I tried to."

"You must try harder," he said. "When it is your time, I will be here."

"And then we'll have forever," I said.

He smiled. "Yes."

"Okay," I said, backing away until I could no longer feel the warmth of his body against mine. "Okay."

Gabriel didn't say anything else. There was nothing else for us to say to each other.

I turned around and saw Daharan standing well away from us, giving us privacy in our good-byes. He could probably hear every word, but it was nice that he was willing to give us the illusion of being alone.

He rose into the air, beckoning me. I looked back one last time at Gabriel, and saw one tear on his cheek, glistening in the yellow sunlight. Gabriel never cried. That almost broke me, almost made me turn back, almost made me beg Daharan to leave me there.

Almost.

I knew that I didn't belong in the land of the dead. I knew there was no one else to save my city except me. But as we flew away, it seemed that my body was rending in two, my heartbreak manifesting as physical pain. My breath was short; my chest hurt.

"Why did you take me there?" I asked Daharan. I think we were both surprised by the anger in my voice.

"I know Gabriel's death was sudden, that you were unable to bid him good-bye. I believed it would give you peace if you were to do so."

"All you did was rip the scab off a healing wound," I said. Yes, I'd had time with Gabriel that I had not expected to ever have again. But it was almost worse now, knowing he was there and I was not, knowing that I had to leave him behind.

I was also more than a little conflicted by the discovery that he was watching over me like a guardian. I'd always thought his voice in my head was some figurative manifestation of my unconscious, not Gabriel *actually talking* to me from beyond the veil.

Part of me felt warm and comforted by the knowledge that he was making sure I was all right. But the other part of me felt like my privacy had been violated. How could I move on with my life, have a relationship with anyone else, knowing that Gabriel was watching me?

Of course, my illusions of privacy were probably just that. Daharan, Puck and Lucifer all seemed to have much more information about my daily doings than they ought to. Every second of my life was likely observed in somebody's crystal ball.

It is very disheartening to think that your life is not your own. And my life had not been my own for a very long time now, no matter what notions I might have had otherwise.

Daharan and I did not speak again until we reached the portal. It was cut into the side of a tree, like a passage to another world in a fairy tale.

I turned to Daharan, trying to ignore the part of me that wanted to pick a fight with him. Daharan wasn't really the type to rise to the bait.

"Will this bring me back to Chicago?" I asked.

Daharan nodded. "Not only to Chicago, but to your home, as long as you fix the place clearly in your mind before you go through."

I took a deep breath, stepped forward. "See you on the other side, then."

I disappeared into the tree before Daharan had a chance to say or do anything. This portal experience was more like the usual for me. My head felt like it was being smashed between two cast-iron pans.

I burst out of the portal and immediately fell onto the sidewalk, rolling to a stop on my side. I breathed in the smell of the city, that indefinable mixture of cooking food, car exhaust and . . . smoke?

Daharan came through the portal, materializing like a shimmering ghost, already on his feet. I sat up slowly, looking around. At first I didn't realize where I was. Then I became aware of three things.

The first was that it was much, much warmer than it had been when I left Nathaniel. The trees on the street had leaves, and flowers had blossomed in front yards. The air had the scent of spring.

Second, my belly seemed to have grown exponentially while I passed through the portal. The minuscule bulge below my belly button had become a legitimate roundness. I could feel the heft and weight of my child in there, no longer just a tiny flutter. He was pushing and rolling inside me.

Third, I was standing on my street, in front of my house. Except that my house was no longer there.

10

THERE WAS A CHARRED RUIN WHERE MY HOUSE USED
to be. I walked forward slowly, as if in a dream, my hand
on my belly. Under my fingers my child wiggled and
stretched.

The two-flat that I had lived in since I was a child was
nothing but a few blackened bits of rubble. The house had
been so thoroughly destroyed that not even the foundation
remained. There was a pit where my home used to be. The
grass in the front and back was completely burned away,
exposing the dirt beneath. Even the shed was gone. Every
last shred, every physical remnant of my life, had been
destroyed.

I had a moment where I was grateful that Beezle was
no longer living in the house. He would have been inside
when this . . . this . . . whatever it was had happened. But
Nathaniel could have been inside, and my heart clenched in
fear. Nathaniel. Where was he?

"What happened here?" I asked, and my voice sounded lonely in the night. "And how long were we gone?"

Daharan and I were the only two souls out on the street. The lamplights burned, and so did the lights inside other houses. Everything seemed like it had gone back to normal in Chicago. I could hear the sound of a sitcom on television drifting from the open window of my neighbor's house. Farther down the block I could see traffic on Addison zipping back and forth. Somebody's dog barked. It was like the vampires had never come, like everyone had returned to their normal lives and forgotten.

But my house was gone. It was *gone*. It was stupid, really, to cry over it. I was still alive, right? My baby was safe. And almost everyone I cared about had left the building long before this had happened. Samiel, Beezle, J.B., Chloe—none of them would have been here. I wasn't certain about Nathaniel. I didn't want to think about it. I didn't want to think about losing someone else to death unless I was sure.

But my pictures of my mother, the blanket that Beezle slept in, my favorite sweaters and the brush that Gabriel had used on my hair on our wedding night . . . All those things were gone. The books I'd read as a child, Gabriel's clothes hanging in the closet, any tangible proof that I had lived, that I had memories. It was all gone.

It seemed like too much on top of everything else. My home had always been my safe haven, the place where I could find refuge when everything else was falling apart. Now there was nowhere for me to go. I was breaking to pieces inside. Soon there would be nothing left of me.

I realized that this was what my enemies wanted. They wanted to break me, to make me helpless. Just the thought of it hardened me. I was not helpless. I would not break. My eyes were dry. I would find out who did this and they would pay.

"What happened here?" I asked Daharan again.

"I was with you, Madeline. I do not know," he said. "But I can use a spell to discover the answer."

"Then do it," I said, and my voice was cold.

Daharan gave me a mildly reproving look, but said nothing. He raised his hands up. I went to stand beside him.

What happened next was a lot like watching a film in reverse. I saw everything that had happened on this spot from the moment we emerged from the portal backward. At first, there wasn't much happening. People walked by; dogs peed on the remains of my lawn. Kids dared one another to climb down into the pit where my house used to be.

The leaves on the trees seemed to shrink down to buds, and then disappear altogether. Samiel and Chloe stood before the charred bits of the building. Beezle sat on Samiel's shoulder. They were speaking, but I couldn't hear what they said.

Then they were gone, and J.B. was there on the sidewalk with his hands in his pockets, tears running down his face.

And then I saw the house, surrounded by darkness and fury and covered in flame. The Retrievers were scorching the earth in their rage. They would make sure that I had no home to return to.

Because I was watching time run in reverse, it seemed that Nathaniel stumbled toward the Retrievers, then knelt on the sidewalk on his hands and knees, coughing up smoke. Nathaniel staggered back into the burning building.

I knew now that he'd escaped, and I was grateful. And

I knew that the Agency had caused this. I had given most of my life to them, to a job that I'd hated and never asked for. When I had broken their laws through no fault of my own, they had sent the Retrievers to take me. When the Retrievers couldn't find me, they'd destroyed everything they could in my stead. I'd had *enough*.

"You don't need to show me any more," I said.

Daharan dropped his hands, and the vision of the house burning, surrounded by furious Retrievers, disappeared.

"What will you do now, Madeline?" he asked.

Part of me wanted to go downtown to the Agency and burn the whole thing to the ground. The other part of me recognized that this was a dark-side thought, and that my argument was not with the Agency but with a select few members of it. So I reined in my impulse to destroy things.

The world was getting more dangerous by the minute, especially for me and for my child. Emotion wasn't enough to carry me through anymore. I had to think, to use my brain.

It was a lot harder to think when my home was gone. I'd always perceived that I was safe there. Supernatural creatures could not cross a threshold without an invitation, and that was powerful magic.

Without a threshold I was vulnerable to more than Retrievers. I could get a hotel room, but the threshold just wasn't as strong. So many people moving in and out of the same space didn't create the same sense of home. And if I was in a hotel, you could bet that some freaky thing would come looking for me there, and that would mean that ordinary people would wind up as collateral damage. I had no idea where Nathaniel was staying. I didn't think that Chloe and Samiel would let me bunk with them, since Samiel had moved out of my place because it was unsafe. There was nowhere for me to go, unless . . .

I looked sharply at Daharan. "Do you think Lucifer knew this would happen? He can see the future, right?"

"He can see aspects of it, yes," Daharan said. "So can we all."

"So he knew—you all knew—that I would wind up homeless?" I asked.

"I did not know this," Daharan said. "Your future is a gray thing to me, despite the familial bond that I feel with you. But soothsaying is not my best skill in any case. That is what Alerian excels at."

"Alerian knew for sure," I said, thinking hard. "Possibly Puck. And almost definitely Lucifer."

"What are you thinking, Madeline?" Daharan asked.

"I'm thinking that it would suit Lucifer very well if I had nowhere to go and no safe place to be, and therefore was forced to come knocking at his door, seeking shelter," I said.

"Well, what do you know? She can use her brain every once in a while," said a familiar voice behind me.

I turned slowly, disbelievingly. Beezle was there, a few feet away, flapping his wings so that he was eye level with me in midair. It hurt to see him, to remember the way he'd left when I'd needed him.

"What are you doing here?" I asked, and my voice was hard and cold.

I expected a smart remark, some typical Beezle off-handedness. Instead his face was grave as he said, "I've been checking back here off and on, looking for you. Everyone thought you were dead. But I knew you'd be here, sooner or later."

"J.B. would know that I wasn't dead," I said, fighting the emotion that had surged with Beezle's sudden appearance. He was the first creature I wanted to see, but the very last one that I'd expected. "He would have seen the order for my soul to be collected if I was."

"Sokolov did show him an order, one that said Bryson collected your soul after you fought the Retrievers and lost," Beezle said.

"But you didn't believe it," I said.

"Pfft. I'd never believe you were dead if I didn't see the body myself," Beezle said. "Are you my girl or not? I made you too stubborn to die."

"Am I your girl?" I asked, very quietly, afraid of the answer.

"You know you are," Beezle said.

He flew to me then, put his little arms around my neck, and the tears were back. "I'm sorry. I'm sorry I left you. If you ever tell anyone I said this, I will deny it to my stone-turning."

I laughed then, and patted his back, and kissed his head in between his horns. "I missed you."

He pulled away, wiping his eyes. "Yeah, yeah. Enough with the waterworks. The Retrievers are going to be back for you as soon as Sokolov realizes you've returned."

"I will take care of the Retrievers," Daharan said.

Beezle flew up to my shoulder. It was comforting to feel his weight there again. He stared at Daharan for a long time, then said, "So, another of Lucifer's brothers, eh? What do you want from Maddy?"

Daharan spread his hands. "Nothing. I have come only to assist my niece in her struggles, which are primarily the fault of Lucifer."

"Just trying to clear the family name?" Beezle asked skeptically.

Daharan nodded. "I can arrange for the Agency to call off the Retrievers."

"And how will you do that?" I asked. "The Agency is pretty convinced that they are a law unto themselves. Puck and Lucifer have both indicated to me that even they don't mess with the soul collectors. And the Agency likes to take a hands-off approach with the other supernatural courts. I learned that from J.B. Basically, the Agency's got a you-don't-bother-us-and-we-won't-bother-you attitude."

"Except where you're concerned," Beezle said.

"Yeah, I don't know what makes me so special," I said.

"You're special because you have managed to piss off an incredibly diverse collection of powerful beings," Beezle said.

"Through no fault of my own," I said.

"Fault doesn't come into it," Beezle said. "The fact remains that you attract attention, and a lot of it. And the Agency doesn't like that."

"I do not like it, either," Daharan said. "I will be having words with my brother on the subject."

"Oh, to be a fly on the wall when *that* conversation happens," Beezle whispered.

"And won't it attract more attention if you go storming in to the Agency and ask them to leave me alone?" I said to Daharan.

"I will not ask," he said.

Daharan smiled, and for the first time I realized why his brothers were afraid of him. He exuded a tangible sense of menace, of power, that would not yield to any persuasion. He was the strongest of them all, and the most implacable.

His magic was born in fire, and fire was the most pitiless force in the universe. Fire did not discriminate. It could not create. It could only destroy.

I looked into his eyes and I knew that if Sokolov and the Agency did not give him what he wanted, they would burn.

Beezle knew it, too. "Are we okay with this?" he asked in a way that let me know he was *not* okay with this.

"Don't harm the Agents," I said. "They're just foot soldiers. But Sokolov, and Bryson . . ."

"You can feel free to grind them into little pieces if you like," Beezle said. "Even I don't see any point in trying to redeem the two of them."

"I will find you again, Madeline," Daharan said.

Then he took to the air. I watched him go until the night covered him and I could see him no longer.

"So," Beezle said. "Do you think the manager at Dunkin' Donuts would let us sleep in the back room if we paid her enough?"

"We are not living anywhere you would have twenty-four-hour access to doughnuts," I said. "You're heavy enough as it is. What's Samiel been feeding you?"

Beezle shrugged. "Whatever Chloe eats, mostly. She's an eating machine. You wouldn't think that a person that little could eat so much, but she can give me a run for my money. I've never seen anyone eat so many tacos in one sitting."

"So you've been gorging yourself while I was half-starved on a distant planet?" I said. "Nice. Very nice."

Beezle flew off my shoulder so he could look critically at my figure. "It doesn't look like you haven't been eating."

"That's the baby, you idiot," I said.

He grinned. "I know, I know. Actually, you do look kind

of thin—other than the basketball hanging off the front of you, that is."

I rubbed the new roundness in my tummy. "It's not basketball-sized yet. It's more like softball-sized."

"That's not a slow-pitch ball," Beezle said. "That's a Chicago sixteen-incher."

"Enough about my belly," I said. "Don't you want to hear what I've been up to?"

"Only if you feed me first," Beezle said. "I haven't eaten in at least a half an hour."

"I don't think these pants came with a platinum card," I said, digging into my pockets. To my great surprise, I found a twenty-dollar bill in one of them.

"Neat-o," Beezle said. "Do you think it will do that every time?"

"Probably not," I said. "I can get you a slice of pizza."

"One slice?" Beezle whined. "You have twenty whole dollars. You can do better than one slice."

"That's my offer. Take it or leave it," I said.

"Oh, fine," Beezle grumbled. "But it better be deep-dish."

"Let's walk to Art of Pizza," I said.

"Walk?" Beezle said dubiously.

"You're going to be carried no matter what, so I don't know why you're complaining already."

"No, it's not that," Beezle said. "Well, of course I will be carried regardless. But I meant that you would be pretty conspicuous walking around with those wings. People are very curious around here about creatures that look different. Some of them are kind of on edge. So you might want to veil those things."

"I keep forgetting. I'm still not used to having them," I admitted as I dropped a veil over my wings. I started down the street, Beezle nestling more comfortably into my shoulder. "Wait a second. If people are still on edge, what are you doing flying around in public?"

"Oh, nobody thinks I'm a threat," Beezle said with a touch of smugness. "In fact, most children and adults find me adorable, and they're thrilled to know that cute little fantasy animals actually exist."

"Cute little fantasy animals," I repeated. "So they haven't actually taken the time to get to know you, then."

"A lot has changed here," Beezle said soberly.

"How long was I gone?" I asked.

"Three and a half months," Beezle said.

"So it's May," I said. "What happened after I got rid of the vampires?"

"Oh, the National Guard came in, and the Army. They made a big fuss on TV about scouring the streets for remaining vampires. Politicians got on the news and made pretty typical left-and-right pronouncements depending on their persuasion. Emergency funding was sent to the city, which was immediately squandered in backroom deals. In the end, Chicago was declared vermin-free and the government took the credit for making the streets safe again."

I snorted. "Well, I can't say that I'm surprised."

"I'm surprised that they thought they could get away with it," Beezle said. "Most of the world has seen the video of you turning into a supernova and making the vampires go boom. Nobody could believe the mayor when he got up in front of the press and thanked everyone but you."

"He doesn't know who I am," I said uneasily. "Why would he thank me?"

"Oh, he knows," Beezle said with relish. "I told you before you left that people would ferret out who you were. It took about three and a half seconds for your identity to be posted all over the Internet. You're a total folk hero, like Robin Hood."

"You told me that people would be terrified of me, that they would show up at my house with torches and pitchforks," I said. "That was why Chloe and Samiel and you left."

"No," Beezle said. "*They* left because they were worried about torches and pitchforks. I left because I was afraid you were becoming a monster."

"And that fear has just magically gone away?" I said.

"No," Beezle said. "But I think I should stay and make sure you don't transform completely from Jekyll to Hyde."

"You're going to be my Jiminy Cricket?" I asked.

"Do you want me to start singing 'Give a Little Whistle'?" Beezle asked.

"Absolutely not. I've heard you sing and it's not an experience I'd like to repeat. Ever. Again."

There were a few people out walking on Lincoln as we headed south toward the six-way intersection at Ashland and Belmont. Most of them barely noticed me, although one middle-aged guy walking a perfectly groomed poodle did give Beezle a double take.

"What are people saying about the existence of vampires?" I asked Beezle. "Have other creatures revealed themselves, too?"

"Besides me, you mean?"

"I don't think your coming out is that significant in the grand scheme of things," I said. "What about the wolves? The fae? The fallen?"

161

"Jude, Nathaniel, Samiel and you were all on television fighting the vampires in Daley Plaza, remember?"

"Of course," I said. That had been before I'd gotten my new wings, before Nathaniel's legacy as Puck's son was revealed, before I'd traveled through a portal to another world. But I would never be able to forget the sight of vampires streaming from the subway tunnels and out of manhole covers, infecting the city like a cancer.

"So because the four of you were on TV looking very supernatural, people kind of knew that there were other creatures out there besides vampires. There's been a lot of chatter on Facebook about what myths could actually exist."

"How do you have time to fool around on Facebook with your eating schedule?" I asked.

"I know how to eat and type," Beezle said. "Anyway, overall the response has been more positive than you'd expect. There's a lot of curiosity."

"Curiosity can be just as dangerous as anger or fear," I said, thinking of the doctor at Northwestern who had seen Nathaniel's wings and *coveted*.

That guy had wanted to take Nathaniel away to a lab and perform experiments on him. He couldn't be the only one who would want to take an angel or a vampire apart and see what made him tick. I shuddered. I was glad Beezle had made me cover my wings. I didn't want to end up on an operating table with my insides on the outside just because some scientist wanted a Nobel Prize.

Beezle continued. "Anyway, who'd have thunk that a generation of people prepared by supernatural TV shows and movies would be so completely receptive to the existence of actual vampires and werewolves and so on?"

"Yeah, who'd have thunk?" I said dryly. "So has any group formally introduced themselves?"

"Not yet," he said. "Wade is considering it. They are holding back because of Therion."

"He's dead," I said. "I don't think his opinion should come into play."

"It's not his opinion they're worried about," Beezle said. "It's the way he went on TV and announced he was taking over everything, and lots of people were eaten up before and after his presentation."

"Wade is so harmless. He looks completely ordinary," I said. "All he has to do is go on the air with his beautiful wife and adorable child and say that he's going to live and let live. Everyone will love him."

"It's his beautiful wife and adorable child that concern him," Beezle said. "He doesn't want to see his family harmed if the gamble fails."

"I thought most people were accepting," I said.

"They are," Beezle said. "They're accepting of the idea that there might be interesting creatures among them. But that doesn't necessarily translate to welcoming an entire population of something that could potentially kill them."

"Humans do a very fine job of killing one another when magic is not involved," I said.

"They don't *usually* slaughter each other in the streets and then eat each other's faces off," Beezle said. "So while there is human curiosity, there is also trepidation. A lot of supernatural creatures think it's best to ease into things."

"Introduce themselves to a small group, hope that the response is positive?" I said.

"Pretty much," Beezle said. "There are anecdotal tales

of wolves and fae coming out to their workplaces or their sports teams, things like that."

"And?" I asked.

"Most responses have been positive," Beezle said.

"Most?"

"There are bigots everywhere," Beezle said sadly. "And they like to kill what they don't understand."

"So you think I should continue to hide my wings," I said.

"For now," Beezle said.

I stopped on the sidewalk next to the Art of Pizza's plaza. There was a rock music school next door, and a tiny parking lot. The restaurant was bright and bustling. Large glass windows fronted the building. I could see people picking up take-out orders, others gathered in groups in the informal seating area. Delivery drivers rushed in and out.

"Beezle," I said. "If I'm a folk hero, won't people recognize me?"

"Nah," Beezle said. "You had really short hair in the first picture that Therion showed on the vampire broadcast."

"People are going to be fooled by the length of my hair?" I asked.

"You were also covered in blood," Beezle pointed out. "And you were wearing that stupid coat."

"That stupid coat keeps me warm," I said. "Or it did. It got burned up, along with the rest of my stuff. What about the video of me destroying the vampires? I had long hair then, and no blood on me."

"But you have wings in that video," Beezle said. "And they are covered up now. So people might *think* they recognize you, but they won't be sure. It will be like an Angelina Jolie sighting."

"I don't think it will be anything like an Angelina Jolie

sighting," I muttered, but I crossed the parking lot and entered the restaurant anyway. I couldn't hide out from the world, and anyway I had nowhere *to* hide.

I'd thought I'd just slide up to the counter, order a couple of slices to go and get out, like a regular person. But I'd forgotten that I had Beezle on my shoulder. All it took was one person noticing my gargoyle. A murmur rose in the restaurant as men and women pointed at him. My cheeks reddened as I stepped up to the counter.

"One thin-crust mushroom and a sausage deep-dish to go," I said to the short Latino guy working behind the counter.

I have to give the guy credit. He didn't even blink. Or maybe he was just so focused on getting through the order and to the next person that the presence of Beezle on my shoulder didn't really register.

It took only about a minute for him to get my slices and ring up the order, but it felt like an eternity. I could feel the stares of the curious burning into my back. Beezle seemed unaffected by the whole thing, adopting the attitude of a celebrity who knows he's been identified but wants to pretend otherwise.

I collected my change and the container holding the pizza and headed for the door. I pretended I had tunnel vision and focused only on the exit. Almost there. Almost . . .

A young man a few inches taller than me wearing a Muse T-shirt and a pair of worn-out jeans slid in front of me just as I was about to push the door open. His blue eyes were alight with excitement.

"Hey," he said loudly. "Aren't you Madeline Black?"

11

I DUCKED MY HEAD AND TRIED TO STEP AROUND HIM. "No, sorry; you must have mistaken me for someone else," I mumbled.

He put his fingers on my shoulder to stop me. "No, I think you are," he insisted.

My temper flared when he put his hand on me. I know he didn't mean me any harm, and even if he did, it would be nothing for me to squash him like a bug. But nobody pushed me around. Not even an insignificant human.

I let my power surge up, so that my eyes would change. Then I lifted my head so he could see it.

"Get your mitts off me and get out of my way," I said in a low voice.

"Whoa, check out your eyes," the guy said.

"He doesn't have enough brains for self-preservation," Beezle said to me. "You ought to blast him just on principle."

"I thought we were against harming the innocent?" I said under my breath.

"Some people are too stupid to live," Beezle said.

I looked up at the guy in my way, who was staring at me like he was hypnotized. "Move now or forever hold your peace."

"Jack, move," another guy hissed. He was seated at the counter that ran along the front window, overlooking the parking lot. The counter seating was right next to the front door.

Jack stepped out of the way, finally. I pushed open the door and went into the lot.

"See if he's following me," I said to Beezle.

Beezle twisted on my shoulder. "His friend is arguing with him. Jack's collecting up his stuff to run after you."

"We're going under a veil," I said. "Stay still."

I pulled the veil over us just as Jack and his friend emerged into the parking lot. They both stood there blinking.

"Did you see . . . ?" Jack asked.

"No," his friend said firmly. He grabbed his buddy's shoulder and steered him back inside. Jack looked back several times, obviously hoping to see me.

"No one was going to recognize me, huh?" I said. I walked back toward the six-way intersection to find a bench to sit on while we ate.

"How was I to know that Jack Dabrowski would be in Art of Pizza at that very moment?" Beezle complained.

"Wait—you knew who that guy was?" I said.

"Of course I did," Beezle said. "He's got a blog that collects all the supernatural sightings in Chicago. He's been

167

doing it since before the vampire invasion. Once upon a time he was considered a crackpot who saw ghosts."

"And now he's a viewed as a high priest, right? All the people who made fun of him know he was correct, that there really are things that go bump in the night."

"He's the reigning authority on anything out of the ordinary," Beezle said. "And he's been a very vocal advocate of yours."

"I guess he wasn't aware that I was supposed to be dead."

"Oh, he knew. He just didn't believe it," Beezle said.

"Why? All the evidence indicated such. He didn't have a personal relationship with me. Why would he think I wasn't dead, and more importantly, why would he care?"

"He wants you to take a leadership role in Chicago. Something high profile, like mayor."

I stared at Beezle. "Did you investigate him to see if he was an agent of Lucifer?"

"He's not," Beezle said. "He just really, really thinks that you should use your powers for good. Be the human face of the supernatural world. People already like you. They already think you're a hero because you wiped out the vampires. He might have a point."

"No, he doesn't," I said firmly. "I am not running for public office, or turning into some kind of mouthpiece for supernaturals. I might as well walk around wearing a T-shirt with a target painted on the front and back. All I'd be doing is making it easier for one of Titania's men to assassinate me while I stood on a platform at a press conference."

"That's true," Beezle admitted. "Dabrowski isn't exactly in full possession of the facts. He just thinks you did something heroic and therefore—"

"I should be punished for it?" I asked.

"I don't think he views it as punishment," Beezle said.

I dropped the veil when I found a very weatherworn bench with a yellow "Your Ad Here" sign on the back rest. There was a boarded-up storefront behind it with a cell-phone carrier name on the crooked sign. Every third or fourth business had been completely abandoned, and it wasn't just a product of the bad economy. It seemed like a fair number of people hadn't bothered to return to Chicago after the vampire devastation. I couldn't say that I blamed them.

Beezle flew off my shoulder and landed on the seat, rubbing his hands together in anticipation as I opened the take-out box.

"You *will* use utensils," I said, pulling a rubber-band-wrapped package with a fork, knife and napkin out of my pocket.

"You're using your hands," Beezle whined as I removed my slice from the box.

"I did not get deep-dish," I pointed out.

"Oh, fine," Beezle grumbled. He climbed inside the container and started cutting into the crust. "Now tell me everything that happened to you."

I started with Alerian's appearance on the beach. Beezle hadn't been around for that. Then I told him about the Retrievers attacking the house, the portal that Nathaniel had made (prompted by Puck), my experiences on the other world, and Puck's deception. I told him about Daharan and the need to pass through the land of the dead. I told him that I saw Gabriel again, although I didn't fill in the details.

"So, Puck wanted you to go to this other planet and get rid of the giant insects," Beezle said when I was finished.

His stomach was splattered with tomato sauce. I took the unused napkin and wiped him down like a child.

"Yes," I said. "Although I don't know what Titania's going to say when she finds out all the Cimice are gone."

"Where did they come from in the first place?" Beezle asked. "If Lucifer closed the ways in and out except for that one portal, how did the Cimice even manage to get there in the first place?"

"Daharan said that if you had enough power, you could just manage to open a portal there. I assume Titania has enough power to do such a thing. Or maybe Lucifer just didn't do a very good job of sealing the place up."

"Yes, but why?" Beezle asked. "It doesn't make any sense. She would have to move the Cimice across the ocean to get them off that planet and into Chicago. Why not leave them on the world that they originally came from?"

"Maybe she had a bone to pick with the fae that lived there," I said. "It did seem like the Cimice were using their battles with the fae as some kind of training."

"It still seems inefficient to me," Beezle said. "And why is Puck so concerned about it, anyway?"

"He said that if Titania released the Cimice in Chicago, it would be tantamount to the Faerie Queen declaring war on Lucifer. Lucifer would be forced to respond. Puck says it doesn't suit him to have the two of them at war. Yet."

"I don't know about that, either," Beezle said. "He hates Lucifer. And he can't have enjoyed pretending to be less powerful than Titania for all of these years. What's he playing at? What's his long game?"

"Don't ask me," I said. "I tried to think through all possible angles but I'm pretty sure I failed. I don't have the right kind of brain for Puck-logic."

"Well, now I'm back so the rightful order of things can be restored. I'll do the thinking; you do the smashing," Beezle said.

I collected up our garbage and stood. Someone touched my shoulder.

I spun around, grabbing the person's wrist and wrenching him to his knees before he realized what was happening. I twisted the arm around the person's back.

"Ow, ow, ow!" Jack Dabrowski said. "Dude, you're breaking my arm."

I kept him in position, especially when I realized who it was. "What are you doing here? Did you follow me?"

"How could I follow you?" Dabrowski protested. "You disappeared."

"Don't parse the question," I said, giving his arm a tug. He let out a little bark of pain. "You were looking for me."

Beezle landed on my shoulder and gave Dabrowski a good hard stare. "I told you he was too stupid to live."

"Are you . . . Are you going to kill me?" he asked. "I wasn't doing anything."

"I'm sure that's not true," I said. "What happened to your friend?"

"He left," Dabrowski said. "He thought I should leave you alone."

"He was right," I said. "How much of that conversation did you hear?"

"None of it," Dabrowski said quickly.

"He's lying," Beezle said.

"I know," I said.

"No, I'm not! I didn't hear a thing. I just saw you sitting there and wanted to talk to you," Dabrowski said.

He tried to pull away from me, but no human was

stronger than an angel, even one with blood as diluted as mine. I held him firmly in place. I had a strong suspicion that he'd not only heard my conversation with Beezle but had recorded it. He was an investigator, after all. And the last thing that I wanted was for my personal business to be broadcast all over the Internet.

I pulled Dabrowski to his feet and grabbed his other arm. "Beezle, search him."

"Eww," Beezle said.

"Just check his pockets for a recording device," I said.

Dabrowski started struggling in earnest, which confirmed my suspicions. Beezle flew around and patted the front of Dabrowski's jacket.

"You can't do this," he said. "You have no authority to check my pockets and take my stuff."

"That's where you're wrong. I have the right to a private conversation," I said.

I was irritated with myself for not considering this possibility even after Beezle had told me that Dabrowski was interested in me. I'd been too happy to be reunited with Beezle and too involved in our conversation to pay attention to our surroundings. Any one of my dozens of enemies could have walked up behind me and slit my throat before I'd have realized what happened.

"The public has a right to know," Dabrowski said as Beezle emerged triumphantly from the guy's front coat pocket holding an iPhone aloft.

"Please do not try to disguise your invasion of my privacy as journalistic integrity," I said. "You're a blogger. You're not writing an investigative piece on public corruption for the *Chicago Tribune*. I'm a private citizen."

"You stopped being a private citizen the day you blasted

all those vampires into oblivion on live television," Dabrowski said.

"I didn't plan on having the event broadcast," I muttered. "And it doesn't matter, anyway. Just because I was witnessed doesn't mean I belong to you, or to anyone else."

"Someone with powers like yours should be out protecting people," Dabrowski said. "You have a responsibility to the citizens of this city."

"Don't you talk to me about responsibility, boy," I said furiously, spinning him around and grabbing him by the lapel. "You have no idea what I've done, what I've sacrificed, while all of you were safely sleeping in your beds dreaming of sugarplums. I was fighting a war before any of you even knew the war existed."

"And the public should know that," Dabrowski said. "They should know that someone is out there working for them. You should be on all the morning shows, letting people know that all supernatural creatures aren't killers."

I smiled, and I knew it was not a nice smile. "What makes you think I'm not a killer?"

Dabrowski paled. "You don't kill people. You save them."

"How old are you?" I asked casually.

"Twenty-seven," he said.

"Would you like to make it to twenty-eight?"

Beezle had been busily tapping away at the screen of the iPhone while this conversation was occurring. "Listen," he said.

He held up the phone and I heard my voice and Beezle's, as clear as day.

"You didn't hear a thing, huh?" I said to Dabrowski.

He swallowed. "What are you going to do?"

"Drop the phone, Beezle," I said.

173

Beezle released the phone, and I blasted it with nightfire as it fell to the ground. There was nothing left of it except a few microscopic fragments.

"My *phone*," Dabrowski moaned. "That phone cost four hundred dollars!"

"You can send me the bill," I said as I released him. "And that will teach you not to mess with things you don't understand in the future."

"You should be grateful, really," Beezle said. "Just think. That could have been your head."

Dabrowski fell to his knees, picking up the tiny pieces that remained of his phone. Then he stood up and faced me, fire in his eyes. "I don't care about the phone. Everything that just happened is going to be all over the Internet in an hour."

"Listen to me, Jack Dabrowski," I said. "If you continue your pursuit and harassment of me, if one word of anything I said or did is printed on your blog, you will regret it."

"You think you can threaten me and get away with it?" Dabrowski said.

"Yes," I said simply.

"Do not mess around with her," Beezle said. "She has this addiction to fire. I don't know where it came from. But she might just decide to burn your house down."

"With you in it," I added.

Dabrowski shook his head. "I can't believe you're like this. I thought you would be nicer."

"I don't know why you thought that," I said. "The only thing you've ever seen me do is kill things."

I turned and walked away then, leaving Dabrowski staring after me.

Beezle waited until we crossed the street and we were

well away from the nosy blogger before speaking. "So, what are we going to do about that problem?"

I shrugged. "Burning down his house sounds like a great idea."

"You're not serious," Beezle said. "I thought you were just throwing your weight around to scare him."

"I wouldn't burn it down with him inside," I clarified. "But if he becomes too much of a liability, I will definitely make sure that he realizes he's going to suffer."

"And there's the dark-side Maddy I know and despise," Beezle said.

I stopped short and pulled Beezle off my shoulder, settling him in one of my palms so I could look him in the eye. "It's not dark side. I'm trying to help that kid."

"Help him by wrecking his house? Didn't someone else just do that to you?"

"Yes, they did," I said. "And I am grateful that it was only the house that burned, and not me, or my loved ones. What do you think would happen to Dabrowski if he had eavesdropped on one of my conversations with Lucifer? Or if he had stumbled upon one of the fae? What do you think Focalor would do to Dabrowski if he caught him spying?"

"He'd have his head ripped from his shoulders," Beezle said reluctantly.

"Yes," I said. "Unceremoniously and without warning. He's all excited because his lifelong theories have been proven true. But he's messing around in things he doesn't understand. The supernatural world is no place for a mortal."

"So you're protecting him," Beezle said.

"And myself," I said. "I can't do what needs to be done if I'm being trailed by a band of groupies."

"And what needs to be done?" Beezle asked. "Seems to me like you're a soldier without a war at the moment. You wiped out those bug-things that were supposedly going to invade. Daharan is taking care of the Agency/Retriever problem. The vampires are gone and the humans are learning how to play nice with things they don't understand."

"There's still the pending problem of Lucifer and Evangeline's child," I reminded him. "And the fact that Titania probably still wants to kill me for defying her several times in a row."

"Oh, she does," Beezle assured me. "My contacts in the court have told me that she curses your name several times a day, particularly now that Bendith has left."

"Bendith left his mother's court?" I said.

That was interesting. I returned Beezle to my shoulder and continued walking north on Lincoln. We passed by Wishbone, a southern-cooking restaurant that always had delicious smells wafting out. The odd mixture of middle-class professionals and low-income students with a penchant for organic eating came and went from the Whole Foods across the street. Sweaty-faced gym-goers emerged from the YMCA. Everything seemed normal, like there had never been a crisis at all.

I remembered going to the YMCA once. I'd had to collect a soul there. I'd also made a grand pronouncement about losing thirty pounds and a noisy commitment to regular exercise. That hadn't happened. The only regular exercise I got was swinging my sword arm.

"Yes, Bendith was particularly close to Oberon," Beezle said, drawing me back to the conversation. "So when he found out that his mother had betrayed his father by sleeping with Puck, he got pretty upset. I guess he wanted to bring Oberon with him when he departed the court but Titania forbade it."

"But she couldn't stop him from leaving," I said.

"No, she couldn't. It was probably better for her, in any case. He'd been stirring up the courtiers, speaking out against her."

"And there's already a segment of the court that doesn't fully support her, right?" I said, recalling something Beezle had told me long ago, before my first visit to Titania's realm.

Beezle nodded. "So while Bendith's departure was a blow to her authority, it probably was better than the alternative."

"Having her son lead a rebellion against her?" I guessed.

"Exactly."

"And she'd like to lay all of this at my door," I said. "Why do I get blamed for everything?"

"It's so much easier to blame you than it is for Titania to admit that perhaps she shouldn't have made her husband a cuckold," Beezle said. "Look, there's Dinkel's."

"You just had deep-dish pizza. You're not getting a pastry on top of it."

"You have change in your pocket. I know you do," Beezle said.

"So Titania will probably try to kill me again soon—that's what you're saying?" I asked, trying to steer the conversation back on track.

Beezle stared longingly across the street at the piles of sweets in the bakery window as we passed.

"No," I repeated.

"You're no fun anymore," Beezle said.

"Do you know where Bendith went after he left Titania?" I asked.

"Nope," Beezle said. "It's like he disappeared into the ether."

"Do you think she might have had him killed?" I asked, alarmed. I didn't want one of Puck's children murdered. I would probably get blamed somehow. Plus, Nathaniel seemed attached to Bendith. They were half brothers, after all.

"Nah, he's her only son," Beezle said.

"My father tried to kill me," I reminded him.

"Titania only has the one child, and it's difficult for the fae to breed. Presumably she would cherish him more, even when he was being disobedient. Your father had other children, so it wasn't such a big deal to him to get rid of one," Beezle said.

"Another child," I said.

"Other *children*," Beezle repeated.

I stopped in the middle of the street again and glared at Beezle. "Really? Really? You're dropping this on me *now*?"

"What?" Beezle asked. "I always thought you would assume that Azazel had other kids. The fallen boink pretty much anyone willing that they can find. And as you discovered, all they have to do is look at a woman suggestively and she gets pregnant."

I gritted my teeth and summoned up all of my patience. I had considered the possibility that Azazel might have other kids. But it was one thing to have a suspicion and another to have that suspicion confirmed by someone who should have informed me sooner. "Do you *know* the identity of any of these children?"

"No, not offhand," Beezle said. "But they're sure to be

out there, lurking. Some of them may even be angry with you for killing your father."

"That's just great," I said. "Another nebulous threat that will manifest at the least opportune moment."

"Yup, when you least expect it," Beezle said cheerfully.

"Do you care at all about the possibility that I have siblings who might show up to kill me sometime in the near future?"

Beezle waved a little clawed hand in dismissal. "Nah. I'm sure you could take them."

"I'm not sure if I should be touched by your confidence or worried about your cavalier attitude toward my health and well-being," I said.

"Look, you killed Ramuell. After coming back from the dead, no less," Beezle said, ticking points off on his fingers. "You defeated Baraqiel. You survived the Maze and the Grimm. You found out who was stealing memories and you massacred a whole bunch of demons and giant spiders along the way. You beat Amarantha and Violet in a fight to the death. You killed the Hob, Antares and Azazel, who was not the least of the fallen. You wiped out an entire population of vampires, for crying out loud. You unlocked your magical legacy from Lucifer and now there isn't a whole lot out there that's stronger than you. I'm absolutely certain that if some mysterious brother or sister showed up, you could take them down without blinking."

It was fairly horrible to hear a list of creatures that I had killed recited like Beezle was naming a few of his favorite things. In every case I'd either been protecting the greater population of humanity from a dire threat or just trying not to get slaughtered myself. But when all the incidents were listed out like that, one thing became pretty apparent.

I was a killer. No matter how you prettied it up, no matter how much I tried to justify it, I was a killer. And with that much blood on my hands, how could I *not* go dark side?

My hand covered the bulge in my belly. What would my son think of a mother who killed demons instead of baking brownies?

I'd been walking on autopilot, and therefore found myself back in front of the charred ruin of my house.

"Oh, yeah," I said. "No home to go to."

I sat down on the sidewalk and crossed my legs.

"It's kind of depressing, isn't it?" Beezle said.

"Kind of," I said. "What are we supposed to do now?"

A voice spoke from the darkness. "Why, go home with me, of course."

12

I CAME TO MY FEET SO SUDDENLY THAT BEEZLE LOST his balance and fell off my shoulder. He fluttered in an irritated way beside me. J.B. emerged from a shadow beside a tree farther down the street.

"J.B.?" I squinted my eyes at him. I'd been fooled by demons' masks before. My hands curled into fists, and I readied my power.

He halted his approach, holding up his hands in a sign of surrender. The streetlight glinted off the metal rims of his glasses.

"Maddy, it's me," he said. "Don't blast me into oblivion."

Beezle gave J.B. a good hard stare. I knew he was checking all the layers of reality to make sure that it was actually my former boss standing there and not something pretending to be him. I felt acutely vulnerable standing near the ruins of my house, knowing that a threshold would keep me safe from those kinds of attacks. If it was a demon disguised as J.B. and I was in the house, all I would have to do was make sure not to invite him in. But without the threshold I'd have to engage in a fight with anything that wanted to have a go at me.

After a very long moment, Beezle said, "It's him."

I breathed a sigh of relief and started toward him, then stopped. The last time I'd seen J.B. we had said some very ugly things to each other. Yes, he had called me later and tried to warn me about the Retrievers, but the argument we had seemed to hang in the air, echoing in the space between us.

"Maddy," he said, and I heard the hoarseness in his voice, could see the telltale gleam of unshed tears in his green eyes. "I thought you were dead."

"How could you believe anything Sokolov would tell you?" I said. "You know he's a liar. You know how much he hates me."

J.B. took a tentative step toward me, shoved his hands in his pockets like he didn't know what else to do with them.

"I thought he wouldn't be able to lie about a death," J.B. said. "It's a bureaucracy. Paper is sacred. If it's written on a piece of paper, then it must be true."

I laughed, despite everything. "Not everyone is as honest as you."

"I'm not even as honest as me," J.B. said, referring to the argument we'd had on the beach. "I'm sorry I didn't tell you about what the Agency knew of Lucifer and his plans."

"You could have saved me a lot of grief," I said.

"And myself, too," J.B. said. "I mourned you."

I almost unbent then, almost ran to him and embraced him. But there was an awkwardness between us that hadn't been there before. It would take a long time to mend this tear.

"I am sorry you had to go through that," I said, and despite everything, I was sorry. It's a horrible thing to lose someone to death, and I knew that better than anyone. "How did you know that I was back?"

J.B. jerked a thumb in the direction of the downtown offices of the Agency. "Your uncle showed up."

"What did he do?" I asked, a little afraid of the answer.

"He menaced," J.B. said. "And then Sokolov invited him up to the boardroom to talk to certain members of upper management."

I peered in the general direction of the offices. "Well, I haven't seen a fireball exploding into the sky, so presumably he hasn't blown the whole place up with everyone inside."

"He's going to make sure they call off the Retrievers," J.B. said. It was a statement, not a question.

"Yes," I said.

"How do you do it?" J.B. said. "How can you break every rule there ever was and get away with it?"

"First of all, I don't break them on purpose. Second of all, I don't get away with anything, believe me. Whatever I do, I always pay for it. Always."

Silence fell again. Beezle cleared his throat significantly. "So, you were going to give us a place to sleep?"

J.B. looked like he'd dropped into deep thought, and he shook his head like he was coming out of a fog. "Uh, yeah. It's going to be a little crowded with Nathaniel and Bendith there, too, but we'll make it work."

"You have Nathaniel and Bendith with you?" I asked. "How did that happen?"

"Nathaniel had nowhere to go once the house was burned down and we thought you were dead. He didn't feel right returning to Lucifer's court now that he's been revealed as Puck's son."

"Yeah, that would not have been a good idea. Lucifer and Puck seem like they're unreasonable about one another."

"And then Bendith tracked Nathaniel down, because he left his mother's court—"

"We know," Beezle said in a bored voice.

"You do?"

"Beezle's on Facebook," I said. "So Bendith tracked down Nathaniel, and?"

"And he wanted to stay with his brother, and I didn't have the heart to turn him away," J.B. said. "Especially now that he's more vulnerable away from Titania's court."

"Has he got fae assassins coming after him or something?"

"Yes, exactly," J.B. said.

"I thought Titania wouldn't kill her own child," I said accusingly to Beezle.

"She wouldn't," Beezle said. "It's got to be Titania's enemies trying to punish her."

"That's what I think," J.B. said. "But we've got him pretty well hidden. Right now they think he's just disappeared into thin air."

"How did you hide him?" I asked.

"It was some pretty nifty magic on Nathaniel's part," J.B. admitted. "Nathaniel combined his blood with Bendith's and then used magic to disguise Bendith's essence with his own. So if anyone tries to track Bendith magically, they'll come up empty. The only power signature he exerts now is Nathaniel's."

"That is some powerful magic," Beezle said. "And it's a lot like what Michael the archangel did all those millennia ago, to disguise Lucifer's children and his bloodline through Evangeline so thoroughly that even the Prince of Darkness himself would not be able to find them."

"Nathaniel's pretty frightening, actually," J.B. said. "He's got an unbelievable amount of power now. The only thing that's holding him in check is you."

"Me?" I said. "What have I got to do with it?"

"When someone they love dies, men respond in one of two ways. They smash everything in sight, or they break inside. Nathaniel broke. And if he hadn't, there probably wouldn't be a city for you to return to, because he could level Chicago with a look."

I shook my head. "I don't understand. Why would Nathaniel think I was dead? He sent me through the portal so I would be safe. He knew where I went."

J.B. shook his head. "Actually, he didn't know where you went. It seemed he was taking telepathic instructions from Puck and he wasn't really thinking at the time. He assumed that Puck didn't mean you harm, so he did what his father said. Then I came home with the news that Sokolov had been crowing about your death at work. Nathaniel believed you had died in the place where he sent you."

"You know, I used to think you guys were smart," I said. "And you're both pretty powerful. So how did you get fooled by such a simple ruse?"

"Someone was making sure they were fooled," Beezle said.

I nodded. "That's what I think, too. And there's only a few characters that have that kind of power."

"Alerian, Daharan, Lucifer and Puck," Beezle said. "Titania and Oberon. Probably a few others. But those are the usual suspects."

"So we have to figure out why one of the usual suspects wanted everyone to think I was dead, and then went to the trouble of laying out a spell to make sure that nobody questioned it."

"Welcome home to your newest conspiracy!" Beezle chirped.

"Someone wanted me out of the way," I said.

"Lots of creatures want you out of the way," J.B. said. "The trouble is narrowing it down."

"Let's see," I said, tapping my finger on my chin. "Puck sent me to an alien world, and went to the trouble of making sure I stayed there to kill off an entire population. I vote for Puck."

"Daharan was there, too," Beezle reminded me. "Who's to say he's not in on the conspiracy?"

I shook my head. "Daharan wouldn't do that to me."

"How do you know?" J.B. asked.

"I know," I said.

"Maddy . . ." J.B. began.

"No," I said. "Don't say that I'm being naïve, or that I just met him. I *know*."

"Don't argue with her," Beezle stage-whispered. "She's pregnant."

"Pregnant doesn't equal brain damaged," I said. "Or deaf."

"Puck could also be doing work for Titania," J.B. pointed out. "He said he was acting of his own accord, but that doesn't mean anything."

"Yeah, and Titania is highly motivated to get rid of you," Beezle said. "Plus, the whole thing kind of has the feel of a faerie plot, doesn't it? They're always putting you in a new game board and watching to see if you get killed."

"You think Titania told Puck to send me to that place, and Puck used Nathaniel as his vessel because my uncle knew I would trust him?"

"That's faerie logic at work right there," J.B. said. "Titania wants you dead, but she would prefer that the actual bloodletting be done by someone else."

"And Puck tried to throw me off the scent by saying that Titania didn't want him there, that she was planning on using the Cimice for mass destruction?"

Beezle nodded. "She probably wanted the Cimice dead for some queenly reason of her own and decided to use you to take care of them for her."

"So, worst-case scenario—I kill off a bunch of her enemies. Best case—I kill off her enemies and die in the process," I said.

"Sounds about right," Beezle said.

"No, it doesn't," I said. "Something's not fitting together here. I met one of the Cimice. It beheaded a woman right under the Southport El platform in the middle of the day and I chased it down and killed it. And before I killed it, it told me that it was the vanguard of millions and there was nothing I could do to stop it."

"Maybe Titania was going to use them for something and changed her mind?" Beezle asked.

I put my hands over my ears. "Enough. Enough guessing. We have too few facts to work with here. The Cimice are dead. I'm not. That much is true. I don't know who was actually responsible for sending me to that place, but I'm not even sure it matters at this point."

"It matters if your actions there started knocking down a chain of dominoes and we're going to feel the effects of it later," J.B. said.

"Should I confront Puck directly and demand that he not lie to me? That will be really productive, I'm sure."

J.B. took off his glasses and rubbed his eyes. "You're right. There's no point in going over and over it right now. You two come back to my place and get some sleep. Maybe Nathaniel or Bendith will have some insight."

J.B. pushed out his wings. Beezle landed on my shoulder. I glanced around quickly before I took off.

"I was keeping an eye out for him," Beezle said under his breath as I followed J.B. into the sky. He flew a little ahead of us, like he wanted some time to think, and I let him go. "Jack didn't come after us once you'd threatened him, and he was nowhere nearby when we were talking."

"Thanks," I said. "I was so surprised to see J.B. that I forgot where we were—again. We have to stop having important conversations in the middle of the street. A regular human might have called the cops if they heard us discussing murder and mayhem."

"Especially since you look weird," Beezle said.

"Your tact is overwhelming," I said.

"I don't mean your face is weird or whatever," Beezle said impatiently. "It's your wings. You spent so much of your life as an Agent with the ability to tuck them away when you wanted to blend in. You don't have that now. And I think that you keep forgetting that your wings are visible all the time now."

"I do keep forgetting," I admitted. "I keep forgetting that I've changed."

I put my hand over my belly. What was going to happen when Titania discovered I was pregnant? Or Amarantha? Even as a ghost she'd displayed an uncanny knack for causing trouble, and she'd worked with my enemies before. There was no hiding the baby now. I wasn't completely sure how big a normal woman's belly was at three months, but mine looked bigger than it was supposed to be.

"Beezle," I said. "Was my mom's stomach this big when she was three months pregnant with me?"

"No way," Beezle said vehemently. "Either your kid is really big-boned or he's growing faster than normal."

"How much faster, do you think?" I asked in a small voice.

"I don't know," Beezle said. "Why?"

"I'm not ready to deliver this baby," I said.

"Most women feel that way," Beezle said. "Giving birth is a scary thing."

"I'm not scared of the process," I said. "I'm scared of what's going to happen after the baby is born. He's going to be much more vulnerable. How will I keep him safe?"

Beezle put his little hand on my cheek. "I don't know how you'll do it. But I know that you *will*."

I nodded, unable to speak. I would do whatever it took to keep my child safe. Of that, I was sure. But would "whatever it took" be enough? Titania, in particular, would love to take my baby from me and raise it as her own. Faeries are crazy about human babies. You only had to read a few old folktales to know that. And for her to take a baby of Lucifer's line would be an unprecedented coup.

Of course, Lucifer would be unable to allow such an insult to pass. And then he would have to go after Titania. There would be a war, and my child could be killed in the cross fire. But Lucifer's pride would be satisfied.

I shook my head to try to clear away such thoughts. My

baby wasn't born yet. He hadn't been stolen away. He was still safe and snug inside me. I just had to make sure that I didn't get killed.

That was a tall order these days.

I was so caught up in my own worries that I didn't notice where we were until Beezle nudged me in the side of my neck with his elbow.

"What?" I asked.

"Don't you want to go *with* J.B.?" Beezle asked.

I saw J.B. descending toward the sidewalk in front of his building in the Loop. He lived in a condo in Printers Row, a short distance from Agency headquarters. It was a nice little area bordered by some slightly sketchy streets. Like a lot of places in Chicago, the haves rubbed right up against the have-nots.

"Veil your wings," J.B. called.

"Right," I said, and did so.

J.B. aimed for a shadowy spot on the street, away from foot traffic, which was fairly sparse this time of night.

"I could eat a horse," Beezle said as we touched the sidewalk.

"You just *ate*," I said. "You haven't even given your body a chance to digest that pizza yet."

"Yeah, but Hackney's is right over there," Beezle said, pointing toward the next street. "I can smell the burgers."

J.B. punched a key code in at the front door of his building and held the door open for us. He automatically checked his mailbox on the way in, collecting a couple of envelopes and throwing the catalogs into a small wastebasket underneath the boxes.

He started up the stairs to the fourth floor.

"Stairs?" Beezle said. "No elevator?"

"I don't know why you're complaining," I said. "You've never walked up a set of stairs in your life. You've always been carried."

"It's psychological pain," Beezle said. "It's hard for me to watch you expend that much energy."

"Uh-huh," I said.

J.B. paused when he reached the door. "I wonder if I should send you outside, and then send him out."

I cocked my head to one side. "Why?" I asked.

"Because I don't know how he's going to react, and I would hate for my condo to be destroyed."

It was kind of weird standing there with J.B. like this, with him more or less acknowledging that Nathaniel was my boyfriend. Which he was, and he wasn't. And it was even weirder that the two romantic rivals had been sharing the same living quarters for the last few months.

I started to speak, to tell J.B. that maybe it was best if Nathaniel and I went outside anyway, as I wasn't particularly interested in an audience for our reunion. But the front door flew open, and Nathaniel stood there.

I remembered the first time I met Nathaniel, standing in the doorway of my father's ballroom. He was golden and arrogant and perfect, and I'd hated him on sight.

Now he was silhouetted in another doorway, his hair dark instead of gold, his eyes no longer icy blue but the same jewel-bright shade as Puck's. Instead of looking polished and tailored, he wore a flannel shirt and jeans that looked like they were falling off his frame.

I didn't hate him anymore. I wasn't sure what I felt for Nathaniel. That had been the problem we'd had before I left, before he thought I died. But I was happy to see him. That, I couldn't deny.

He was thinner, a lot thinner, and he looked tired. But he saw me, and his eyes blazed.

Beezle flew off my shoulder to J.B.'s. "Umm, we'll just . . . get out of your way."

Nathaniel stepped into the hallway. His feet were bare, but he never hesitated, his eyes never leaving my face. J.B. and Beezle slipped into the apartment behind Nathaniel and quietly closed the door.

I stood still, and I waited. My insides were all jumbled up, in need and confusion. This was what he did to me.

He put his hands on my face, like a blind man, feeling my cheeks, my nose, my eyebrows.

"You're alive," he said.

I nodded. I wanted to crack a joke to lighten the tension, but I couldn't be flippant in the face of his emotion. He'd thought I died, and it was just sinking in now that I hadn't, that the last few months of grief need never have been.

"You're alive," he repeated.

And then his mouth was on mine, devouring, almost punishing. It was like he was trying to crawl inside me, trying to breathe the same air I was breathing. He was marking me, claiming me as his.

I was breathless, and he was relentless, and I welcomed it. And then I remembered Gabriel. My lust turned to confusion. Gabriel was dead. I was alive.

But he was watching me. He'd said so.

"Nathaniel," I tried to say, but it came out a jumble of syllables.

He kept kissing me, like he couldn't stop, like an addict reunited with his drug of choice.

I pushed at his shoulders, and he finally got the message.

He pulled away from my mouth, leaned his forehead against mine, looking into my eyes.

"I thought you were dead," he said. "Sokolov told J.B. you were dead."

"I know," I said soothingly, taking his hands in mine. This wasn't the time for a heart-to-heart about Gabriel, or the future of my relationship with Nathaniel.

But I was going to have to make some kind of decision soon. Would I continue to live in the past, with the memory of Gabriel? Or would I let Nathaniel in?

"Sokolov told us you were dead," Nathaniel repeated.

The air around him seemed to change, to crackle with electricity. His hands dropped away from mine and curled into fists.

"I will tear him to pieces," Nathaniel said, and when he spoke he didn't sound like Nathaniel anymore.

He sounded like Lucifer when he was in Prince of Darkness mode. He sounded like something not of this earth, something not human at all—which he wasn't. He was the son of Puck and an angel of the host, and there wasn't a drop of humanity inside to temper his rage.

"Nathaniel, don't," I said, grabbing his shoulders. His fury was a palpable thing, heat pouring from his body. "Don't make it worse than it already is. If you kill Sokolov, the Agency will not be able to ignore you anymore. They'll come for you."

"Let them come," Nathaniel said. "I will destroy them all."

"Nathaniel," I said, my hands on his face, trying to draw him back to me. "Don't bring grief upon yourself for my sake. I'm here. I'm alive."

"I would do anything for your sake, Madeline," Nathaniel

said. His jewel-blue eyes burned. "I would slaughter a thousand enemies for you. I would tear the sun from the sky for you. I would defy the laws of the universe, reorder the galaxies, stand against Lucifer and his brothers in defiance, if that was what it took to keep you safe. I will not lose you again. I will not."

"You won't," I said. "You won't."

"You cannot make such a guarantee," Nathaniel said.

"Neither can you," I said softly. "Death comes for us all."

I kept my hands on his face, my eyes on his eyes. "Nathaniel. For me. Do not do this, because I am asking you not to."

"Madeline," he said, and his voice broke. The heat of his anger receded a little. "Do not ask me to lay aside my vengeance. They deserve to suffer. They hounded you and harried you and sent the Retrievers to take you."

"But you saved me," I said, and kissed him very gently. "You sent me away. You saved me."

"I thought I had killed you," he said, and one single tear fell. "I wanted only to keep you safe, and I thought I had sent you to your doom."

"You didn't," I said. "I survived. I always do."

"And you truly do not wish me to take vengeance upon Sokolov for your suffering? He is responsible. He should pay."

His eyes searched mine. I knew he wanted me to let him loose upon the Agency, but I couldn't do it.

"Someday someone might have to take care of Sokolov," I acknowledged. "But not today."

"I would feel better if you would let me smite him," Nathaniel said sulkily.

I laughed. He looked like a toddler who'd just been

denied a trip to the candy store. "I know it would be satisfying to break him into little pieces, but no."

"I will respect your wishes, Madeline," Nathaniel said. "For now. But know this—Sokolov will receive no more chances from me."

I understood what Nathaniel was saying. The next time Sokolov tried anything, Nathaniel *would* grind him up and spit him out.

And no amount of affection for me would stop Nathaniel again.

13

I HAD TO MAKE PEACE WITH THIS. IT WASN'T THAT I necessarily objected to removing Sokolov. He had tortured J.B. He had sent Bryson after me and Nathaniel, and we'd been shot out of the sky and nearly killed. He'd sicced the Retrievers on me and caused me a lot of grief generally.

And I wasn't that bothered by one more death. Maybe that was a dark-side thought, but it was true. Especially the death of someone who had worked very hard to make himself my enemy.

I didn't want Nathaniel to incur the wrath of the Agency. I didn't want him to be hunted as I was.

But I also couldn't ask him to sit by over and over and watch the woman he cared about suffer at Sokolov's hands.

So I had to make peace with this. Nathaniel would not be leashed by me again, and I couldn't ask him to be.

He watched me expectantly, waiting for my answer.

"I understand," I said finally.

"Good," he said, and kissed me again. It was a warmer kiss, full of promise, and when it was over he took my hand. "Now you can come inside and tell me what has happened to you."

"And you can tell me what's happened to you," I said. "You look like you haven't eaten a thing since I left."

"You are also thinner," Nathaniel said.

"But I was on an alien planet and I didn't know what food was edible," I said.

Nathaniel shrugged. "Eating was not a priority."

"It was for me," I said. "But I thought I was only gone for a few days, not three months."

Nathaniel pushed open the front door. Bendith, J.B. and Beezle were seated around a coffee table, arguing over something. I realized in that moment that I had never been inside J.B.'s condo. He had been in my house a ton of times, but I'd never seen his living space.

It was more or less what I would have expected of J.B. Color was pretty much nonexistent—everything was gray or black. Wall-to-wall carpeting was gray. A galley kitchen opened into a wide living/dining area, with a hallway leading off behind the living room, presumably toward bedrooms. The kitchen was pristine, and looked like it had never been used.

Tall windows on the opposite side of the front door were covered by dark gray shades that completely blocked out any ambient light from the street. There were tall lamps set at intervals around the room. The dining room had a square table made of something shiny and black, surrounded by four chairs.

The living area was arranged in a perfect rectangle, with a sofa on one side, two chairs divided by an end table on the other and the coffee table in the center.

There were no photographs, throw blankets, flowers, books, or anything personal of any kind. It looked like a show floor at Crate and Barrel, except with less warmth.

It was kind of shocking to think that three men had been living in the space. I would have expected a spare sock on the floor or a dirty cereal bowl in the sink, at least. There was nothing. Just a perfectly perfect, almost inhuman space.

Bendith and J.B. sat on the couch a few feet apart, and Beezle was perched on the coffee table, which looked like it was made of the same stuff as the shiny laptops in the window at the Apple store. I realized that Beezle was standing in front of a stack of take-out menus, and that the argument was about whether or not to order food.

"Maddy said you just ate," J.B. said. "You're not going to get me in trouble."

Bendith had looked up when we walked in. I saw his eyes lock on Nathaniel, like a child who was waiting for his parent to come home. He glanced at our joined hands uncertainly.

I knew that Bendith was very attached to Nathaniel. Bendith and I had not had positive interactions in the past. He, like so many people I knew, had tried to kill me. He had to be wondering about his welcome now that I'd returned. But I wasn't going to bring it up unless he did. I had enough uncomfortable personal conversations looming on my horizon.

Nathaniel shut the door quietly behind us. I dropped his hand and crossed my arms, glaring at Beezle.

"I told you that you don't need any more food. You just had pizza. We are not getting takeout."

"Other people might be hungry," Beezle said. "Bendith said he would eat if we ordered Chinese."

I looked at Bendith, who shrugged. "Fae have large appetites."

"If Bendith wants food, he can have some," I said to Beezle. "But you're not getting any."

I rubbed my forehead, abruptly tired. I'd been through the wringer today. "Look, J.B., is there somewhere I can lie down?"

He got to his feet, immediately solicitous. "I'll put you in the spare bedroom. Just give me a second to change the sheets."

Nathaniel led me to one of the empty chairs. "Have you overexerted yourself again today?"

"Not in the way you're thinking," I said.

But I had been reunited with my dead husband, and then taken away from him again. And then I'd returned home to find out three months had passed and my house was gone.

All in all, it had been an emotionally stressful day, if not a physical one.

"Where shall we sleep if Madeline is going in the spare bedroom?" Bendith asked.

Nathaniel looked surprised that Bendith would show such poor manners by asking the question in front of me. He frowned at his brother.

"I am certain that appropriate arrangements will be made for everyone," Nathaniel said with a finality that indicated the subject was closed.

Bendith muttered something under his breath that I

couldn't hear, but Nathaniel could. He'd gotten super hearing when he had come into his legacy from Puck.

His disapproving frown changed to thunderous anger in an instant. "Apologize to Madeline."

Bendith gave his brother a truculent look. "She didn't hear me."

"But I did," Nathaniel said.

"Sorry," Bendith said to me. He didn't sound like he was sorry at all.

"Accepted," I said quickly, before Nathaniel could make a bigger deal out of the situation.

Bendith was acting like a brat, but it wasn't surprising. He was the only son of a Faerie queen who had likely cherished him beyond belief, and therefore spoiled him. And the fae, despite their endless age, seem more immature than most supernatural folk. Except for J.B., but then, he was half-human.

J.B. emerged from the hallway and beckoned me toward him. Nathaniel helped me to my feet.

"I'm okay," I said gently.

He kissed my forehead and sent me on my way. I'd half expected he would follow me, or at least help me to the room. But he apparently wanted a further word with Bendith out of my hearing.

J.B. raised a brow questioningly as I joined him. I shook my head.

Not now, I mouthed.

I followed him down the gray-carpeted hallway. There were two closed doors on either side.

"That one's mine," he said, pointing to the right.

He opened the other door and showed me into another

drab room. The comforter was black; the sheets were gray. More gray window shades covered the windows.

"Jeez, J.B. Who decorated this place? A prison warden?"

"I like black and gray," he said.

"Can't you at least open the window shades? It would be nice to have some ambient light," I said, sitting on the bed.

"Not unless you want to see Amarantha looming over you all night long," J.B. said. "She has a horrible habit of hanging outside the window and screaming like a banshee if she can see you asleep inside."

"She's still hanging around doing that?" I asked. "I'd have thought she'd have run off with her tail between her legs after I blasted her out of your bloodstream."

It was the wrong thing to say. It reminded both of us that things weren't exactly right. Amarantha had possessed J.B., had nearly stopped his heart from the inside. I'd saved him, but in the aftermath we'd argued. And he'd left.

"Uh, yeah," J.B. said, trying to cover the awkward silence. "She disappeared for a while, but now she's back again."

"Has she seen Bendith?" I asked.

If she had, then no amount of magic could hide Titania's son from his enemies. Amarantha would report straight to whoever would listen. They wouldn't need a spell to track Bendith down. They could just lie in wait outside J.B.'s front door.

J.B. shook his head. "We've been careful. Bendith's been veiled whenever he leaves the building, and the shades are drawn whenever we're inside."

"Are you sure?" I persisted.

"Nobody suspects he's here," J.B. said reassuringly.

"But she might have seen me arrive," I said. I stood up

and swayed a little as blood rushed to my head. "I can't stay here. I'm putting you in danger."

"Maddy, you're practically dead on your feet. You have nowhere else to go. Just calm down," J.B. said. "I'm sure you'll be safe here for one night."

I wasn't so sure about that. "Fine," I said. "One night."

J.B. looked like he wanted to argue further, to ask where I was going to go tomorrow. But he didn't say anything.

"I'll see you in the morning," he said instead, and left the room.

I undressed down to my T-shirt and underpants and crawled under the sheets. It felt unbelievably luxurious to be in a real bed, with real pillows and a real mattress, especially after sleeping in a tree branch, on a platform exposed to the elements, on a beach, and in a sling while flying through the air carried by a dragon.

I passed out immediately. At some point in the night another warm body slid in beside me. I woke briefly as Nathaniel put his arm around my waist and spooned up against me, his breath in my hair. Then I slept again.

I was dreaming. In my dream, something exploded. It seemed muffled and far away. A woman was screaming. I could smell smoke. Nathaniel was shaking me, his voice urgent.

"Wake up!" he said.

I was in his arms, the air cold on my bare legs, and he was carrying me to the window.

"What's happening?" I asked, still groggy.

"Somebody bombed the building. It could come crashing down anytime," Nathaniel shouted. As if to illustrate his point, several chunks of plaster fell from the ceiling.

"Beezle," I said. "I won't go without him."

"He's with J.B.," Nathaniel said. "They had to get Bendith. He can't fly."

Nathaniel gave the window a good hard glare. The shade flew up, the glass exploded outward and the warm spring air came in. Nathaniel flew outside just in time. I could hear the building shaking on its foundation. I was reminded of the mountain crashing down on the Cimice, burying the evidence of the massacre I'd created.

It was still dark out. I was surprised. It seemed like I'd slept for a long time. But the clock on the bank down the street told me I'd been out for only a couple of hours.

Nathaniel stopped in the air and turned around. J.B. was right behind us, carrying Bendith under the shoulders. Beezle was perched on J.B.'s shoulder.

Nathaniel muttered something. I felt a veil drop over all of us. In that small spell I could feel the strength of Nathaniel's power now, how much he'd changed in the time that had passed. J.B. was right. Nathaniel could level the city with a look if he wanted.

And that meant that if he decided to do something like that, I was the only person around with power enough to try to stop him. Emphasis here on "try," because while I had a pretty big repository of power, I had only the smallest fraction of Nathaniel's skill. I had a lot of magic, but I couldn't access it with ease the way he could.

We floated down to the street. It was a good thing we were under a veil. Nathaniel was wearing nothing but pajama pants, and I was the next-best thing to naked. Bendith looked like his pride was smarting from being carried. He pulled away from J.B. as soon as his feet touched the ground.

The window Nathaniel had broken for our escape was

on the back of the building, so we were standing in the alley and had no way of knowing what was happening in front. Smoke poured from the lower windows, and I could hear things crashing inside. Sirens blared, approaching fast.

"Do you think everyone got out of the building?" I asked. Nathaniel was still holding me. Normally I would feel resentful of this, but at the moment I was happy that I wasn't walking in the alley muck in my bare feet, as he was.

"We have to check," I said.

"No," Nathaniel said. "We have to get you away from here as quickly as possible."

"So you think this is because of me?" I asked.

"No one tried to blow up the building until you were in it," J.B. said.

"I told you that it wasn't safe for me to be there," I said.

"I thought we could get through one night," J.B. said. "But someone must have seen you go into the building with me."

"Who, though?" I asked. "And where are they?"

Nathaniel frowned. "You're right. If this was a plot to drive you out into the open, where you would be vulnerable, then the enemy should be lying in wait. But they are not."

"Anyone coming after you would have to know that just setting off some charges in a building wouldn't take you down," J.B. said. His gaze took on a faraway look, a sure sign that he was thinking hard. "Maybe this doesn't have anything to do with you."

"You're taking this awfully well," I said. "Your home is probably going to be destroyed."

J.B. shrugged. "You're out of there. Other than that, there wasn't anything special inside that I cared about."

"We still have to make sure that everyone is okay,"

I said. "Even if this isn't about me, the chances are good that the explosion was meant for one of us. We can't let innocents die just because they're caught in the cross fire."

"You're not going back in there," J.B. said.

"She does not have to," Nathaniel said.

He held me out to J.B. like I was a baby being passed to a relative. This time I did resent his high-handedness.

"Put me down," I said.

Nathaniel complied without argument. I shivered as my bare feet touched the concrete. J.B. looked disappointed that he wouldn't have a chance to carry me around while I wasn't wearing any pants. I may not have had a lot of dignity at that moment, but I wanted to preserve what little I had. I would stand on my own two feet. Even if I was standing in rat poison and the remains of last week's garbage.

"Just so you know, you're not going in that building alone, either," I said to Nathaniel. "So don't get any funny ideas about being a hero."

"I have no such ideas," Nathaniel said. "I am simply going to scan the building and see if there is anyone alive inside. And it is easier for me to concentrate when I am not holding you."

"You can do that? Scan the building like an X-ray machine?" I asked. Nathaniel was getting more terrifying by the moment.

He went very still, his blue eyes staring at J.B.'s former abode. Then he floated up to the roof and began descending slowly, methodically scanning each floor.

"My brother can do anything," Bendith said with obvious pride.

"You could probably do it, too," Beezle said, landing on my shoulder. "If you just applied yourself."

"I apply myself," I muttered.

"Yeah, you apply yourself to breaking and smashing," Beezle said. "Not even remotely as cool—or as useful—as being able to check if anyone's alive without going into the building."

"Breaking and smashing has its place," I said, stung.

"Not as often as you think it does," Beezle replied.

"It must not have been a very big charge," J.B. said. "The building would have collapsed otherwise."

"I thought it was going to," I admitted.

"I don't know why you thought that," Beezle said. "There's magic protecting this building."

J.B.'s eyebrows winged up to his hairline. "There is?"

"Yeah," Beezle said. "I always check every building Maddy goes in."

"You do?" I asked. "That's news to me."

"Home guardian," Beezle said.

"Well, you never seem like you're doing that much at home, so why would I think you were at work when we're elsewhere?"

"Touché," Beezle said. "But the fact remains that there is magic protecting this building."

"I wonder who put it there," I said.

Beezle shrugged. "J.B.'s mom probably laid it in to keep him safe."

J.B. snorted. "That would require maternal feeling. My mother lacked that even when she was alive. And if she had put protective spells on my home, she would certainly have found some way to remove them after she thought I'd betrayed her by siding with Maddy so often."

Beezle shook his head. "These spells have been embed-

206

ded in the brick. Once done, it would be very difficult to undo."

"Who would care enough to do that if not your mother?" I asked J.B.

He shrugged. "I don't know. The fae have never shown much affection toward me in general. Even the members of my own court don't think much of me. Of course, that's probably because I spent so much time here instead of there."

"Well, whoever put those spells there saved the building," Beezle said. "The explosion probably would have taken the whole thing down otherwise. Right now magic is holding it up."

Bendith had been completely silent during this exchange. He cast me the occasional sidelong look, though, like he was wondering how to get rid of me.

Nathaniel landed beside me, but his gaze was still focused on the building. He seemed like he was staring into the ground now.

"There is a basement in this structure, yes?" Nathaniel asked.

"Yeah," J.B. said. "It's got storage areas and some maintenance stuff."

"There is no one in the rest of the building. The fireman went through while I was scanning. However, at this moment there are about forty creatures alive in that space," Nathaniel said, pointing down.

"Creatures?" I asked.

"I cannot tell what they are, but they are definitely not human."

I looked at the others. "I don't think we can leave them there without investigating."

"Why not?" Bendith asked. "They are not humans to be saved. Not that I consider humans worth the effort, but you apparently do."

"Yeah, I'm unreasonable about saving my own kind," I said.

"They are not your kind," Bendith pointed out. "So why do we need to waste our time poking in the business of these creatures?"

"Because it might be forty vampires waiting for a signal to start chowing down on the population," I said.

"Or it might be demons," J.B. said.

"Or zombies," Beezle said.

I raised an eyebrow at him.

"What?" Beezle said. "There could be zombies."

"The point is that something is in the basement that is not supposed to be, and we're the only ones who know about it," I said. "We check it out. Whatever is down there should have heard the explosion and smelled the smoke. Just about everything in the world has a sense of self-preservation when it comes to fire. So why are they still down there?"

"I do not care why they are there. I am not about to put myself in danger for something so foolish," Bendith said.

"Then stay outside if you're going to be useless," I said. I addressed J.B. as I pointed to a metal door on the ground floor. "Is that the maintenance door? Does it lead to the basement?"

He nodded. "It's usually locked."

"That's not a problem for me," I said. "I'll just do the Hound thing and then let you guys in."

I went to the door, and tried not to feel self-conscious about the fact that I was wearing nothing but underpants and a T-shirt, and there were three guys standing behind me looking at my butt.

"You're going to have to wait here for a second," I said to Beezle.

He flew off my shoulder, hovering in the air beside me.

"Be careful," he said.

"I will," I said.

"No, you won't," Beezle said. "But it makes me feel better to say it."

I placed my hand on the door and said the words. "I am the Hound of the Hunt, and no walls can bind me."

The door went fluid, and I slipped inside. It was pitch-black, and that worried me. There should have been a safety light on. The smoke was thicker down here, closer to the source of the explosion.

I fumbled for the handle of the door in the dark. My fingers touched a dead bolt, and I turned it until it opened and then pushed the door open.

Nathaniel and J.B. had approached the door and were standing right on top of it when I swung it outward. Beezle immediately shot inside and took up his usual perch on my shoulder. Bendith stood several feet away with his arms crossed like a sulky child, spotlighted in the glare from the streetlight.

"Bendith," I called softly. "Will you at least come over here and hold the door open while we're inside?"

"I do not see why I should," Bendith said.

"Bendith," Nathaniel said. He didn't raise his voice, but there was steel there.

Titania's son slouched across the alley to the door and leaned against it, resuming his crossed-arm posture. "Happy?"

"Delighted," I said. I gestured to the other two to enter.

Nathaniel immediately took up a position in front of me, and J.B. behind. I rolled my eyes.

Nathaniel lit a very small ball of nightfire. In its faint light we could see the empty maintenance hallway, and a set of dark stairs leading to the basement. There's something ominous about steps disappearing into an underground darkness. Everyone knows that there's nothing good in the basement. The basement is where secrets hide, horrors lurk.

And my own experience had taught me that monsters were definitely waiting for me.

Nathaniel sent the nightfire ahead of us. The little ball of light floated over the steps, showing that there was nothing waiting there for us. We proceeded cautiously down after it.

About halfway down, the smell hit me. My stomach roiled and I gagged.

"Don't puke," Beezle whispered. "You'll definitely attract attention if you puke."

I covered my nose and mouth. "What is that?"

It smelled sort of rotten, but also had a sharp, ammonia-like tang to it. It reminded me of something, but I couldn't think of what. It seemed like I had smelled it recently, but it hadn't been exactly the same. I couldn't put my finger on it.

"We definitely know someone smelly is in there," J.B. said.

I reached for my sword, and realized I didn't have it. It was lying on top of the pile of clothes I'd discarded next to the bed. I was loaded with magic, but I still felt strangely helpless without the sword.

The aura from the nightfire seemed a small thing, pathetic against the encroaching darkness. We had no hope of sneaking up on whatever was in the basement. The nightfire might as well be a beacon announcing our presence. It still seemed wiser to have light than go without.

Nathaniel reached the bottom step.

14

I READIED MY MAGIC FOR AN ATTACK. WE ALL TOOK AN inward breath as he passed under the doorway and into the room.

Nothing happened. I hurried after him, so that he wouldn't be alone if some horrible thing came snarling out of the darkness. The smell was overwhelming now. I was worried we were about to stumble onto a pile of dead bodies stored here since the vampire invasion. Nathaniel paused for a moment, directing the nightfire around the room so that we could see all around.

It was a pretty standard-looking storage area. The room was long and rectangular. There was a maintenance supply closet to the right. J.B. quickly checked the door to confirm that it was locked. The rest of the space was filled with floor-to-ceiling cages in two rows on each side. Each space was padlocked and stuffed with items that people didn't want or need inside their condos. Bikes, kayaks, Christmas decorations—it all seemed safe and normal and not menacing in the least.

"What the hell is *that*?" J.B. said behind me.

I glanced back at him and saw him pointing toward the floor at the end of the storage rows. Nathaniel turned up the luminescence on the nightfire with a wave of his hand. The shadows receded, and we could all see what J.B. was indicating.

Some kind of green slime coated the floor at the very end of the room. It glistened like a live thing in the blaze from the nightfire.

"Oh, no," Beezle said. "The last time there was viscous liquid, a bunch of us ended up inside a chrysalis."

"Shh," Nathaniel said, and began moving forward cautiously. J.B. and I followed. I wondered whether Bendith was still holding the door open upstairs, or whether he'd gotten bored and decided to wander away.

"But you weren't in the chrysalis, so what do you care?" I asked softly.

"There are not enough red shirts here for my liking," Beezle said. "I might end up getting cocooned just because there's no one else around. I'd climb inside your pocket but you didn't bother to put any pants on."

"And thank the gods above and below for that," J.B. murmured behind me.

"How can you think of sex at a time like this?" I hissed.

"I'm a guy. And you're not wearing pants," J.B. said. "It's kind of hard to concentrate on imminent peril while I'm walking behind you, actually."

"Will the three of you cease?" Nathaniel said in an

undertone. "Why do we not simply dispense with all caution if you are going to bicker so loudly that we cannot hear danger approaching?"

The three of us subsided, chastened.

The path between the storage areas was just wide enough for two people to walk side by side. I moved up so that I was at Nathaniel's shoulder.

He glanced down at me like he wanted to argue, and I shook my head.

"You're the one who doesn't want to bicker," I whispered.

He gave me a brief smile at that. He was so thin now that his face looked like carved stone in the nightfire glare. There was not an ounce of softness on him anywhere, just muscle and bone and fierce blue eyes.

There was now one storage space between us and the stuff all over the floor. I held up my hand so everyone would stop.

"It's coming from there," I said, pointing to the last storage area.

We couldn't see what was inside because the lockup beside it was stuffed to the gills with junk. But it was very apparent that the slime was leaking from something inside the last space.

I summoned a ball of nightfire to hurl at anything that might pop out at us, and wished I held my sword instead.

The three of us crept closer. I winced as my bare feet touched the goop on the floor. The last storage area came into view.

"That . . . is . . . disgusting," Beezle said.

"What are they?" I asked.

The space was filled with dozens of hanging sacs

roughly the size of footballs. Each one was attached to the cage by a kind of looped tentacle that protruded from the top. They were connected to one another by a long cord, almost like a vein with nodules jutting from it. Each sac was dripping slime, and some of them were wiggling, as though the living creature inside was shifting.

I automatically put my hand to my newly swollen belly, covering it protectively. My baby fluttered beneath my touch.

"Whatever they are, they don't belong here," J.B. said.

"Quick, get a form," Beezle said. "I'm sure you'll need to file some paperwork on this."

"Why does everyone think I love paperwork?" J.B. said.

"Because you do," Beezle and I both said together.

"So how do we kill them?" I asked. "It looks like they're all connected to that vein. I bet it's some kind of sustenance for them."

"We're just going to kill them without knowing what they are?" J.B. said. "They haven't done us any harm."

"J.B., anything that grows in the basement in a slime-covered chrysalis is not going to make nice with humans," I said. "We should count ourselves lucky that they're still inside and not out running around on the street. I don't think people could handle another panic so soon after the vampire attacks."

"But it seems wrong to just slaughter something so help-less," J.B. said.

"Better them than us," I said.

"Can we at least find out what it is we're killing before we kill it?" J.B. asked.

"How can we do that?" I said.

"Hang on," Beezle said, giving the colony a good hard stare. "It looks like some kind of green insect, kind of praying mantis-y, but not exactly the same."

"Green insect?" I asked, dread filling me. "Nathaniel, can you put that nightfire closer to one of the cocoons? I want to try to see the shape of the creature inside."

Nathaniel sent the nightfire close to one of the closer sacs. A shape was silhouetted inside the slime-covered membrane. The shape of a Cimice. I knew suddenly why the smell had seemed familiar. The stink of the insects had pervaded the air around the mountain, but it hadn't seemed so strong then, as the space wasn't enclosed.

"I don't understand," I whispered. "How did they get here?"

"Who?" J.B. asked.

"The Cimice," I said. I started to explain about the Cimice, because I hadn't had a chance to really tell Nathaniel or J.B. about my adventures, but Nathaniel cut me off.

"The gargoyle explained," Nathaniel said.

He frowned at the colony of eggs, for that was what they were. Tiny little eggs holding tiny little Cimice that would grow into mating pairs. I remembered what Batarian and Sakarian had said about how quickly the creatures bred. They could overrun the city in no time.

"We have to kill them all," I said.

"Yes," Nathaniel said. "If they are as dangerous as you say, then we have no choice."

We both looked at J.B. He nodded with obvious reluctance.

"If we have to do it, then let's do it," he said. "But how did they get here, in this building?"

"Good question," I said. "Who put them here, and why?"

"There are no clues to be found here," Nathaniel said. "Except only the obvious one, that this is somehow linked to Titania or a member of her court."

"Yeah, but what's the point? Are they after J.B., or Bendith, or me?"

"Maybe it's got nothing to do with you at all, solipsist," Beezle said. "Maybe this is just a convenient launching place for an attack."

"And it just happens to be the building in which J.B. lives?" I asked. "Color me skeptical. Plus, this isn't exactly a strategic location."

"Why not?" Beezle asked. "It's close enough to the Loop to cause chaos, and far enough away that it's not under the same tight security as most of the other buildings."

"And maybe I would get blamed for missing the threat under my nose," J.B. said. "Titania is still technically my sovereign, and she would love to have an excuse to take my crown away and put her own puppet on the throne in my court."

"Let us destroy these creatures and then worry about where they came from," Nathaniel said.

"Yeah," I said, staring at the mass of eggs. "My first instinct would be to set them on fire. But how do we do that without burning the whole building down?"

"Where's your sword?" J.B. asked.

"With my clothes," I said.

"Madeline," Nathaniel said. "When you killed Azazel, did you not reverse his death spell and send it into his own blood?"

"Yes," I said. "But how will that apply here?"

"If you create a similar spell, you could send it through the first egg," Nathaniel said. "If the spell were sufficiently powerful, it would follow the cord that binds all of the creatures together and kill all of them."

"I don't know," Beezle said. "This seems kind of subtle for Maddy."

"I can do subtle," I said.

I'd halted the momentum of Azazel's spell and thrown it back to him. I'd done something similar when I'd cast Amarantha from J.B.'s body. But in both cases I was basically acting as a slingshot, hurling the magic back at the person who had created it.

But then again, I had figured out how to take out the colony of Cimice by using their blood. This process wouldn't be that different. I'd just be finding a different way into the spell.

I'd used my powers to defend myself. I'd killed when I thought there was no other choice. I knew that the Cimice were like a time bomb ticking away down here in this basement, and that people would be unable to defend themselves from these creatures.

This was really the same argument that I'd made to justify the killing of the Cimice on that alien world. And I had done it. To prevent human deaths, to protect the innocent.

So I would do it again. Because it was the right thing to do, or the closest thing to right, and everyone present seemed to agree that it was the best course of action. But it seemed like it was getting too easy for me to justify making the decision to take life away.

"I can assist you," Nathaniel said. "I will combine my power with yours to ensure there is enough force to eliminate all of the creatures."

That gave me pause. Every time Nathaniel and I combined our powers, we ended up half-naked on the floor. Of course, we were both already half-naked, and this was hardly a sexy spell. We were going to kill together. It wasn't supposed to be an arousing act.

"Okay," I said. "How do we do this? I don't even know where to begin."

"What do you normally do when you create a spell?" Nathaniel asked.

"I don't create spells," I admitted. "I just throw as much power as I can at whatever is in front of me at the time."

"I told you it was too subtle for her," Beezle said.

"It is not. She has performed a task like this before," Nathaniel said. "Which gives her an advantage over me. Using magic is similar to using a muscle. Once you have used a certain kind of power, it will be easier for you to use it again a second time."

"So I just need to remember what it felt like to push the death spell into Azazel, and it will all come back to me, like riding a bike?" I asked.

"Precisely," Nathaniel said. "There is nothing complex in creating magic. You simply need will and focus. Consider your task, and then determine how best to execute it. When you are ready, I will assist you by giving you some of my power."

"Okay," I said, taking a deep breath. I was nervous, and they were all staring at me, which made it worse. "Can you not stare at me with the weight of your expectations?"

J.B. and Nathaniel both smiled and obediently looked toward the ceiling, but Beezle gave me a pointed stare.

"What?" I asked.

"Are you sure this is a good idea?"

"I can kill them now or I can kill them later, after they've done some damage. I'd prefer to do it now, before anyone gets hurt."

"Yeah, but this is dark magic," Beezle said. "This isn't like anything you've done before."

"Are you sure about that?" I asked. "Because when I wiped away all the vampires in one fell swoop, you seemed convinced that was pretty dark."

"And it was," Beezle acknowledged. "But should you be making it a habit?"

"What else am I supposed to do?" I said. "No one else knows about this. No one else can take care of the problem. It has to be me. It always has to be me. So let me *be*, Beezle."

My gargoyle opened his mouth again, but I shook my head.

"No," I said. "I'm going to do this. I have to do this. So be quiet."

I closed my eyes. I'd never made a complex spell from scratch, but I had done quite a bit of shooting-from-the-hip magic in the past. In every case I had done exactly as Nathaniel had said—I'd considered my task and executed it.

First I needed to weigh the amount of power required. This wasn't like bringing down a mountain, or even like destroying all the vampires. In both cases I'd summoned the depths of my magical energy and let it explode outward. I didn't want anything to explode right now. I wanted to concentrate the magic in a steady stream.

I needed to kill every single one of the Cimice eggs. But I didn't have the stomach to make the creatures blow up inside the membranes or anything like that. So I wanted something that would just quietly stop their hearts beating.

I summoned my magic and my will, and then I did something I'd never done before. I went deeper. Ever since I'd come into my legacy from Lucifer, I had deliberately avoided exploring the full dimensions of my powers. I suspected that there were things I was capable of doing that I didn't want to know about.

I was right. As I sank further into the well of magic inside me, I saw powers almost incomprehensible in their scope, powers that could destroy the world and remake it in the image I chose. There were dark things buried there, cruel impulses, death without reason or mercy.

This was what it felt like to be Lucifer, to have the energy of all the galaxies at your fingertips, to feel that those around you are small and mewling things, things that could be swept away in an instant, without thought, like clearing a chessboard with a swipe of the hand.

I was afraid of that darkness, and part of me wanted to leave it there. But the other part of me, the part that grew stronger every day, embraced it. This was what I was born for. This was who I was meant to be.

And I knew what to do.

I walked forward, almost in a trance. Beezle flew from my shoulder. Nathaniel reached for me, but I ignored him. I touched my hand to the lock on the door and it melted to the floor. J.B. gasped behind me.

The door opened without my touching the handle. I entered the space until I was surrounded by the Cimice eggs. Slime dripped on my face and hair, but I hardly noticed.

I found the egg at the center of the room and placed my

hand upon it. My power spread outward until I could feel every creature in the web. I could sense the pulse of life in all of them, the tiny throbbing hearts. They were all there, beneath my fingertips.

Far away from me, Lucifer rested on his throne, his head in his hands. He lifted his head slowly, and he smiled.

And nearer, the dragon inside Daharan woke up. As it did, something inside me responded, something lit with flame.

I pushed death through my hands, and into the first egg. I knew the moment its heart stopped. The spell continued without my guidance, seeking the next heart, smothering it beneath a cloak of darkness. The vein that connected all of the eggs together shriveled and blackened, and any dead membrane shriveled as well, so we could see the course of the spell moving through the creatures, killing them one by one.

I could feel them dying, but it did not grieve me. The Cimice were nothing to me. This was just a diversion for someone as powerful as I.

"Madeline," Nathaniel said behind me.

I turned and met his eyes. He had approached to within a few inches, watching me cautiously. J.B. and Beezle were wide-eyed in the corridor.

"Madeline, you are on fire," Nathaniel said.

I looked down at my body, slowly, in wonder. I was engulfed in flame. It danced over me, covered me in its flickering warmth, but my skin did not burn. My T-shirt and underpants were gone, but I didn't feel vulnerable. I felt powerful. I *was* powerful, and here before me stood my equal. I could sense the strength inside Nathaniel, more than enough to match my own.

I walked toward him, the Cimice forgotten. His eyes blazed, jewel-bright in the firelight.

"Nathaniel," I said, and it was like he was in a trance, hypnotized by me.

I reached up, put my arms around his neck, and covered his mouth. As soon as our lips touched the darkness inside me roared up, engulfing Nathaniel and me. Only our lips touched, but we were joined in blood and bone and essence, the magic that pulsed inside us twining together.

Together we could do anything. We could lay waste to Lucifer's dominion. We could take over the world.

"Maddy!"

J.B.'s voice. Beezle's voice. Far away. They didn't matter. All that mattered was Nathaniel and the power inside me that hungered to be used.

"Maddy! You're burning him!" J.B., more insistent.

I thought about making him disappear. I could do that. He was like a fly buzzing around, annoying me.

Deep inside my consciousness, I could feel Lucifer nodding in approval.

Then I was suddenly shocked by wet and cold, and Nathaniel was pulled away from me.

I wiped my hair out of my eyes. Beezle hovered nearby, holding a bucket still half-full of water. J.B. held Nathaniel under the arms. There was a ring of burned flesh on Nathaniel's chest that circled up to his neck. Parts of his face were scorched, too, where my mouth had touched him. His lips were blistered.

"Gods above and below. Nathaniel, I am so sorry."

Every trace of darkness and magic had been smothered by the shock of having water thrown on me. I shivered, abruptly conscious of my nakedness. I tried to cover myself with my hands. J.B. politely averted his eyes.

"Do not worry, Madeline," Nathaniel said softly, his gaze on mine. "I can be healed."

"But what if J.B. and Beezle weren't here?" I asked. "What if I'd burned you to death and you never even realized what was happening?"

My body was covered in goose bumps, but it wasn't just from the cold. I was feeling the aftereffects of the magic, like shock running through my system. And I was scared. I'd touched the darkness inside me before, but I had never embraced it so thoroughly.

I didn't ever want to do that again. But now that it had been awakened, it was like the power was a living creature inside me. It hummed just under the surface of my skin, waiting to be called again.

Even worse, I could still feel Lucifer's approval.

I definitely was not interested in doing anything of which Lucifer would approve.

"Well, it looks like you managed to take care of the Cimice problem," Beezle said. "In a typically overboard fashion, that is."

I glanced around the room. You could hardly tell that there had been a network of slimy, dripping eggs a few moments before. All that remained was a few blackened, shriveled fragments. Most of the eggs had disappeared completely, nothing remaining except some flakes of ash on the floor.

J.B. released Nathaniel's arms. "I'll go out the back and up to the window of the condo and get your clothes. Stay here."

He disappeared into the darkness as he passed out of the glow of Nathaniel's nightfire, which still floated above us.

Beezle floated in the air between Nathaniel and me, a disapproving look on his face.

"Don't say anything," I warned.

"I could just dump the rest of this water over your head, since you deserve it," Beezle said.

"Why didn't you go with J.B.?" I asked.

"Because I think the two of you need monitoring," Beezle said.

"It was me that was the problem, not Nathaniel," I said. "I lost control of my power."

"I don't think so," Beezle said. "I think you knew exactly what you were doing. And you were enjoying it."

"I didn't expect it to be like that," I whispered. "Nathaniel, I'm sorry you got hurt because of me."

"He was enjoying it, too," Beezle said.

"Do not presume to know my feelings, gargoyle," Nathaniel said.

"You may have marginally improved as a person, but deep down you're still a guy who loves power. That was why you wanted Maddy in the first place, way back when Azazel arranged a marriage between you. Don't lie to me and tell me that you didn't feel the call when she looked at you," Beezle said. "I could see it happen."

"Madeline may tolerate your interference in her business, but I do not have to," Nathaniel said.

"Yeah, that's what I thought," Beezle said, smirking.

I approached Nathaniel, a little embarrassed. "I should heal you."

He put his hand on my chin, lifting my eyes to his. "Do not hide from me. You did not mean me harm."

"But I did it anyway," I said. Everything inside me was a tangle. "I don't know who I am anymore."

"I know who you are," he said softly. "You are Madeline Black, as you have always been."

I placed my hands on his neck, his lips, making the blackened, blistered flesh disappear.

I heard the sound of pounding feet, and we turned to see J.B. running down the hall between the storage spaces.

He stopped in front of us and dumped an armload of clothing on the floor. My sword clattered to the ground.

"Get dressed," he said. "Bendith's gone."

15

NATHANIEL SWORE. "WHOEVER SET THE CHARGE ON the building must have known he was inside."

He yanked a shirt and jeans from the jumble of clothes and pulled off his pajama pants. He wasn't wearing any underwear beneath but he didn't seem self-conscious in the least.

Beezle turned away, covering his eyes with his hands. "For the love of the Morningstar, don't do that without warning me. I've seen enough naked humans for one day."

J.B. had collected my jeans and shoes, but my underwear and shirt had burned up in the heart-of-darkness incident. I put on the jeans while he scooped a plaid flannel shirt out of the pile.

"I brought you one of mine," he said, trying to look everywhere except my chest.

"Thanks," I said, pulling it over my head, as it was already buttoned. I felt better once I was covered by the shirt. J.B. was a lot taller than me, so the tail hung to the middle of my thighs. "Was there any sign of a struggle outside?"

J.B. shook his head. "No. It's like he just disappeared into thin air."

Nathaniel finished dressing, pulling on a pair of well-worn black leather boots. "It could not have been the assassins, then. They would not have bothered to take him away."

J.B. nodded grimly. "They would have killed him and left him there so we could see that we'd failed."

"Somebody took him," I said as I put on my own boots. "I don't think he would have left of his own accord, do you?"

Nathaniel paused. "I suppose it's possible he ran off in a fit of pique."

"I noticed that he wasn't too happy about my arrival," I said.

Nathaniel directed the nightfire back toward the stairs and we all trooped in that direction. Beezle took up his usual position on my shoulder.

"No, he was not," Nathaniel admitted. "However, I still need to find him. If Bendith is out on his own, then he is vulnerable."

"Doesn't he have magic of his own?" I asked. "He can't be totally helpless. He's Puck and Titania's kid, after all."

"He does have abilities," Nathaniel said. "But they are woefully underdeveloped. It seems that Titania deliberately prevented him from nurturing his power."

"She was afraid he might realize he was related to Puck and not Oberon if he used his magic too much," I guessed.

"Precisely," Nathaniel said. "I have attempted to help

him access more of his magic, but it is difficult to overcome centuries of neglect."

We spilled out into the alley, all of us braced for the possibility of attack. There was no one there. It seemed unusually silent, especially after the excitement of the explosion. I'd half expected the place to be crawling with assorted emergency personnel. But there was no one around. The scent of smoke pervaded the air, and the sky appeared to be lightening.

"Better get under a veil," I said. "We don't want to attract attention."

Nathaniel dropped a veil over all of us, but somehow managed to manipulate it so we could still see one another. His power was noticeably stronger than before, and the darkness that lingered beneath my skin quickened in anticipation.

No, I thought, pushing it back. I wasn't a time bomb waiting to go off. I was Madeline Black, just as Nathaniel had said, and I controlled my power. It would not control me.

But Beezle was a little bit right when he said that you weren't totally out of control before, wasn't he? You liked it. You liked feeling all-powerful.

I pushed the thought away. My heart was still my own. I did not belong to Lucifer. I would not.

"Now what?" Beezle said.

"I can trace Bendith," Nathaniel said. "We have a blood connection, so it is a simple thing for me to follow him."

Nathaniel closed his eyes. I could feel the pulse of his magic spreading outward, searching for a trace for Bendith. J.B. raised his eyebrows at me, and I knew that he could feel it, too.

And I was as strong as Nathaniel, maybe stronger. It was a terrifying, seductive thought.

Nathaniel's magic pulsed again, and there was something different about it, almost as if he were frustrated.

"What is it?" I asked.

"I cannot feel him," Nathaniel said, and I could hear the strain in his voice. "I have been able to sense his presence since we met in Titania's forest."

"Since your eyes changed and you both realized that Puck was your father," I said.

"Yes. I am always aware of him," Nathaniel said. "However, now that I realize it, I lost him when you were, ah . . ."

". . . on fire and kissing you like she wanted to devour you?" Beezle said innocently.

"I am going to make sure you never eat hot wings again if you keep this up," I said.

Beezle mimed zipping his mouth shut.

"In any case, he must have disappeared then," Nathaniel said. "But I did not realize it because I was distracted."

"So there are two options," I said. "He left this world for another, or someone is deliberately hiding him from you as you were hiding him from everyone else."

"The list of suspects strong enough to do that is pretty short," J.B. said. "I'm looking at two of them."

"And obviously you can eliminate the two of us from your suspect roster," I said.

"So that leaves Lucifer, Puck, Alerian, Daharan, Titania and maybe a few of the fallen," Beezle said.

"I don't think we want to go around quizzing any of them to see if they have alibis," I said.

"What happened to Daharan, anyway?" Beezle asked.

"I thought he was going to smack Sokolov around and then come back to you."

"He didn't have anything to do with this," I said.

"Maddy—" J.B. began.

"No, I know he didn't," I said. "I don't know how to explain it to you. I'm not more closely related to him than I am to Alerian or Puck, but I feel more connected to him. I know that he didn't take Bendith."

J.B. looked skeptical, but Nathaniel looked thoughtful. "I wonder why the two of you have bonded so strongly."

I shrugged. "I don't know why. I just felt it as soon as I looked into his eyes. It's like he's my guardian angel."

Saying it made it seem true, and right. Daharan was my guardian. He was supposed to watch over me.

"I can tell you this," I continued. "Puck got really, really angry about it."

"That makes sense," J.B. said. "Puck has been trying to maneuver you into his corner, away from Lucifer. He can't be happy that this other sibling has popped up out of nowhere and staked a claim on you."

"This is all very well," Beezle said. "But what are we going to do about Bendith if Nathaniel can't track him?"

"Let's think about this logically," I said. "Who has the most motivation to take Bendith away from you and hide him?"

"Titania," J.B. and Nathaniel said together.

I nodded. "That's what I think, too. So it looks like we're making yet another unscheduled trip to Titania's court."

"Are you sure that's a good idea?" Beezle asked. "You've, um, wrecked a lot of her stuff."

I'd burned down a lot of her forest, killed off several of her magical guardians, and diminished her husband to his original fairy form. Yeah, you could say I'd wrecked a lot of her stuff.

Of course, she'd tried to kill me several times, so I considered us even.

"Would it even be productive?" J.B. asked. "I don't think Titania would hurt Bendith. She just wants her son back. And if we went to her court, something bad and irrevocable is likely to happen."

"That happens a lot around Maddy," Beezle said.

"You're probably right," I said reluctantly. "But if Bendith doesn't want to be there, I don't think we should leave him there against his will."

"We are also assuming that Titania will not harm him," Nathaniel said.

"I don't think she would kill her own son," J.B. said.

"I agree," Nathaniel said. "But that doesn't mean she will not harm him."

"Yeah, and Titania is a very creative torturer," J.B. said.

A shadow passed over J.B.'s face, and I knew he was remembering when Titania had captured and punished him for not making me fall in line.

The thought of a mother harming her own son made me sick. I put my hand over my belly, felt my child safe and secure inside me. I could never hurt my kid. I really did not understand immortals at all.

I rubbed my face. "Let's think. Obviously it would be dumb to go charging into Titania's court. She's got the advantage there. But it's also the most likely place where she would hold Bendith, isn't it?"

J.B. looked thoughtful. "Not necessarily. She has boltholes scattered all over the place. She even has some in Chicago. I've met with her here a time or two, back when my mother was alive."

"It's unlikely that she came here herself to collect Bendith," Beezle said. "She would have sent some flunkies to take care of the problem."

"Especially because this is considered Lucifer's realm," Nathaniel said. "The old ones are very careful not to cross into one another's territory without permission."

"So Bendith might be here," I said. "Then again, he might not."

"Let's work the problem," J.B. said. "We'll eliminate her known addresses here, and if we can't find Bendith that way, then we'll do it your way."

"My way?" I asked.

"Yeah, we'll illegally cross into Titania's territory, tear up some monsters, burn down a few buildings, threaten the queen, and grab Bendith and leave," Beezle said.

I really wished I could argue with him, but that was probably the way it would work out.

"Where is the most likely place Titania would take Bendith?" Nathaniel asked.

"She keeps a condo in Water Tower Place," J.B. said.

I shook my head. "Too visible. There are shoppers and tourists all over that area. If Bendith tried to make a break for it, he could easily disappear into the crowd. We're probably looking for something more out of the way."

"Hmm," J.B. said. "I think there's a place on Damen, down near that Kinzie Industrial Corridor."

I knew the place J.B. was talking about. There was a whole lot of nothing that way. There were some condos built by hopeful developers who wanted the area to turn into a happening neighborhood and some large warehouse buildings. Foot traffic was light, and most people drove through that part of the city without stopping.

"If she wanted to stash him for now and move him later, that would be the place," I agreed.

"And we're all sure that Titania is the one who took him?" Beezle said. "We could be heading out on a wild-goose chase."

"We have to start somewhere," I said impatiently.

Beezle held up his hands in surrender.

"Let's go," I said.

We took to the sky, heading west toward the industrial corridor. The city below looked more or less normal. Maybe there were fewer cars on the streets than before. Maybe the pedestrians walking on the sidewalk were a little more alert, a little less involved in their smartphones. But all in all, it seemed like Chicago had snapped back pretty well after the vampire attacks. The resilience of the human mind is an amazing thing.

None of us spoke as we flew. My own brain was too busy working to talk.

We had all been so preoccupied by my momentary descent into darkness that we'd forgotten three important facts. Someone had put the Cimice in J.B.'s building. Someone had set an explosive in the building. And someone had put layers of protection in the structure.

Given the number of enemies that I had, it was by no means a sure thing that the same person had set the explosion and planted the Cimice. Since Titania already had an association with the insects, then she was the obvious suspect regarding the eggs. But she wasn't the only suspect.

My own darling uncle Puck could have put the Cimice

in J.B.'s building for some twisted reason of his own. Or he could have been working at Titania's behest.

The explosives were a different story. There was something very unsubtle, very un-fae, about an explosion. It felt more like something a demon would do.

And that opened up the probability that Focalor was out and about trying to cause trouble. He was still pissed at me for humiliating him in front of Amarantha's court. I'd also killed Azazel, his partner in rebellion, and caused him to completely lose status in Lucifer's court by exposing his treachery.

Yeah, Focalor was a good bet for planting the explosives. But how had he known I was in the condo? Or was he trying to get at me by hurting J.B., and the plan backfired because of the protective spells on the building?

And who had set the protective spells in the first place?

Too many questions, not enough answers.

Nothing big was happening, as it had been when Azazel was massing his troops or when the vampires attacked. There was no obvious problem for me to attend—as Beezle had said, I was a soldier without a war. But all these little things added up made me uneasy. And I still wanted to know why Puck had wanted me away from the city for a few months, killing Cimice on a foreign world. He had plans of his own, and I hated to think that I had inadvertently helped him fulfill those plans.

I felt the kind of anxiety that you feel when you know a storm is coming, and you can't do anything about it.

We seemed to be on the leading edge of something huge. All the players were moving into position, but I didn't know yet what part I was to play in the game, or where the other players were going to move next. I was never good at predicting what immortals might be up to at the best of times, but I felt more blind than usual.

There were too many factions with their own agendas. My agenda was just to make sure that I survived and kept my baby safe. Oh, and to make sure no "normals" got caught in the cross fire.

J.B. and Nathaniel had gotten a little ahead of me while I was ruminating. Beezle had fallen asleep on my shoulder and was snoring softly.

J.B. paused in midair, looking down. "I can't remember exactly where it is. But it's in this area."

He pointed toward a two- or three-block radius.

I shook my head. "We can't go around knocking on doors. Can't you remember anything about the place?"

"I didn't want to be there at all, because it was an official function. So I wasn't paying close attention. And all the buildings kind of look the same," J.B. said.

I had to agree with him. All the structures looked like brick boxes cut out of a mold, especially from up here.

"I can scan the buildings for signs of the fae, as I did when I checked your residence," Nathaniel said.

"Seems almost as inefficient as knocking on doors," Beezle said.

"What if," I said slowly, thinking it through as I spoke, "instead of scanning for signs of the fae, you scan for dead space?"

Nathaniel looked at me, recognition dawning as he figured it out. "I understand."

J.B. glanced between us. "You think that because they hid his magical signature, he just won't appear?"

"It makes sense," Beezle said. "Unless Titania was with

them—which is unlikely—the kidnappers would be using a bottled, quick-and-dirty spell. Titania wouldn't be able to put a lot of complexity into that kind of spell."

"Like when Nathaniel protected Bendith by hiding his magical essence with his own," I said.

"Exactly," Beezle said. "That's complex magic. Titania wouldn't be able to throw that kind of spell on a charm and hand it off to one of her flunkies. She could, however, put a more limited version of that spell on or in an object that a soldier could use to cast it."

"Like a cloak," I said. "Just enough to cover him up, make it harder for us to track him."

"Yes," Beezle said. "So, for a change, Maddy actually has a good and sensible idea. Look for dead space. All of you can do it, and we'll be able to get this over and done with quickly."

"Do you have a pressing appointment?" I asked.

"Yes, with a pumpernickel bagel, cream cheese and lox," Beezle said.

We all stared at him.

"What? It's breakfast time," he said.

"Spread out a little," I told the other two, ignoring Beezle. "Then we can each take a section. You can help, too, Beezle. You can look through the layers of reality for signs of a magic spell."

Beezle flew off my shoulder, grumbling something about overworking an old gargoyle.

"I'm sure that old gargoyles shouldn't be eating exciting things like cinnamon rolls and sausage pizza," I called after him. "If you're that infirm, I should probably limit you to porridge and prunes."

"You wouldn't dare," Beezle said.

I raised an eyebrow at him. "Help, and stop complaining."

"You might actually be sincere about this," Beezle said. He flew a little distance away, glancing back over his shoulder like he wasn't sure whether to take me seriously or not.

J.B. and Nathaniel had already flown a short distance away, spacing themselves out so they could cover the whole area. I concentrated hard, sending my power out as I did when I was searching for the portal on the alien world.

To my surprise, I found what I was looking for almost immediately. Directly below me was a nondescript brick building with a few grills on the roof, indicating that it was a residence. And on the top floor, I could sense the presence of exactly the dead space for which I was searching.

"Hey," I called to the other three. They all looked up at me, and I pointed at the spot I had found.

"Are we still under the veil?" I asked Nathaniel. His magic was so light and nonintrusive, it was hard to tell.

He nodded. "Although it may not protect us from the fae. They are likely to see through it."

"It's not the fae I'm worried about," I said. "It's early, and people will be getting up for work. I don't want anyone to see us landing on their neighbor's roof."

J.B. nodded. "And we have to make sure that the people in the building are unharmed."

"So that means no tearing around, smashing and burning," Beezle said pointedly to me. "I'd like to see you manage that."

I decided it was best not to rise to the bait.

Nathaniel concentrated hard on the place I had indicated. "There is no need to worry. There are only two in the room besides Bendith, and no one else is present in the building."

"Really?" I asked. "Isn't that weird?"

"Perhaps they made sure that the humans were sent away before Bendith was kidnapped. It is an easy thing for the fae or the fallen to do. Human minds are very malleable. You simply set a spell so that any person who crosses the threshold suddenly decides to take a vacation, or stay late at work, or spend several hours shopping."

I frowned. "I've never known a fae to care that much about the safety of humans."

"Hey," J.B. said in an insulted tone.

"You're about as much fae as I am fallen," I said impatiently. "You know and I know that we're more human than anything. But you're missing the point. Why would they send the humans away?"

"It might not have had anything to do with their safety," Beezle pointed out. "Maybe they just didn't want anyone to notice that they're holding Bendith there. Humans might be very malleable, but they're also very nosy. And they have a tendency to ask questions."

I shook my head. "Yeah, but a fae would be able to glamour a human so that they would be distracted, or forget. They wouldn't need to remove the people altogether. And I know that somebody must live in that building, because I don't think faeries are that fond of barbecue."

"So what are you thinking?" J.B. asked.

"There's something going on here besides Bendith's kidnapping," I said. "I can't put my finger on it. But there are all these little things that aren't adding up. This can't possibly be as simple as Titania wanting her son back."

"Wouldn't you do anything if you thought your son was taken from you?" Beezle asked.

Yes. Yes, I would, I thought. And I would probably do it with a lot less restraint than Titania has shown.

"We will approach cautiously," Nathaniel said. "I cannot leave my brother there. He will expect me to come for him."

For a moment I thought Nathaniel was Gabriel, and that he was talking about Samiel. They seemed so similar in that moment that my heart ached.

"Okay," I said. But something was nagging at me. This didn't feel right.

Beezle snuggled into the front pocket of my flannel shirt, which flopped loosely around me. Just his eyes and horns peered out over the edge. J.B., Nathaniel and I flew to the street level, landing on the sidewalk in front of the condo.

"I do not sense the presence of any special magic," Nathaniel said. "Only the two inside with Bendith."

He moved toward the front door. I halted him with a tug on his sleeve.

"What if it's not Bendith?" I asked. "What if it's something else?"

"Madeline, I must see," Nathaniel said. "If it is him, I cannot leave him."

"I understand," I said, but my entire body tingled with tension.

I didn't know why the others weren't as concerned as I was. Usually I was the one rushing forward, heedless of danger. But everything about this felt like a trap. We had tracked Bendith too easily. The magic used to conceal him seemed clumsy, more of a lure than an effective cover.

Nathaniel climbed the steps to the front door. I think we

all expected it to be locked, but it opened when he tugged on the handle.

I shook my head from side to side. "Uh-uh. That's an invitation. Whatever is in there *wants* us inside."

"How many times have you gone into a dangerous situation because you felt you must?" Nathaniel asked. "And I have always stood at your side."

"I know," I said. "But this is different. There's something larger at stake."

"What is at stake?" Nathaniel asked, moving through the lobby and up the stairs. I followed him, with J.B. taking up the last position in line.

It was too quiet. There should have been the sounds of people moving around inside their residences, the smell of the morning's breakfast cooking on the stove. It seemed a haunted place, and cold passed through me like a shade.

"I don't know," I said, frustrated. "But we shouldn't go any farther. Once we do, all the dominoes will fall."

As I said this, I knew it to be true. Whatever happened next would set off a chain reaction that would affect everything.

"Daharan," I whispered. "Help me."

There was no answer. I had felt him earlier, when I'd used my power to destroy the Cimice eggs. But now I did not feel the strand of connection between us. It was like he was hidden from me. I'd felt this way before, when Lucifer had left our world for another. Had Daharan disappeared into another dimension after he'd confronted the Agency? And why would he do that when he'd told me that he would return to me?

My sense of dread increased with each step we took up the stairs. We reached the top floor. There were two apartment doors on either side of a small landing. A window hung between them, facing the street.

Nathaniel turned automatically toward the door to the right. I was so tense I felt sick. This was wrong. But I couldn't leave. Nathaniel had put himself in danger for my sake more times than I could count. I couldn't leave him. And J.B. wouldn't leave me, so we were all in this together.

It seemed that time slowed, stretched out with unbearable tension. Nathaniel reached for the doorknob, turning it under his fingers.

The door swung open. We had just a moment to see the tableau before us. Bendith was tied to a chair, the cords wrapped around his body. His mouth was gagged. His blue eyes, the exact mirror of Nathaniel's, widened when he saw us. On either side of him were two fae I did not know, both trussed up like Bendith.

Bendith began shaking his head and trying to shout through the gag. Nathaniel started to step over the threshold.

I sensed it just an instant before it happened.

"Nathaniel, no!" I cried, grabbing his arm, pulling him back.

And then the world exploded.

16

I HAD JUST A SECOND TO THROW A PROTECTIVE SPELL over the four of us. J.B. slammed into me from behind, wrenching me away from Nathaniel. He sped toward the window with me in his arms as the blast from the explosion licked at our heels.

We burst through the glass just ahead of the flame. I twisted out of his grasp, turning back to see Nathaniel emerge, unscathed, from inside the flame. My spell had worked. It had kept him safe.

There was a tremendous sound of impact as the flame reached the gas lines in the building, and the whole thing suddenly went up in a huge fireball.

Beezle peeked over the edge of my shirt pocket. "That's magnificent, even for you."

"I didn't do that," I said, irritated. "It's just a coincidence that the building exploded. Someone else set a charge or a spell before we even got here."

Beezle looked dubious. "Seems too convenient that someone else used your modus operandi. It's almost like they knew you were going to be here."

Nathaniel flew toward us like he was drunk, his face haggard and shocked. I met him in the air, taking his hands.

"Bendith," he said hoarsely. "I could not . . . I could not . . ."

"I know," I said.

Bendith was dead. Titania's son was dead.

The sky above us turned a sickly, poison green. Clouds rolled in, swirling in a frantic circle above our heads.

"She's coming," I said. "The dominoes are falling."

I felt a strange calm as I said this. The knot that had pulled so tight inside me was gone. The thing I had feared had happened. There was nothing left to do now except deal with the fallout.

"She?" Nathaniel said. He seemed numb, too wrapped in his own grief to realize what was happening.

"Titania," I said.

The air around us crackled with tension, and then we heard it. A scream, a howl so complete in its pain that I felt it in the marrow of my bones. It started off softly, like it was far away, and then gathered in volume and intensity until I was forced to cover my ears so that they would not bleed, and still I could hear her, feel her screaming inside my brain and my heart, the grief of a mother who has lost her only child.

That grief went into the heart of me, into that place that lived every moment in fear for the life of my own son. Titania had been my enemy from the start, but I was sorry for her, more sorry than I could say. No one should have to feel pain like that.

Was this what Lucifer felt when he thought he'd lost

Evangeline and his sons all those years ago? I thought with a sudden flash of insight. *Or, worse, had he actually felt this way when I'd killed Baraqiel and Ramuell?*

I hardly ever credited Lucifer with human feeling. God knows he had more children than could possibly be counted, and the ones I had met were pretty monstrous. But maybe that didn't mean he loved them any less.

And just because it wasn't in his nature to howl and rage at the sky didn't mean that he wasn't furious with me for killing them.

I don't know why this had never bothered me before. Maybe it was because I was pregnant that I finally realized how it felt to be a parent, or maybe it was because Lucifer always acted like he cared about me. Everyone always talked about how obsessed he was with his bloodline, and I was part of that bloodline.

But a granddaughter several times removed couldn't possibly hold the same rank as a child would in his heart.

J.B.'s voice broke into my reverie. "Um, maybe we should leave. Because Titania is going to be pretty upset, and like Beezle said, you've got a reputation for setting things on fire."

"She's going to blame me," I said. It was strange how calm I felt as I said this. "Someone set me up. Someone manipulated us into coming here so that we could take the fall. Bendith was never taken by Titania's men in the first place. Someone else's agenda is at work here."

J.B. tugged at my arm as the sky darkened more. "If you know you're going to get blamed, then isn't it better to leave the scene of the crime?"

"She'll just chase me," I said faintly, looking at the sky. "There's nothing I can do to stop this."

A showdown between Titania and me had been brewing for a while. She'd tried to kill me several times by proxy, but I didn't think she was going to sit on her throne and try throwing a monster at me this time. She would want to feel my throat being crushed beneath her hands.

"Take Beezle," I said, passing my gargoyle to J.B. "And get away. I'm going to try to lead her toward the lake, so nobody gets hurt."

"Except you," J.B. said.

"I won't let her kill me," I said, covering my belly with my hand. "I have too much to live for."

Nathaniel finally seemed to come out of his shock-induced coma. "You are not going to battle the High Queen of Faerie."

"You don't get to decide," I said. "The two of you are talking like I have a choice here. She's going to think I killed Bendith. It doesn't matter what the truth is, that I had nothing to do with it. I'm on the scene, and she hates me anyway. She's going to hound me until I'm dead, no matter what. It's better if we have this out now, while it's just Titania. If I wait, she'll raise an army against me and then I won't have a prayer."

Nathaniel grabbed me by the shoulders. "You don't have a prayer now. She is an ancient thing, older even than Azazel. Even with all the depths of your power, she is stronger than you can imagine."

"But she's also mad with grief," I said softly. "She won't be thinking clearly. I will be."

Nathaniel dropped his hands to his sides, his face shocked. "You mean to try to kill her."

"You can't," J.B. said. "You could take out the whole

city. Killing something that old and magical would be like setting off a nuclear bomb over Lake Michigan."

"I can diminish her," I said. "Like I did with Oberon."

"This is ridiculous," J.B said.

"I agree," Nathaniel said.

Beezle only watched me with sad, steady eyes. "Maddy's right. She has to do this now, or else Titania will never give her peace. But, Maddy . . ."

I waited for him to finish, my eyes on his.

"Don't forget who you are," he said finally.

"I won't," I promised, and kissed his forehead. "Now, go. I'm going to head toward the lake before the Wicked Witch appears."

"Are you so sure she will follow you?" Nathaniel asked.

"Yes," I said. "She'll look for traces of magic, and she'll know I was here. And once she knows that, she will follow me."

"I do not want to leave you alone," Nathaniel said. "I sent you away from me once, and I thought I lost you forever. You cannot ask me to stand by and let you take this risk on your own."

"You have to. It's me she wants, me that she will engage. You'll just get in the way," I said, pushing him toward J.B. and Beezle. "I won't die."

"Do not make promises you cannot keep," Nathaniel said. "Everything dies. You should know that better than anyone. You told me so yourself."

"I do know," I said. "But I won't let Titania kill me."

He reached for me, but I backed away, shaking my head. "I'm not going to kiss you good-bye. Because I am going to come back."

I turned away then, speeding east over the city and toward Lake Michigan. I wished I felt as confident as I seemed. There was a very good chance that Titania would tear me to shreds. But I had to try to deal with her now, while she was grieving and presumably not thinking straight. I might never have a shot otherwise.

The storm in the sky grew, reaching its tentacles across Chicago. The city below was coated in green light.

I passed over the Loop, a busy hive of people hurrying to work. The El rumbled along its various tracks. Cabs discharged harried passengers in front of office buildings. No one seemed in the least concerned that a major unscheduled storm was brewing.

The sailboats had returned to the harbor with the advent of spring, and the boats were rocking on their moorings as the lake was whipped up by the atmosphere.

I wondered whether Alerian had returned to the lake, and whether he would help me if I needed it. I knew next to nothing about my mysterious uncle, but I didn't get the same feeling of warmth and comfort from him that I got from Daharan. I didn't think he would be inclined to stick his neck out for me, especially since he didn't seem to like Lucifer much.

None of his brothers seemed to like Lucifer much, come to think of it.

I kept going until I was well away from the shore, and still I flew. I didn't want Titania anywhere near my city. The people of Chicago had suffered more than enough already.

When I glanced behind me and saw that the skyline was nothing but a speck, I stopped and turned around. My heart was pounding furiously in my chest. I floated high above the surface of Lake Michigan, and wondered just what the hell I thought I was doing here.

I didn't have the least idea of how I would defeat Titania. I just knew that I had to. This wasn't just about my life, no matter what I'd claimed to Nathaniel and J.B. It was about my baby.

My pregnancy wasn't hidden anymore. Now that her son was dead, she wouldn't be satisfied with just killing me. She would want my child, the tangible proof that she had defeated Lucifer's favorite, that she had obtained an advantage in her ongoing battle with the Morningstar.

So she wouldn't kill me. Not right away. She would keep me like a breeding animal until the baby was born. Then she would take my son and kill me by inches, letting me live my final moments in agony, knowing that my child would grow up calling her "Mommy" instead of me.

Maybe I *was* getting better at figuring out what immortals wanted.

The storm above the city had chased me over the lake, the physical manifestation of Titania's seeking magic. I waited.

There was no warning. One moment I was alone, fluttering my wings to stay aloft in the increasing wind, and the next moment she was there before me.

Her face was as unearthly and beautiful as always, even when frozen in a white mask of rage. She was dressed in unyielding black, and it only made her beauty more perfect, more unreal.

"Madeline Black," she said, and in her voice was all the power that she had kept suppressed for centuries.

This was an ancient being, perhaps older than the Earth itself. She had been toying with her court and with mortal lives to keep amused as the eons passed. Like Lucifer, she hadn't bothered to exert herself for time untold. But now she was angry, and grieving, and all of that magic was building inside her, waiting to punish me.

"Titania," I said. "I had nothing to do with his death."

"If you did not, then why did you run from me?" she asked. Her voice was pitched low and full of malice.

"Because I knew you would think I killed Bendith," I said. I gathered my energy. I didn't want to be the one to strike the first blow. I was still hoping—in a vague, naïve sort of way—that this wouldn't turn into a fistfight. But I wanted to be prepared for whatever Titania might decide to do.

"You were there," she said. "You, and Amarantha's whelp, and that fallen angel that Puck fathered."

"Yes. We were looking for your child," I said. Something in me grasped at straws, hoping she would believe we were there for benevolent reasons. It didn't seem likely. Titania had thought the worst of me from the start. As I gathered my energy, I touched the place of darkness inside me, the place that had nearly overwhelmed me. I did not want to go to that place again. But I would, if I had to. I could not let Titania take my son.

"You were looking for him so you could kill him?" Titania said. "Spare me your lies."

"Titania," I said. "It doesn't have to end this way. I never sought to be your enemy."

"And yet you have behaved as my enemy from the start. You murdered Queen Amarantha, one of my subjects. You killed my Hob. You diminished my husband. Time and again, you have defied me, made me look the fool in front of my own court. And now you have taken my son from me."

"I did not," I said. "Someone made sure that you would

think that. I might be guilty of all the other stuff, but I didn't kill Bendith. Why would I?"

"To hurt me, of course," she said. "To lay me low."

"I don't care that much about you," I said. "I don't want anything to do with you. I'm not interested in having you as ally or an enemy. I just want to be left alone. That's all I ever wanted."

"And your wish shall be granted," Titania said. "After I cut your child from your belly, I will bury you alive at the bottom of the sea, on a planet at the far end of the universe. There will you die slowly, alone, secure in the knowledge that it was your own actions that brought you there."

"You won't take my child," I said, my anger flaring. Thus far I'd managed to remain relatively calm in the face of Titania's magic, in the face of her threats. But when she spoke the very words I had thought only a few minutes before, my temper surged. Nightfire lit on both of my palms.

To my surprise, Titania laughed. It was a high and mirthless cackle, the cry of a heartbroken witch.

"Do you really think that you can defeat me with such small and pathetic spells?" she said. "I have seen galaxies rise and fall. You are nothing but a blip in the universe, and your power is nothing to me."

She lifted her hand, palm flat, and blew air across her fingers at me.

I tumbled backward across the sky, caught in the gale of a hurricane wind. There was no way to right myself as the world went spinning. Titania's laugh trailed behind me.

The wind abruptly stopped, and I plummeted toward the lake. I managed to pull my body up just before I crashed into the cold depths below.

The nightfire in my hands had been extinguished by

Titania's wind. I looked wildly around for the Faerie Queen, but she seemed to have disappeared.

I did a quick search of the area for a trace of magic that I could follow. I didn't want Titania to sneak up on me again. But there was nothing. The Faerie Queen had appeared without warning, and disappeared just as quickly.

She hadn't even really used her power on me, and I'd been completely neutralized. Somehow, despite all the odds against me, I'd always managed to defeat my enemy. Even when I'd fought Azazel, I'd been sure I could find a way.

But I was outclassed here. Everyone had warned me that tangling with something as old as Titania was a bad idea. Too bad it took me so long to realize it.

The attack, when it came, arrived without warning. One moment I was searching the air for Titania. The next moment pain was arcing through my body. It was like I had been set on fire from the inside out, but it was a small, subtle fire. It wormed in between the layers of muscle and nerve. It made me want to scream and tear at my clothes, claw at my skin until it bled and I let the burning thing that was underneath *out*.

Titania blinked into sight a few feet in front of me. She'd been covered under a veil so thorough that I hadn't even been aware she was using magic. My own spell hadn't found a trace of her.

She had one hand raised, and her eyes were focused with laser intensity on mine. I could feel her hate. She wanted me to bleed, and she wanted to watch.

The pain was agony. I couldn't fight this. Fire was the weapon I used on everyone else. It had never harmed me before, and a part of me felt vaguely betrayed. I couldn't smash it or hit it or knock it down. I could barely even think straight. The fire had sped through my spine and up to my brain, seeping into the layers of cortex, setting off all the synapses like a triggered minefield. Pain exploded in my head, and I did scream then. Blood gushed from my nose in a torrent.

I had to get away from her, get away from the pain. But I couldn't even move, and I realized she was holding me in place, keeping me still so she could torture me. I hung in the air like a rag doll, suspended only by Titania's will, unable to do anything more than writhe in agony.

There had never been any hope for me, really. It had always been a matter of time before I was caught and pinned like a struggling butterfly by one of these creatures.

As I thought this, my son shifted in my belly, his little wings fluttering in distress.

My son. My son. I couldn't let Titania win. I couldn't let her take him away. That thought centered me, gave me the clarity I needed to think through the pain.

There was no chance of my reversing the spell on Titania as I had with Azazel. This magic was much more powerful, and much more invasive. I needed to get her to stop.

Then I needed to find some way to make her hurt as much as she had hurt me. It was the only thing she understood.

I could offer her compassion in the face of her loss and she would simply spit it back at me. I could try to explain, try to broker a peace with her.

There was no point. Titania had decided long ago that I was her enemy. And every time I had selfishly refused to let her hurt me, or humiliate me, or kill me for the amusement of her court, I had only compounded her notion that I existed only to defy her.

So many of my choices seemed to come down to this.

I could kill, or I could be killed. It was not the life I wanted for myself, or for my child. But it was the only life I had, and I couldn't let Titania take it away.

She laughed like a mad fiend as I grew visibly weaker. Blood was still running from my nose and the loss was making me feel dizzy and sick. I pulled my focus together, reached deep inside me for my magic.

And touched the black heart inside of me, the swirling, dark mass of power that threatened to consume me.

I could use that power, and survive, and possibly be someone else afterward, someone that Beezle had warned of, someone that may not be recognizable as Madeline Black.

Or I could let Titania keep me locked in a cage for the rest of my short life while she poked me with sticks.

When I thought about it that way, there really wasn't much of a choice at all.

I'm sorry, Beezle.

I plunged into the darkness.

17

THE PAIN DISAPPEARED IMMEDIATELY. TITANIA WAS still throwing the spell, but I could no longer feel it. My mind had retreated to a place where her magic could not harm me, a place that was cool and dark and seething with coiled energy waiting to be loosed.

I lifted my head and looked into the eyes of the Faerie Queen. Shock spread across her face. She had been convinced that I was broken.

And I had been. But now I was born anew.

I wiped the blood from my face with my sleeve. "Stand down, Titania, High Queen of all Faerie. Or be destroyed."

"Do you truly believe you can defeat me?" she asked. "The power of the Morningstar is diluted inside you. You are nothing but a pretender to Lucifer's line."

"I warned you," I said steadily, and never took my eyes from her face. "When you are crying out for Oberon at the end, remember that I warned you. I gave you the chance to leave."

Then I let the darkness inside me surge up. Magic filled my every pore, racing through to repair the damage wrought by Titania's spell. The storm above us disappeared as abruptly as it had arrived, and the clouds blew away to reveal the blazing sun and the fresh blue sky of a spring day.

The heart of my power was the sun, a sun covered by the moon in a burning eclipse. I'd never truly understood this before. I had always held back, always been afraid of unleashing the full extent of my power.

I was no longer afraid.

When I'd touched the dark heart inside me in the basement, I'd felt intoxicated by the power, so overcome that it had set me ablaze. Now it felt like the power and I were one, that it moved easily within me. It would not harm me, or overtake me. It would do as I bid.

I flew toward Titania and wrapped my arms around her before she realized what was happening. Her arms were locked in my embrace. I let the darkness flow from me until it covered her, smothered her, drowned her magic in mine.

I turned the two of us upside down and arrowed toward the churning waves of Lake Michigan.

"What are you doing?" she shouted, her face furious. I could feel her magic pulsing weakly against me, but it was a small thing battering against a castle wall.

I said nothing, only held her tight to me. The darkness wrapped around her again, smothering the light that burned inside her.

Her white skin grew sickly gray, and the sparkle faded from her beautiful jeweled eyes.

"How can this be?" she said.

Then we broke the surface of the water, and went under.

It was as dark as the ocean here in the depths of the lake, and just as strange. Silence surrounded us, and still my magic worked my will without direction. The seeping, oozing darkness continued to bind Titania like a cocoon.

She struggled feebly against me, but she could not fight this. This was not a blazing magic that she could battle with her own power. This was as insidious and inevitable as the night itself, a creeping shadow that gave her no quarter.

I swam deeper, unaffected by the lack of oxygen, until I reached the very bottom of the lake. Then I removed one arm from Titania, but she no longer struggled. Her eyes were closed, and her face was still and gray as stone.

I blasted a hole in the bottom of the lake, prepared to drop Titania in it and then bury her forever. Then I hesitated. The black spell had pushed Titania's magic to the limit, but it was still not completely doused. There was still a little flicker of flame inside her. I could sense it, like a moth battering against a streetlight. If I left her alive, she would find a way to return, to take up where she had left off.

I couldn't leave her alive. And I would never have an opportunity such as this again.

But the problem of the magical blowback remained. I didn't want Chicago to be leveled by an earthquake when Titania's magic was released.

Send her through a portal.

I don't know whether it was my own thought, or a thought directed by the magic working through me, or a message from Lucifer or Puck or Gabriel. It didn't matter, really. I knew what I had to do now.

I closed my eyes, sent my power reaching out into the far-distant galaxies of the universe, looking for a broken place, a place that would not be harmed by Titania's destruction.

When I found it, a place light-years from my own blue planet, I fixed its location in my mind. Then I opened a portal in the silt at the bottom of the lake, a special portal that looked like a window. On the other side of it, I could see a gray rock floating in space, circling a dead star.

I concentrated on the little light flickering inside Titania. Then, with one final push of magic, I crushed it out.

I dropped Titania through the portal just as she started to come apart.

I watched as the High Queen of Faerie disintegrated, piece by piece, into motes of dust on the surface of that faraway place.

Suddenly there was a tremendous explosion, like a star going supernova. I heard nothing. I felt nothing. I could only see the burst of light through the portal.

When the starburst was over, the little gray rock floating in space was nothing but a memory.

And so went Titania. I wondered who would rule Faerie now that Bendith and the queen were dead, and Oberon was diminished.

I swam to the surface of the lake and flew up into the blue sky, turning my face to the sunshine. The darkness still swam inside me, a live thing, and I knew that a line had been crossed. I would never be able to rid myself of it. The shadow was a part of me now.

Inside my heart, I could feel Lucifer radiating his approval.

I flew toward the city. I should have been elated, but instead I was just exhausted. Titania was gone, but I still had no home to return to. I had embraced the darkness inside me to save myself and the life of my child, but what price would I pay?

Anything that made Lucifer happy couldn't be a good thing.

I turned north, automatically heading toward the site of my old home. Maybe I could pitch a tent in the yard or something. I was nearly to the lakeshore when I saw three figures flying toward me.

I paused and peered at the people coming into focus. It wasn't Nathaniel or J.B. It was Bryson, and two other Agents I didn't know. They were dressed in the black military fatigues of the Agency retrieval unit.

I rubbed my forehead tiredly. "Really? I have to deal with this now?"

I waited for them to reach me. Bryson looked surprised when he saw that I wasn't going to make them chase me; then his expression grew wary. They stopped a few feet from me in the air, almost as if we had accidentally met on the street.

"Madeline Black," Bryson said. "You are under arrest for defying the law of the Agency and willfully crossing into the land of the dead. You have fraternized illegally with a dead soul. You will submit to our authority and return to the Agency for sentencing, or else you will have the Retrievers set upon you."

"Okay," I said.

Bryson's eyebrows winged up to his hairline. "Okay?"

"Okay, call the Retrievers," I said. "Bring your armies. Do whatever you want. But I am not going with you."

"You are not a law unto yourself, whatever you may think," Bryson said angrily.

"Oh, yes, I am," I said.

Bryson indicated to the other two with a shake of his head that they should grab me.

I gave them a look. "I just killed one of the oldest creatures in the universe. Are you sure that you want to be the one who tries to force me to come back to the Agency with you?"

Bryson's lackeys paused and glanced at each other.

"Captain . . ." one of them began.

"I will call the Retrievers if you will not do your duty," Bryson said, with the air of a magician pulling his best trick.

The other two visibly cowered at the thought of being in the presence of the Retrievers. I tried flying around Bryson, who grabbed my arm.

"Where are you going?" Bryson shouted. He was starting to look a little unhinged, like he just couldn't believe that I would ignore him so completely.

"I told you, do what you want. The Agency has no authority over me anymore," I said, shaking him off like he was a flea.

"I am going to enjoy watching the Retrievers eat your soul," Bryson hissed through his teeth.

He pulled a small silver whistle from his pants pocket and put it in his mouth. He blew into it, but I didn't hear anything.

"You use a dog whistle to call the Retrievers?" I said.

"I have watched from afar as you have defied the Agency, defied the very laws of the universe," Bryson said. "You cast off your Agent's mantle, the sacred charge that was given to you. You entered the realm of the dead and brought forth a soul even when you knew that it was forbidden. You do as you please, over and over, and I am sick of it. Now I will watch the Retrievers tear you to pieces, and I will enjoy it."

I don't know whether it was my intense exhaustion or the artificial boost I was getting from my acknowledgment of the totality of my power, but I just couldn't get that worked up about the arrival of the Retrievers. Which was strange. They had been the bogeymen under the bed for as long as I'd been an Agent, and I'd fled through a portal to another world just so I wouldn't have to tangle with them.

But now I couldn't care less. "Let them come," I said to Bryson.

"Agent Black," one of the other Agents said.

I looked at him. He was young, muscular, and looked like the type who was dedicated to his job. His eyes were worried.

"I'm not an Agent anymore," I said to him.

"But . . . shouldn't you be running? Or fighting? Or something?" he said. "The Retrievers are pretty bad."

"I know," I said softly. "I've seen them before."

"You have?" the third Agent said.

I nodded. "And a whole lot of other stuff that no one should ever have to see."

A street strewn with bodies after Ramuell had destroyed it. A cave full of imprisoned nephilim, calling for my blood. My own body missing its heart, my soul floating high above my broken shell.

A maze comprised of my darkest fears and deepest secrets. A room full of children tied to machines that took away their memories.

Gabriel falling, his blood pooling in the snow.

A plaza piled high with bodies, and vampires pouring from the dark underground into the sunlight.

More demons and monsters than I could count dying beneath my sword.

Antares. Ramuell. Baraqiel. Amarantha. Therion. Azazel. Titania.

Alerian rising from the ocean. Puck's eyes flashing with mischief. Lucifer smiling.

Yes, I had seen a whole lot of stuff no one should ever have to see.

"But, Agent Black—" the first Agent said again.

"She's not an Agent," Bryson spat. "She is a rogue, and should be treated as such. Stop trying to help her or you'll be cited for insubordination."

I looked at the first Agent and shrugged. "Don't worry about me, kid."

The Agent's face hardened. "It's not right, sir. She's pregnant."

"Pregnant with a monster," Bryson said. "Her child will be a plague upon the world."

I shook my head. "Seriously, Agent . . ."

"Hill," the first guy said.

"Hill, don't get yourself into trouble with the Agency," I said. "It's not worth the aggravation."

Hill tilted his head to one side. "You're really not worried about the Retrievers."

"Nope," I said.

I put my hands in my pockets and turned south. That was the direction they were coming from. I could feel them now that they had entered our dimension. I didn't know where they were kept normally, but it wasn't on our plane of existence.

Hill and the other Agent backed away a little from me. Bryson watched me avidly, practically salivating.

I started to whistle.

The Retrievers approached, their pace quickening. I sensed their anticipation. They longed for a soul to take, for a purpose. They had spent so long inside their prison.

"The Retrievers are your prisoners?" I asked Bryson.

"If we did not imprison them, they would run rampant over the world, devouring souls," Bryson said dismissively. "We allowed them their lives. Now they can fulfill their desires in the service of the Agency."

"You need to stop hiding behind the Agency like it's some kind of untouchable institution," I said. "You guys have made plenty of mistakes. And one of them was trying to chain creatures that should never have been chained."

"You sound like you feel sorry for the Retrievers, Agent Black," Hill said.

"I do," I said softly.

As they got closer and closer I could feel their pain, the centuries they had suffered in the Agency's prison. Even now, when they were allowed to run free, chains bound them so that they would be forced to return to the place they hated.

Darkness appeared in the distance. The Retrievers would be here at any moment.

When I saw the Retriever at my house, just before I'd leapt into the portal, I'd had a sense of something huge and horrible, something impossible for the human mind to understand. They sped toward us as giant, inky black shadows, contorting in monstrous shapes.

I pulled my hands from my pockets, and held them out in front of me in supplication as the Retrievers drew near. The creatures howled as they approached, their maws open, ready to devour me.

And then they stopped.

The dark magic inside me poured from my hands, reached out to the Retrievers. The creatures seemed confused. They were supposed to attack me. I poured my compassion into the darkness, and settled it over them like a balm. One of them whimpered, and the three creatures seemed to shrink in confusion. Now the Retrievers looked like nothing more than miserable, confused dogs. They looked like oversized mastiffs, blacker than the night before the dawn.

In this form it was easy to see the silver cuffs that each Retriever had around two legs. The cuffs were held there by the magic and power of the Agency. These were the bindings that forced them to return to their prison after they did the Agency's bidding.

I studied the spell for a moment, and then waved my hand at the Retrievers. The cuffs disappeared into smoke.

The Retrievers approached me cautiously, wound around my ankles, sought affection from my petting hands. The new magic inside me let me know what they were feeling. They had not been free for eons, and I had given them this gift. They would serve me willingly. They would destroy every member of the Agency if I asked them to.

I have to admit that I was tempted, just for a moment, to set them on Bryson. As soon as I had this thought, they turned on the Agency's captain, growling. Bryson backed up several feet, shock and terror on his face.

"No, no," I said to my new pets. "Stay."

Hill stared at me in amazement touched with fear. The third Agent had fled some time after the Retrievers arrived.

"Go back to the Agency," I said to Bryson. "And tell

Sokolov that if he comes after me again, I'll deliver the same punishment to him that he would have given to me. The Retrievers are mine now."

"Your heart is as black as Lucifer Morningstar's," Bryson said. "One day, someone will bring you to heel."

"Possibly," I said. "But it won't be today. And it won't be you."

Bryson and Hill took off in the direction of the Agency. Hill looked back once over his shoulder at me, floating in midair, surrounded by the Retrievers that were supposed to destroy me.

"Now, what am I supposed to do with the three of you?" I murmured. "I hope you don't like pizza, because I don't think Beezle will share."

I continued flying north again, toward the place where my house used to be. The Retrievers loped along in the air beside me. It seemed that the more doglike I thought of them, the more doglike they became. Their ears and heads grew more defined, and they all let their tongues loll out as they ran.

I flew over my street, unsure what I was doing there. I just wasn't sure what else to do with myself. After I defeated the big bad monster, I always went home. This was where my home was, even if the house was gone.

Except that the house was there.

I landed on the sidewalk in front of the building. It looked just like the house I'd grown up in. The porch was painted red, and the paint was peeling. The bricks over the second-floor window were crumbling. Beezle's nest of sticks and blankets was perched on the roof over the porch. Lights were burning inside on the second floor.

I walked forward as if in a dream, wondering whether this was a glamour, a trick. But the steps felt solid beneath my feet. The front door opened when I turned the knob.

I climbed the stairs to the second floor. The carpet was worn in the same places. I reached the top landing, and heard someone moving around inside my apartment. The Retrievers had silently followed me inside, and crowded around me, nudging my legs with their wet noses.

I opened the front door.

Daharan was setting the dining room table. There was an amazing array of food set up there—a roast chicken, mashed potatoes, grilled asparagus. He turned and smiled when he saw me standing in the doorway, but his smile was touched by sadness.

"How?" I said.

"Magic does not only destroy," he said. "I thought that this was the least service I could do for you, especially since . . ."

He trailed off, shaking his head. "Not now. First, you must eat."

I let him lead me to the table. I wasn't aware until I sat down that I was still wet from my dunking in Lake Michigan, and that the water that drenched my clothes didn't smell all that great.

"Um, maybe I should change," I said.

Daharan nodded. "The meal will stay warm for you. I have contacted your gargoyle, and told him that you are well."

"Is he coming home?" I asked.

"Soon," Daharan said.

I went into the hallway to the bathroom, where my shampoo and soap waited for me, just as if the house had never burned down. The same towel was thrown over the rack, just as if I'd hastily left it there the day before.

The Retrievers had trailed me to the bathroom door, and I pointed them back to the dining room. "Wait for me there," I said.

The three gigantic dogs reluctantly returned to the other room. I was going to have to come up with some names for them. I wondered what Beezle would think of the new additions to our household.

I wondered what he would think when he saw the way the darkness had spread inside me.

I showered, dressed in clothes that had magically returned to my closet, and tied my hair in a braid. My belly protruded slightly above my jeans, exposed by a too-short T-shirt. I was going to have to buy maternity wear soon.

Beezle would probably have some choice words about maternity shopping, too.

When I returned to the dining room, I found that Daharan had set my plate with heaping servings of food. The Retrievers were flopped on the furniture in the living room, resting but watchful. All three perked up their ears when I entered the room. Daharan was drinking a glass of red wine, and appeared to be brooding.

"I note you have gained some new companions," he said, glancing at the Retrievers.

"Yes. I'm not really sure what to do with them yet. They seem to want to keep me," I said.

"They will be powerful allies for you," Daharan said. "They will protect your child."

I hadn't thought about that. Any advantage I might gain in keeping my baby safe was a good thing. I gave the three giant dogs an appreciative glance.

"They seem to be getting more doggy by the minute," I said, putting a forkful of chicken in my mouth. It was delicious, perfectly roasted and crisp outside and juicy inside. Beezle would die of happiness if he could get some of this.

"They were born of the same stuff that created the universe," Daharan said. "And they never found a perfect form. Thus they have been malleable, prone to the whims of those who rule them."

"Were they never free?" I asked, glancing at the three dogs.

"Once they might have been. But Michael tamed them long ago, and they were put to the Agency's service."

"Michael?" I asked. "The archangel who was friends with Lucifer?"

"If anyone can truly be friends with Lucifer, then Michael was," Daharan said. "The Retrievers terrorized humans, killing them and eating their souls."

"But Michael showed them mercy?" I asked.

"If you could call what he did 'mercy,'" Daharan said. "He entrapped them, forced them to serve the Agency. The creatures were only acting upon their natures. It is not fair to shoot a tiger simply because it behaves like one."

"Are you saying the Retrievers will be good now that they belong to me?" I asked.

"That depends," Daharan said. "Are you good?"

My cheeks colored. "I think so."

"I am not passing judgment upon you. I am asking if you still believe that you are, as you would say, one of the good guys," Daharan said.

I thought about smothering Titania within a cocoon of darkness.

"I try to be," I said.

Daharan fell silent at this, and I returned my attention to my dinner.

"Aren't you eating?" I asked, shoveling food in my mouth. Everything was amazing, and as usual, I was famished.

"I have already done so," he said, but something in the way he said it made me pause.

"No, you haven't," I said. "Why would you lie about that?"

Daharan looked surprised. "You know when I say a falsehood?"

"Yeah," I said. "I mean, I don't know if I could before. But I can now. Since I . . ."

I trailed off. I didn't know whether Daharan knew about the Titania thing yet. And I was a little afraid that he did know, and that he would disapprove.

"Since you killed the Faerie Queen," Daharan said.

There was no judgment in his tone, only a statement of fact.

"Yes," I said, putting my fork down. "She thought I killed Bendith."

"Of course she thought you killed her son. Because it was arranged so that she would think that."

His voice was still calm, but I could see the anger banked in his eyes. The anger wasn't for me, though.

"Do you know who set me up?" I asked. Whoever it was had a lot to answer for.

Daharan took a large sip of wine, swallowed it, and gazed directly at me. "Yes."

"Are you going to tell me who it is?" I asked.

"I am sorry I did not return to you as soon as you expected me," Daharan said. "So much of this could have been avoided."

"Where were you, anyway? And don't think I haven't noticed that you didn't answer the question," I said.

"I was detained by Alerian," he said.

"Alerian?" I asked, alarmed. "Why? What's he up to?"

"Nothing that he will reveal to me. He simply wanted to see me, as we have been out of contact for many centuries," Daharan said. "But our powers are in such direct opposition to one another that it has a dampening effect on our magic when we are together. You may have felt the connection between us break while I was in my brother's presence."

"Yeah," I said. "I thought you left, went to some other universe or something. It was the same feeling that I used to get when Lucifer went to the land of the dead."

"It was because of Alerian's presence that I did not feel the threat to you when the faerie king's apartment was under attack," Daharan said. "Else I would have rushed to your aid immediately. And if that had been averted, none of the rest would have followed."

"So who was it?" I asked.

"The same person who has interfered so often in your life lately," Daharan said.

"Lucifer," I swore. "I don't know what he's up to, but when I—"

Daharan shook his head. "Not Lucifer. Puck."

18

"PUCK?" I ASKED. I DON'T KNOW WHY, BUT THAT TOOK me off guard. "Puck did this? But why would he kill his own son?"

"He has another," Daharan said.

"Kids aren't usually that interchangeable to their parents," I said.

"I would not know. I have none," Daharan said.

"You don't?" I said, momentarily distracted. "Lucifer's got them coming out of his ears."

"Lucifer is not as discriminating as I," Daharan said. "And my true nature makes it difficult to mate with human women."

I made a concerted attempt to refocus. "Still, even if he does have Nathaniel, it makes no sense for Puck to kill Bendith."

"There is something you do not know about Puck,"

Daharan said. "Many millennia ago he was tricked into binding his life to Titania. He has served her ever since."

I stared at Daharan. "And let me guess. The binding is only broken with Titania's death."

"Yes," Daharan said.

The darkness rose up inside me, swirling as my fury rose. "He set it up to make it look like I murdered his son so Titania would blame me. And he used me to kill Titania and free him from his servitude."

"Yes," Daharan said sadly.

I stood from the table. The Retrievers came to immediate attention in the living room. I stomped through the hallway and into my bedroom. If Daharan had restored everything else in the house, then the object I was looking for would still be there.

On my dresser a bright blue jewel winked like Puck's merry eyes. I grabbed the jewel off the dresser and went back to the living room.

"Puck!" I shouted.

Nothing. He was supposed to come when I called, when I used the jewel.

My power rose up, furious now, and Daharan made no move to calm or stop me. He simply waited. The Retrievers lined up in a row before me and sat on their haunches, as if awaiting my command to attack.

"PUCK!" I said, and pushed my power into the jewel.

"There's no need to shout," he said from behind me. "I'm right here."

I spun around. Puck leaned against the doorframe, his arms crossed, his usual expression of merriment on his face. He was dressed in a pair of jeans and a black Neubauten T-shirt, and he wore engineer boots. His hair had been artfully arranged with some kind of hair product. He looked like he was going to a concert at the Metro.

And while Puck was grooming himself for a night out, I was drawing upon the darkness in my soul to unwittingly kill the Faerie Queen for him.

"I am going to kill you," I swore.

I raised my hand to throw a spell at him, but Puck waggled his finger at me.

"Uh-uh-uh," he said. "I think you'll find you can't do that."

I paused. I was pretty sure that, having taken Titania down, I could definitely put the hurt on Puck, but he seemed very confident.

"Why in the name of all the hells not?" I said.

"Remember what I told you about magic leaving a trace of itself?" Puck said.

Back on the far-distant planet, when Puck had given me a boost of energy when I'd been flagging, he'd told me that the spell would not leave permanent damage. But that it would leave a trace of itself.

A bond. And that I might find that I would be unable to harm him should I ever wish to do so.

"You didn't just arrange Bendith's death," I said. "You arranged the whole damned thing from beginning to end."

Puck twinkled at me. "Of course I did. And let me tell you that it was no simple thing. I had to cull you away from your herd of merry men by sending you to Batarian's world. I had to maneuver you into trusting me, into unleashing the dark power inside you. Without it you never would have been able to defeat Titania. I had to make sure that I left a mark on you so that you could not harm me. And I had to give Nathaniel and Bendith enough time to form a bond so that you would all chase after him if you thought he was kidnapped. So many pieces to arrange, but I must say that I am pleased with the way my jigsaw turned out."

I felt sick to my stomach. "So there never was a threat from the Cimice? Titania wasn't going to unleash them on Chicago? You just put me there and told me that story so I would exercise a part of my power that I had never touched before?"

"Yes, basically," Puck said. "It was a pain to plant the Cimice there, too, with Lucifer's thrice-bedamned portal restrictions."

"And Batarian's fae?" I said. "What of them? Did you even care that they might suffer because you had put an alien species on their planet, in their forest?"

"Oh, those fae were never there in the first place," Puck said dismissively. "They used to be, long ago, but Lucifer killed them all. I simply summoned the memory of them to help convince you to take care of the Cimice. You do so seem to enjoy protecting innocents," Puck said.

I'd told Batarian that his people were nothing more than pawns on a chessboard. But I hadn't realized just how right I was when I'd said that.

"That means you sent that Cimice here to kill Jayne Wiskowski," I said slowly, as I put the pieces together. "All this time, all along, you were leading me here, to this place, so that I would get rid of Titania for you? How dare you? How dare you?"

"How dare I what?" Puck said, and the merriment vanished from this eyes. "Use you? I would have done anything if only it meant that I could be free of that witch. I suffered for centuries at her hand, treated like an inferior creature when my power was far greater than hers. When you appeared in court it was as if you had been sent to me by fate. I knew as soon as I saw you that you would be the one. Only you would have power enough to do it, and only you were human enough to be manipulated into place."

I turned furiously to Daharan, who still sat at the table, watching, saying nothing. "And what did you know of all this?"

"I was not aware of all his machinations. But when Puck broke Lucifer's decree and placed the Cimice on that planet, I went there to attempt to limit his mischief. I did not know he had drawn you into his web. When finally I did know, it was too late to stop it. Events had already been set in motion," Daharan said. "I would not deliberately harm you, Madeline. You must believe that."

I did believe that. I knew it in my bones, because he couldn't lie to me. But my anger surged and seethed inside me with no outlet. I wanted to destroy the one who had done this to me, but by his own prescient behavior I was unable to do so.

I'd never before felt so impotent, so helpless. All along I'd thought I was doing the right thing. But I was nothing more than a pawn in Puck's bid for freedom.

I'd killed the High Queen of Faerie. I'd killed one of the oldest creatures in the universe, because I thought I was protecting the people of Chicago, because I thought I was protecting my child. But none of it had been real, and still the queen was dead.

"Wait," I said. "What else do you get, besides your freedom?"

Puck smiled. "The throne of Faerie, of course. There will be challengers, but none that can match me in power."

"And then?" I asked, dreading the answer.

"I will have an army, of course. I imagine I might need one someday," Puck said.

"To start a war with Lucifer?" I asked. "You had me take one of the most powerful pieces off the chessboard so that you would have an easier path to victory over your brother?"

"Now, little Madeline. What fun is there for me if you know all my plans?" Puck said, and he touched the tip of my nose with his finger.

The three Retrievers came to their feet and growled. Puck looked askance at the dogs.

"I see you've obtained some new pets," he said.

"Yes" I said, enjoying his obvious discomfort. "And I bet that there would be no restriction on Lock, Stock or Barrel harming you, as there is on me."

Puck raised an eyebrow at the names. "It's a good thing I have business elsewhere, then. Until we meet again, Madeline. Daharan."

Puck whirled in a dramatic little circle and disappeared.

I considered calling him back with the jewel and setting the dogs on him just for the fun of it, but I didn't.

Although I wanted to. I really, really wanted to.

I sat down in one of the dining room chairs. The dogs crowded around me, putting their muzzles in my lap. My baby fluttered gently inside my belly, as if he were pleased by the presence of the Retrievers.

Daharan stood. "I imagine you do not wish to see me at this moment."

"You didn't know everything," I said. "But you knew some things. And you didn't tell me."

"I have no children of my own. I wished to protect you," Daharan said.

"But you couldn't," I said sadly. "You didn't."

"The apartment downstairs is empty. Do I have your permission to use it?"

"Yes," I said. "For now."

My uncle walked out of the front door without another word. I heard his footsteps softly creaking on the stairs.

I rubbed the head of the first Retriever, the one I'd named Lock. "I hope that he doesn't sleep in his dragon form. There isn't enough room down there."

"Or enough fire extinguisher," Beezle said from the hallway.

Beezle and Nathaniel were there, both with identical expressions of worry on their faces.

"How long have you been there?" I asked.

"Long enough that you don't have to give us a recap. We know all about the Puck manipulation thing and the killing of Titania thing and the rising of the dark inside you thing," Beezle said. "Ooh, dinner!"

He flew to the table and dove headfirst into the roast chicken.

"I hope you weren't hungry," I said to Nathaniel.

"Give her the thing," Beezle said, his voice muffled because he was inside the chicken.

"What thing?" I asked Nathaniel.

He approached me cautiously, giving the Retrievers an unsure look. They lifted their heads and growled.

"It's okay," I soothed. "He's a friend. It's okay."

Nathaniel continued toward me. I noticed he had a piece of paper in his grip. He handed it to me while Lock, Stock and Barrel gave him the beady eye.

I unfolded the slip of paper. All it said was, "We know who you are, and we know where you are. We are watching."

I turned it over, hoping for something more. "Where was this?"

"On the porch," Nathaniel said. "Beezle seems to think it's from someone named Jack."

Jack Dabrowski, the blogger who wanted me to be mayor, who wanted to broadcast my business on the Internet. Apparently I hadn't done a good enough job of scaring him off.

The Retrievers let Nathaniel put his hand on my shoulder. I covered his hand with my own and leaned my head back against his body.

"Nathaniel," I said. "You need to be careful. Puck killed Bendith to serve his own purpose. I don't think he feels particularly warm toward his children."

"I know," Nathaniel said. "But I am not in any more danger than you. Now that you have killed Titania, you will have many more enemies. You have established yourself as something to be feared, something to dread."

"I am something to be feared," I said. "Puck made me this way. And Puck had better watch his ass."

Beezle stopped stuffing his face long enough to say, "I hope you're not thinking of revenge. Because I think Puck has already proven that he's much better at thinking long-term than you are."

Maybe Puck was better at strategic planning. I was more emotional, more spontaneous. But he had twisted me into this shape and used me like a weapon.

There was no reason why that weapon should not, could not, turn on him.

I smiled, thinking of Puck suffering at my hands.

"Maddy?" Beezle said. "What are you thinking?"

Inside me, the darkness smiled, too.